MW00891032

A View to Die For

Richard Houston

Copyright © 2012 by Richard Houston

All rights reserved. No part of this book may be reprinted, scanned, or distributed in any printed or electronic form without the permission of the author

ISBN-13 978-1481995832
ISBN-10 1481995839

This is a work of fiction. Names, places, and incidents are the product of the author's imagination or are used fitctitiously. Any resemblance to actual persons, living or dead, companies, events or locales is entirely coincidental.

DEDICATION

To my wife, Cherie, who has managed to put up with my daydreaming all these years.

ACKNOWLEDGMENTS

I wish to thank the following people for helping me make this work readable:

Candace Levy – my second set of eyes,
Catherine York-Garcia from www.critiquemynovel.com,
Tom Baker of www.papercpr.com,
Catherine Astofolo,
Shawn Hopkins,
And to all who were kind enough to read my early drafts.

CHAPTER 1

Truman, Missouri. May 16, 2011.

LOCAL COUPLE FOUND DEAD

The bodies of a prominent coin dealer and his wife were found at their lakeside home today. John and Margot Fergusons, owners of the Show Me Gold and Pawn in Liberty, Missouri, had recently retired to the lake after Margot had been diagnosed with lymphoma.

In a statement, Sergeant Bennet of the Fremont County Sheriff's Department said he believes John took his own life after finding his wife had committed suicide. There was, as of this time, no evidence of a break-in.

The envelope was postmarked Truman, Missouri. I would never have bothered to read it had I not been arranging the clutter on my desk. Arranging my clutter and pencil sharpening was my way of getting back to work on my novel. I had thrown the envelope on my desk with the intent of tossing it out with the other junk mail.

I only knew a handful of people in Missouri, and they were all family. They would never send me something like this without a note of some kind and surely, I would think, not without a signature. Whoever sent this didn't want me to know who they were, but why?

I reread it for the tenth time hoping to unravel some clue as to who sent it. It was a copy of an article from the Truman Lake Sentinel. Because of a line running diagonally across the paper, the copy was hard to read. I had seen similar lines caused by defective laser printers.

The mystery of the anonymous letter soon faded when the phone began to ring. I let the answering machine pick it up; maybe

I was old school, but I preferred the outdated device over voice mail. This way I could hear who was calling. This time, it was my neighbor, Bonnie Jones. "Jake, Sweetheart, I hope you don't mind me calling you so late on a Sunday. It's my toilet again. Would you be a dear and stop by in the morning to take a look?"

Bonnie is a widow and also one of my best customers. I should have called her back; it really wasn't that late – seven-thirty according to my kitchen clock – but I knew I would never be able to write another word if I did. She was the kind who could talk for hours about nothing. Then the phone rang again.

"Damn, Fred," I said to my Golden Retriever. "Doesn't that woman ever give up?" But this time it was a telemarketing recording, telling me I had won an all-expense paid three-day cruise. All I had to do was call them back and give them a small deposit with my credit card. Well at least, I thought, it wasn't my mortgage company asking when I was going to catch up my payments.

Ever since being laid off by one of Denver's largest database development firms several years ago, unplugging toilets and dodging creditors had become an art with me. My software engineering job had been shipped to Bangalore right after the dot-com bust, and a year after that, my wife sent me packing. Natalie kept the big house in Castle Rock; Fred and I moved to our little weekend cabin in Evergreen. Being over forty, I didn't have a chance of finding another job in my field, so I went into the handyman business. I'm okay with it. Natalie is doing a great job raising our daughter with her new husband, and I finally had the chance to pursue my dream of writing the Great American Novel. Fred, on the other hand, couldn't care less.

***

It was two o'clock in the morning. Just as Bonnie was kissing me on the neck, the phone woke me. The call even woke Fred up. "Damn, don't they have laws about being harassed in the middle of a dream?" I asked. Fred looked at me with his big brown eyes, the way he always does when I say his name, then started wagging his tail. I let the phone ring the mandatory six times before the answering machine picked up.

"Jacob, where are you when I need you?" My mother was frantic. "Please call me. Your father had another attack, and Megan has been arrested for killing Mike. I don't have anyone else who can help. I need you here, Jake. Please call."

Talk about a wakeup call. I pushed the recall button and noticed Mom had called me from her cell phone. She hardly used that phone; she was paranoid of getting brain cancer from it. "Sorry, Mom," I said when she picked up. "I thought it was another telemarketer. Is Dad okay?"

"His lung collapsed again." Her voice sounded a lot weaker than it had on my machine. "They flew him to the hospital in Columbia, and I'm on the way there now. They'll probably stick that tube in his chest this time, and knowing your father, he'll be back on the lake by the end of the week. It's your sister I'm worried about. She'll go crazy in that jail if I don't get her out soon."

"Well that explains the cell phone," I said. "But what is this about Megan killing Mike?"

"Your sister had nothing to do with it," Mom answered in a much louder voice. "He committed suicide."

"Killed himself?" I asked. "It wasn't another overdose was it?"

This time she even woke up Fred, who had gone back to sleep. "You're as bad as that awful deputy. Everyone assumes she did it just because her last two husbands died. Megan wasn't anywhere near him when he killed himself."

"Sorry, Mom. I didn't mean it that way. I know Megan wouldn't hurt a cockroach. I meant to ask how Mike died, but let's change the subject. Who's driving you to the hospital?" My mother never drove after dark; she had the night vision of an earthworm. "Kevin's not driving? Is he?"

"No, he's still out and isn't answering his phone, and I don't know how to text him. Why these kids don't ever want to talk to anyone is beyond me. Why bother having a phone if you can only text with it? Seems to me it's all going backwards. And for your information, Mister Doubting Thomas, Mike killed himself by driving into Truman Lake; he drowned."

"So who's driving you, Mom?"

"Hal. He's such a dear man. When Amy heard about Megan being arrested, she called to ask if there was anything she could do to help. I wish Megan could have met someone as nice as Hal, instead of Mike. Not that I mean to speak badly of the dead, but her life has been horrible since she married him."

"Hal? Amy?" I asked. "Who are they, Mom?"

"Megan's neighbors of course. You met them last time you were here. Didn't you?" Then she said something to Hal I couldn't quite hear.

"I guess I must be getting old-timers. Hal said he doesn't remember meeting you either. In any case, you could learn a lot from Hal. Maybe he could get you on with that pharmaceutical company he works for."

Lately, my mother's thoughts could get sidetracked and never return to the main spur if I let her go on. I didn't bother to remind her about my chances of getting a programming job at my age when all the good jobs had been shipped overseas. "What about Mike, Mom? I can see why they think Megan killed him, but why suicide? How do they know it wasn't an accident?"

"There you go again. How can you say that about your own sister, Jacob?"

It was obvious that Mother wasn't going to tell me how Mike met his maker without dragging out dirty laundry in front of a near stranger, so I needed to cut the conversation short and call someone who could fill me in on the enigma. "Sorry, Mom, take care of Dad, and I'll get there as soon as I can. In the meantime, I can make a few calls. Do you have the number of the sheriff's office by chance?"

"I need you to put up bail for your sister. I told you, Megan will go crazy in that jail. You could fly out first thing in the morning, and Kevin will pick you up at the airport in Kansas City and take you back to Truman."

"I can't fly, Mom; I have to bring Fred. I'll make some calls in the morning then head on out. I should be there by Tuesday morning." I was already talking to a dead phone. Either my mother had hung up without waiting for a reply or she was out of range of a cell tower. Knowing her, she had cut it short before the phone gave her a brain tumor. Not that it really mattered. I knew she would want to know why I couldn't leave at dawn, so I could be there by tomorrow afternoon.

I slept in until after eight the next morning. I could have got up sooner, but I knew, without at least six hours sleep, I would be too tired to drive twelve hours straight. Besides, the trip would cost at least two hundred dollars in my gas guzzling van, and I only had one credit card left that wasn't at its limit. Before Fred and I could leave, I needed to stop by the bank and cash-out my last CD. Megan would have to wait another day as it would be past midnight by the time I got to Truman. I loved my sister, but I knew another day in jail wouldn't drive her crazy. If anything, it was the jailers who would need the shrink. The trip to Missouri would have to wait until the bank opened. In the meantime, I decided to take care of my neighbor's toilet.

"Well aren't you an early-bird," Bonnie said when she came to the door. Her revealing robe didn't catch me off guard this time. I swore she put it on whenever she thought there was an eligible man in the vicinity.

"Morning, Bonnie. Fred and I have to make a trip to Missouri, so I thought I'd better take care of business before I leave."

"Well then, you better let that big boy out of your van. That's a long drive you have ahead of you," she said. I could see the disappointment in her eyes. "When you're ready, just come on in.

I'll put on some coffee and get decent. You know where the bathroom is." I went back to my van, and while I searched for my plunger, I let Fred out to do his thing.

Watching Fred run free made me realize I didn't have it so bad after all. If I still lived in town, my neighbors would be on their phone to animal control before Fred could finish watering their lawns. But Bonnie's nearest neighbor was half a mile away and out of sight. I wondered if Fred would have this kind of freedom in Missouri.

When I returned to the house, the smell of fried bacon had filled the air. I glimpsed Bonnie in the kitchen as I passed on my way to the bathroom. She was at her stove and either didn't hear me or was too busy cooking to look up. I quickly went through the ritual of unplugging a toilet that wasn't stopped up and returned to the kitchen. "Whatever it was must have worked its way through the plumbing already," I said.

She smiled at me, and then went back to her cooking. "Grab yourself a cup of coffee, Jake. The bacon's almost done and then I'll start on the eggs. I'm cooking it just the way you like it. Not too crispy."

I should have known I couldn't escape from Bonnie in less than an hour. And by the time I left the bank, the traffic on Interstate Seventy was bumper-to-bumper. It was past noon before I stopped for gas in Limon and made the call, despite the sign at the pump warning not to use any electronic device while operating the pumps, to the Fremont County sheriff's office,. It was another ten minutes before I got the sheriff on the line. My cell phone started flashing the dreaded low-battery warning when he answered.

I had to wonder just how small of a town Truman was for me to talk directly to the main man. "Your sister will be arraigned this afternoon," he said after I had explained who I was and why I was calling. "I don't advise her meeting Judge Simons without a lawyer. He probably won't set bail unless she has counsel. You also need to call the funeral home. They need to know what to do with the ashes." Then my phone went dead at the same time the pump quit.

It was one of those gas stations that required cash up front before you could start pumping. I had reached the limit of my sixty dollar deposit. I returned the nozzle to the pump and got back in my van. Fred acted like I'd been gone all day. His tail wagging was shaking the entire van. I was afraid he'd break his tail or slobber all over me as I leaned over to plug my cell into the charger.

We were well past the Colorado-Kansas state line when I tried the cell phone again. I could have used it sooner, but Fred might have objected to the charger's cord. It was plugged in right by the air-conditioner vent where he had chosen to lay his head. The phone refused to connect. Evidently, I was too far from a cell tower.

I was now beginning to doubt my wisdom of leaving so soon. I could have been more effective from my cabin in Colorado than in a dead-zone stretch of Interstate Seventy. So much for new millennium technology, I thought. The task of finding Meg a lawyer so she wouldn't have to face the judge alone would have to wait until I got closer to Hays. Fred, in the meantime, started in with his "I've got to go now" whimper. Maybe the rest area up ahead had a real phone.

When I drove into the parking lot in front of the restrooms, there was an old pickup truck, with a still older camper, sitting there; its hood was open. When they saw me pull in, a young couple turned their attention from the truck toward me. He had been putting water in the radiator, and the girl, who couldn't have been more than sixteen, held a baby in her arms. She started toward me before I was even out of my van.

Fred ran for the nearest tree, and he had his leg raised by the time the girl reached the van. "Could you spare a couple dollars for gas, Mister?" she asked.

It was probably another setup. I read somewhere that more and more people found it easier to panhandle than to work. The article said they could make several hundred dollars a day. But then in this economy, who knows. What if the couple really were down on their luck?

Fred was back before I could answer. "Sure," I said, grabbing his collar. "I'll catch you before I leave, after I've put my dog away." I had the hardest time holding Fred back from the baby. Why he thought all babies need a tongue-bath was beyond me.

After Fred left his contribution on the lawn, I put him back in the van and reached for my wallet. Showing a full wallet to strangers isn't the best of ideas, so I removed a five-dollar bill before I walked over to the girl. She was putting the baby in a car seat and trying to wipe tears from her eyes at the same time. The father, or at least I assumed he was the father, was talking to a man down by the restrooms. I put the five dollars back in my pocket as I approached.

"Where you guys headed?" I asked.

"Kansas City," she answered. "Mike's got a friend who works at the airport there and thinks he can get Mike a job fueling the planes. We ain't got nuthin back in Denver, and we can stay with Mike's buddy until he finds a job."

"This won't get you to Kansas City, but it should help with diapers or something," I said, opening my wallet and giving her a couple twenties.

"Thank you, Mister," she said, staring at my wallet. "Are you going to Kansas City too?"

"Not if I can help it. We're headed for Truman down by Lake of the Ozarks. My GPS keeps trying to route us through KC, but I prefer to take the back roads and avoid the big cities."

"I got a sister in Truman. You should take highway seven out of Harrisonville," she said.

"Well, take care of that little cutie. We better get going," I replied, then turned and headed for my van.

"God bless you, Mister," she shouted as we passed their truck on our way out of the rest area. Fred answered for me with a loud bark.

God must have approved. My phone started ringing before we could merge into traffic. "Jacob, where are you?"

"Hi, Mom. How's Dad doing?"

"Your father is going to be fine. He's out of intensive care and resting now. Why didn't you get Megan a lawyer? I thought you said you would help?"

"Sorry, Mom. I couldn't get a signal."

"Then how come I got through if you couldn't get a signal?"

"Mom, I'm not lying, honest." She had me on the defensive already; she must be feeling her old self again.

"Well, the judge postponed the hearing until she could get a lawyer. When do you think you will be in Truman?"

"I'll use my phone to find her a lawyer as soon as I get to Hays. I should be there within an hour."

"You can do that from your phone? How is that possible, Jacob?"

"The web, Mom," I answered. "I can surf the web and then call the lawyer from Hays. I should have enough left on my credit card to pay his retainer, but I may need help with the bail."

"Seems like a big waste, if you ask me. What's wrong with a good old fashioned phone booth and phone book? It's no wonder your credit card is at its limit. I bet you pay a fortune for that stupid smart phone."

My phone cut out before I could comment on my mother's oxymoron. She may have been right about the new technology if not for the fact that phone booths had gone the way of television antennas, which was another one of her peeves.

Less than an hour later, while eating a burger at the McDonald's in Hays, I found a lawyer. Fred wasn't too happy about staying in the van alone, but I wanted to use my laptop and the free wireless internet access to avoid using up my data download limit imposed on my cellphone plan. The lawyer agreed to help as soon as I could come up with his retainer. It was far more than what I had left on my credit card. I was beginning to wonder if Missouri had any decent public defenders.

"Could you accept a deposit with my debit card, Mister Rosenblum?" I asked. "I can give you the balance in cash once I get to Truman."

His attitude seemed to change instantly. "No problem. Cash always works. I'll have my secretary call you back in a few minutes to get your card number. I better get on over to the courthouse before George leaves for lunch," he said.

"George?" I asked.

"The judge. He's an old friend of mine. It'll take some talking, but I should be able to get him to set bail. Lucky for your sister, you called the right lawyer."

Bail, if there was any, would be another hurdle I'd have to jump when I got to Truman. The lawyer's fee would make my wallet look like the week's biggest loser at Weight Watchers.

Fred would have to wait for his lunch a bit longer. I decided to search the web while I waited for Rosenblum's secretary to call me back. I was curious so see if Megan had made the news. The wire services didn't even mention the small town murder, but my search did produce an article on a Springfield, Missouri television web page. I had chosen the keywords of Missouri, and murder. I found the link on the tenth page of my search results. Who would have thought Missouri would have so much homicide. The article was titled "Black Widow Strikes Again." There was even a video clip of an exclusive report.

"Sergeant Bennet, a deputy with the Fremont County Sheriff's office, said he became suspicious when the victim's autopsy showed he had died by carbon monoxide poisoning and not by the accident," said the reporter. Then she had the cameraman cut to the sergeant.

"That and the insurance company," he added. "I did a little detective work and called Mrs. Carver's insurance company. That's when I had the coroner do an autopsy. The adjuster pointed out that Mrs. Carver's two previous husbands had died in auto accidents after overdosing on medication, the last only two years ago, and she had collected a sizeable amount on those policies."

"How much is the current policy?" the reporter asked.

"One million," Bennet replied.

"Almost double the amount she collected from her last husband," the reporter said, and then cut to an interview shot earlier.

"That bitch stole my husband, and now she's gonna pay." The woman being interviewed was still dressed in her bathrobe and standing outside an old mobile home. All she needed to complete my mental picture were curlers in her hair and runny mascara, but, sadly, she had neither. In fact she was a very attractive woman, much better looking than my sister.

I was surprised they didn't bleep her, but I suppose calling someone a female dog isn't considered swearing in the Ozarks. "I tried to tell Mike she was just a no good bitch, and he better watch his back. But he was always in heat himself and couldn't keep his BLEEP in his pants." That time they did bleep her, but it was obvious what they cut. The reporter was probing for more information when I saw the old truck from the rest area pull into the parking lot. I had parked my van in the back lot under some shade trees for Fred. They must not have noticed it.

The couple was met in the lot by one of the McDonald's workers, a woman; the worker had been waiting by an SUV with Colorado plates. That's when I noticed the Kansas plates on the truck. Something didn't ring true. If this couple was from Denver, why did their truck have Kansas plates? And why hadn't I noticed that back at the rest area?

Although I couldn't hear what was going on, it was obvious the McDonald's employee was upset with the couple. The worker took the keys from the girl and was still yelling as she got into the truck and checked on the baby in its car seat.

My concentration on the show outside was interrupted by another employee. "Would you like a refill on your coffee, Sir?"

"Sure," I responded, somewhat in shock. "Is this a new policy or just Kansas hospitality?"

"What do you mean?" she asked.

"I've never been in a fast-food restaurant that waited on its customers with refills," I answered.

"Really? Where are you from?" she asked.

"Colorado. On my way to Missouri. I hope they are this friendly there."

"Shelia's little sister is from Colorado, too. That's them out there. Sorry you had to see that, but her little sister and her boyfriend are a real pain in Shelia's neck. That girl is always late bringing back Shelia's baby, but at least it's free babysitting."

My phone started to ring, and the waitress took it as her cue to go on to the next table. "Hello," I said.

"Mr. Martin?" Without waiting for me to answer, she continued. "Mr. Rosenblum asked me to run your debit card."

I gave the lawyer's secretary the info she needed, and then waited while she made sure it cleared. By the time she was finished with me, it was too late to catch the couple who had conned me at the rest area. They were already leaving the parking lot in their SUV. I grabbed Fred's hamburgers and headed out the door.

By now, Fred's burgers were quite cold, but he ate them in two gulps when I let him out of the van. I barely had time to get out his water bowl before the burgers disappeared. "That will have to hold you for now, Boy. Drink up. We've got a long trip ahead."

But Fred wasn't quite ready to leave. Next to swimming, there is nothing a male Golden Retriever likes to do more than sniff out the markings of another male dog's claim to a tree. He had to circle it three times before declaring it his own. "Come on, Fred. Let's go get your aunt out of jail."

***

I was beat by the time we got to Kansas City. I had given up fighting my GPS to route me through the back roads of Kansas. It acted like they didn't exist. I had been driving for ten hours straight and still had another two hours to go. The drive across eastern Colorado and Kansas must be the most boring five hundred miles in America. Without coffee and radar guns, I would have fallen asleep at the wheel long ago. It had been four hours since I'd heard from my mother or anyone other than a McDonald's voice asking to take my order. I owe them and the Kansas Highway Patrol my life. But now, I was in traffic worse than anything I had seen in Denver since the rebuilding of I-25, and I was lost. Just as I was looking for a place to pull over and check my GPS, the phone rang.

"Hi, Mom," I said.

"How did you know it was me, Jacob?"

"ESP, Mom," I answered without going into the marvels of caller ID.

"Do you always have to be such a smartass?" she asked. Then in a much softer voice she said, "Where are you now?"

"Sorry, Mom," I said for the hundredth time in the last day. I was on I-435, and I missed the exit to Sedalia. "Looks like I'm headed to St. Louis. Don't worry. I'll check my GPS and should be in Truman in a couple hours."

"Then, I take it, you didn't get a lawyer," she questioned.

"Yes, Mother. I got a lawyer. He is supposed to call once he arranged bail. How's Dad by the way? Can I talk to him?"

"He's sleeping now. I'm going to stay in your father's hospital room tonight, so you need to check on Kevin when you get to the house. Make sure he has something to eat when you get there."

"Mom, I didn't drive seven hundred miles to babysit my nephew. I'm sure Kevin can order fast food as well as I can, or has that new tongue piercing stopped him from talking?"

"Don't start in with me about Kevin. You know it's just a stage he's going through. There's a motel next to the hospital. I'll get a room there for a couple of days until your father is well enough to go home. Please take care of your nephew."

After checking a map, since my GPS couldn't tell me where I was, I saw I had missed the turnoff for US 71 and was going east on I-435. I had an impulse to continue on to I-70 towards Columbia and check in on my father, but then my mother would be furious. I got off at the next exit and went back in search of the wagon path my GPS couldn't find.

It was dark by the time I finally found US 71 and headed toward Harrisonville. From there, I would take Highway Seven on into Clinton and then to Truman. Ironically, it was the route the con artist had suggested back at the rest area.

It was after ten when we got to Clinton; both Fred and I needed to relieve ourselves. Luck was with us when I turned east toward Truman and spotted the golden arches. It was too late to go inside, and there wasn't any grass in the parking lot. I would have to go through the drive-up and find somewhere else to let Fred out. I ordered a couple burgers and a coffee then headed out of town in search of a place to pull over. I found a cemetery a couple blocks down the road. Superstitious people would have been reluctant to stop at a cemetery this late at night, but it looked like the only place to stop before the highway narrowed to shoulder-less two lanes.

"Hungry, Boy," I asked, tossing him one of the burgers. He ate his sandwich before I could even get mine out of the wrapper. "Okay, you can have this one too."

Fred finished the second burger then decided to wash it down, spilling more water than he actually drank. I let him take his potty break at a nearby tree. I suppose I could have done the same had it been anywhere but a cemetery. My break would have to wait. I put Fred in the van and rechecked the map. "Just another thirty miles, Freddie boy. Then another fifteen or so to Megan's, and we can both get some sleep."

Soon after leaving Clinton, Highway Seven turned from a pleasant drive on a four-lane divided-highway to a stomach-wrenching two-lane roller coaster. I now knew why there was a cemetery at the edge of town; this road was a killer. Headlights tried to blind me at almost every rise in the road, and more than once, an oncoming car or truck almost side swiped me. However, the road was nothing compared to the shoulder – there wasn't any. In place of shoulders, the road builders had opted for deep ditches to drain away the water. They thought, I presumed, any driver who was stupid enough to try and pull off the road deserved to be washed away. How Fred managed to sleep through it all is anybody's guess.

I knew enough about Missouri back roads to watch for deer after the sun goes down. Earlier, just before sunset, and before Fred fell to sleep, the deer had started to appear at the side of the road. I would have missed them if Fred hadn't started to bark. At half the size of Rocky Mountain mule deer, he must have thought they were big dogs.

Except for the lights of a car coming up behind me, I was driving in total darkness. The time right after sunset, before the stars and moon make their appearance, is the darkest and spookiest time of night. I should have slowed down, but I was in a hurry to get off the road. Then my cell phone rang; it couldn't have happened at a worse time. The car in my rear-view mirror was coming up fast.

"Hello?" I asked. It was too dark to see the caller ID.

"What? No ESP?" she replied.

"Not tonight, Mom. What's up? Is it Dad?"

"No, Jacob. I called to tell you not to worry about your nephew. Kevin went on to his friend's house when you didn't show up."

"Give me a break, Mom. I'm trying my best. I got lost up by Independence and now its pitch black with deer jumping out all over, and I've got some crazy idiot trying to pass me on a hill."

"Anyway, here's Taylor's address," she said as though she never heard my plea for mercy. "You'll have to go there to get the key,"

"Can you text me the address, Mom?"

"Jacob, you know I don't know how to do that. Let me give you the address and number. Do you have something to write on?"

"Mom, are you trying to kill me? I'm on a road that Evil Kinevil wouldn't try. And there is some nut behind me who is trying to run me off the road. What is it with these Missouri drivers anyway. I'll call you when I get to town. It's only another ten miles or so."

I hung up just in time to see the deer. "Shit," I exclaimed, turning the wheel hard left to avoid the creature. That's when the jerk behind me decided to pass and hit the rear of my van. The impact sent me into a spin toward the other side of the road. My van flew over the ditch and was headed toward a large tree. Then everything went totally dark.

CHAPTER 2

"Am I in heaven?" I asked the angel standing over me when I woke. I had to be in heaven. She was the prettiest woman I had ever seen who wasn't in a magazine or on television. She had midnight-black hair and beautiful violet-blue eyes. All she needed to complete the picture was a pair of wings. But her ID badge confirmed she was human; you can't photograph angels.

"More like purgatory. You've been in an accident," she said, quickly glancing at a monitor to my right. "The doctor left orders to call him when you woke up. I'll be right back."

My angel returned within minutes alongside a guy in a ponytail. I assumed he was an orderly. "Mr. Martin, I'm Doctor Woodward. You have no idea how lucky you are to be alive. Do you remember what happened?"

By now I was fully awake and realized what had happened to me. "How about Fred? Is he okay?" I asked.

"Fred? Who's Fred?" he asked.

"My dog. Do you know where he is?"

My angelic nurse spoke up when she saw the blank look on the doctor's face. "I heard something about the sheriff taking him to the vet in Truman. I'll give the office a call and see how he's doing."

Ponytail cut in before I could thank my angel. "Do you remember anything about the accident?"

"Kind of," I replied, "One minute I'm enjoying the roller coaster ride while talking to my mother, and the next thing I know a deer is trying to mate with my van, all while some idiot is trying to pass me. I almost hit the poor thing."

"Your mother? Was she in the van with you?" My angel asked. I could hear the worried tone in her voice. I didn't think angels were supposed to worry.

"No. On the phone, I meant. I was talking to my mother on the cell just before the accident. Just Fred and I were in the van. God, I hope he's okay. Please let me know as soon as you hear something from the vet."

"There was another car involved?" It was the doctor again. I was starting to wonder if he was some kind of cop in disguise. He seemed more concerned with the details of the accident than my vitals.

"The jerk clipped me when he tried to pass. That's what caused me to run off the road."

"I'm sure Sergeant Bennet would like to hear about the other car. People like that shouldn't be allowed to drive. Well, In the meantime, you need to get some rest," he said. "You had a mild concussion. I'd like to keep you overnight. You should be out of here in the morning."

They moved me out of intensive care and into a room with three other patients. It seems billing had already checked on my insurance. My online discount policy wouldn't pay for much more than a barracks and some aspirin. I had been awake for some time when my angel appeared early next morning. "How are you feeling this morning?" she asked while closing the privacy curtain around my bed.

"Got a splitting headache, but I'll live. Did you talk to the vet?"

She had moved to the other side of my bed to check my urine bag. "Don't worry. He was a little stiff at first, but he is doing great now. He perks up and starts wagging his tail every time he hears a man's voice. He must think it's yours." She reached under the thin blanket and began adjusting my catheter. "Would you rather I call an orderly to do this?" she asked, too late.

"No. But now I think we have to get married," I laughed.

She replaced the blanket and smiled at me. "Do you feel up to any visitors yet, or do you need more rest?"

"Visitors?"

"I believe he said he's your nephew."

"Kevin?" I asked.

"Uh huh. His earrings remind me of my own son."

Her remark about earrings didn't surprise me. Every generation seemed to have its way of rebelling. "Sure," I said. "Send him in." I had not seen Kevin since he went to live with his father when he was eight or nine. He'd been in and out of trouble since then, and when he got busted at twelve with marijuana, his father quickly sent him back to Megan.

It wasn't five minutes later when the curtain slid open again. It must have been Kevin, but I didn't recognize him. "Uncle Martin?" he asked.

I stared at him thinking, *who is this kid?* Not only did he have holes in his ears the size of quarters, he had every conceivable loose piece of skin on his face pierced and ringed. I felt like grabbing the ring in his nose and pulling as hard as I could. Then I heard my mother's voice in my head, telling me not to judge a book by its cover.

"How you doing, Uncle Martin?"

"That sounds like a line from an old TV show. Call me Jake, okay? Sorry if I didn't recognize you. Maybe it's the Mohawk. I don't think I ever saw a Mohican with red and purple hair."

"Cool, huh. You should see how it freaks out all these old farts," he answered.

"Is your grandmother here, Kevin?"

"Na. Just me, Uncle Martin. Grandma's at the reception with Mom and Grandpa. They sent me to fetch you."

"Your mother is out of jail? And what do you mean the reception?" I felt like Woody Allen in *Bananas*. Life, it seemed, had gone on without me and passed me by.

"Yeah. That fancy lawyer you hired got them to drop all the charges," he said. "Mom didn't waste any time putting Mike's urn in the ground, and now all the old people in town are over at grandma's eating her food."

Megan had told me Kevin never took to Mike so his attitude toward his deceased step-father didn't surprise me. "Damn. So much has happened in the last day. How is your grandfather doing?"

"He's cool."

"What's that supposed to mean, Kevin?"

We were interrupted before Kevin could answer. It was my doctor. "You look a lot better than the last time I saw you. How are you feeling this morning?"

"Great," I lied, hoping for a quick release from the hospital. My head was throbbing. "This is my nephew, Kevin. He's here to take me home."

"You're a lucky man, Mr. Martin. No broken bones or lingering concussion. How's your leg? Do you think you can walk on it?"

"Ready for the Boston marathon," I answered, "if you let me out of here."

"Okay then. I would like to do another CT scan in a couple of weeks, but otherwise, I see no reason not to let your nephew take you home."

My wallet and cell phone were not in my room, so I stopped off at admissions on the way out. They had my phone, but they had no idea about my wallet. It must have been their way of ensuring I didn't get away without the requisite paperwork, so they could bill me for services that my insurance company didn't pay. "That doesn't make any sense," I told the clerk who checked me out. "How did you know what insurance I have? You must have seen my insurance card, and my card was in my wallet."

The girl just looked at me like I had asked a Daily Double *Jeopardy* question. She was preoccupied with her desktop printer; it had jammed in the middle of printing my pardon. She was saved from answering when her supervisor showed up. "I believe the sheriff has your wallet, Mr. Martin. He asked me to tell you he would like to see you as soon as you are released." Then without another word to me, she turned toward the clerk. "Sue, switch over to the backup printer until someone can fix yours." And she was gone as quickly as she had appeared.

The clerk kept Kevin busy gawking at her until she got up to retrieve the printout. She was young – about his age – with a gold stud in her nose. "I gotta go out and have a smoke, Uncle Martin," he said after she disappeared into the back room.

I started to watch my nephew light up in the no-smoking area right outside the entrance lobby when I saw my nurse again. She was arguing with an older man; he had parked at the entrance to pick her up. I couldn't hear what they were saying, but he seemed to be upset. He slammed the passenger door before she barely had settled into the SUV. It was a very expensive Mercedes; the kind that would cost me a year's salary when I had been gainfully employed.

"Sorry it took so long, Mister Martin," said Sue, the admissions clerk. She had returned with my release form while I had been watching the show outside.

"No problem," I said and folded the printout, so it would fit in my shirt pocket. Then I smiled at her, trying not to stare at her nose, and left to join Kevin.

"Wonder what that's all about?" I asked my nephew.

He took a final drag on his cigarette before flicking it on the ground, despite the several sand-filled cigarette cans behind him. It was clearly marked with the icon of a crossed-out circle and a smoking cigarette. "That's my friend Taylor's dad. She must be his mom," he answered, starting off toward the parking lot.

"You know her?" I asked, trying to keep up.

"Na. Not 'till now. Taylor said she was a nurse, but I never seen her before. She's never home when Taylor and me hang at his place. But his dad's really cool." I barely heard him. He was several yards ahead of me when he stopped at a beat-up junker parked in a handicap spot close to the entrance.

We had to drive the thirty-some miles from Clinton to Truman in Kevin's '92 Ford Tempo. He said how my van was not going anywhere but the scrap heap, so he would be my wheels as long as I needed. I knew I would be looking elsewhere for a car, or I had to at least learn to ride a bicycle again, assuming we made it to Meg's house. He sped along the same road that had made me a god-fearing man.

The Tempo's air conditioning was blowing hot air. Nothing happened when I pressed the window's down-button. "Sorry Uncle Martin, that button don't work. I gotta lower it for you."

The July air hit my face, hot and humid, with an occasional bug or two, but it felt great. The temperature in the car had risen to well over one hundred.

"Did Mike have a nice service?" I asked, catching a breath of the moist air blowing into the car.

"I guess. Me and Grandpa missed most of it. He started hacking, so I got elected to take him out back."

It sounded like my father was back to smoking his two packs a day. "Maybe the tar from the cigarettes will patch the hole in his lung," I said.

Kevin must have missed out on the family's sarcasm gene. He gave me a blank look then turned his attention back to his driving, just before nearly rear-ending a slower car in front of him. After giving the other driver a one-finger salute in his rear-view mirror, he turned toward me again. "What you going to tell the cops, Uncle Martin?"

"Haven't given it much thought, Kevin. If it wasn't for my wallet, I'd make them wait. I really want to check on Fred first, but I'll need money to pay his bill. And please. I'm not a Martian – call me Jake."

"Huh." he said, his expression going blank again. Either I was showing my age by referring to the old sixties television show, *My Favorite Martian*, or my nephew had some kind of synaptic short circuit.

Except for asking Kevin to slow down every few minutes, we didn't talk much the rest of the trip. He was too busy practicing his stockcar skills, and I was trying to second-guess the sheriff. I couldn't imagine why he wanted to see me. We then passed the accident scene, and I almost freaked out. "Pull over, Kevin!" I yelled.

"Here? There ain't no friggin place to pull over!"

"Then slow down for Christ sake. Okay, pull over by that bridge." There was a scenic turnout right before the bridge crossed the lake. Kevin and I got out of the Tempo and started following some tire tracks back to where my van had jumped the ditch. The tow truck must have come this way to get my van. I hobbled after my nephew who was yards ahead of me. Then I saw tracks leading toward a big oak tree, and another set that hadn't been so lucky. I slid down the bank to where my van had been stopped by the tree, only yards from the edge of a steep bluff. From there it was straight down to the water. The other tire tracks went right up to the edge and disappeared.

"Wow, this is the same place Mike ate his lunch," Kevin said when I caught up with him. "Kind of weird, huh."

"Very weird. I wonder what the odds are that I almost dined here too."

He turned away from the water and looked at me blankly. Then the light went on. "Oh, I get it, Uncle Martin. You meant ate your lunch, too."

"Something like that," I answered while looking past him, toward the road. Several cars had gone by in the time it took us to reach the accident scene, and now one of them was slowing down to watch us. I waved at him even though I hadn't a clue who he was. The driver waved back then sped up.

"What's weird, Kevin, are those tracks by the road."

"Think they were Mike's, Uncle Martin?"

"No. Mike's tracks go straight to the water. Those tracks parallel the road."

"Must have been the ambulance," he said.

Or the people who nearly killed me, I thought and started back toward the Tempo.

CHAPTER 3

Kevin stopped the Tempo at a bank a block from the county jail. He didn't really park the car, nor did he turn off his motor. The bank's thermometer read ninety-nine – and that was in the shade. Compared to the sauna Kevin called a car, it felt great when I stepped out on the sidewalk. "I ain't going nowhere near that jailhouse," Kevin said, still sitting in the car. "You can call my cell when you need me." And then he took off without giving me his cellphone number.

The jail wasn't exactly out of Mayberry, but it was close. The jail and sheriff's office was housed in an old, two-story, brick building right across from the town square, one of those old town squares with a hundred-year-old courthouse, surrounded by all the local businesses. But most of those businesses were gone – run out of town by a new SuperMart in a newer part of town. Now the stores were either boarded up or selling junk they called antiques.

When I entered the building, I half expected to see either Andy or Barney sitting at a big oak desk. But the inside was as modern as any police station I've ever seen. Not that I've been in a lot of police stations, but I've seen my share on television. I went up to the glass window separating the good citizens of Truman from their protectors. "Hi, my name is Jake Martin. Is Sergeant Bennet in?" I asked a pretty bleached-blond clerk, who sat behind the glass.

She sized me up through the window, and then spoke: "He's busy right now. Can I help you?"

"The sergeant left me a message at the hospital to come in and see him. I was in an accident the day before yesterday. I think he has my wallet."

"Can I see some identification, please?" she asked without the slightest sign of how absurd her question was.

"It's in my wallet," I answered. "That's why I'm here. Driver's license, credit cards, and all my money are in my wallet."

"I can't let you in without any ID," she said, reaching for a phone on her desk. "But if you want to wait, I'll let him know you're here."

She waited for me to take a seat at a bench across from her window before speaking into the receiver. I assumed whatever she had to say to the sergeant was not meant for my ears. The bench was either from a church remodel, or it was intended to put the fear of God in me. The back was straight and hard – just like the pews that used to keep me awake during Sunday service. It didn't work.

"Can I help you?" I must have dozed off while waiting. I didn't hear or see the deputy approach.

"I need to see Sergeant Bennet," I replied, noting the weird resemblance to Don Knotts.

"I'm Sergeant Bennet," he said, extending a hand. "How are you feeling?"

"A little sore and a killer headache. Thanks for asking," I said, returning the handshake.

"Heard you almost met your maker. Lucky you had your seat belt on. I hate to tell you how many tickets I give out around here to people who won't wear them. We could use you for a poster child. Speaking metaphorically, that is. I can see you're not a child."

'Metaphorically?' Now there was a word I didn't expect to hear in these parts. Be careful what I say, I thought, this guy is no Barney Fife.

He led me to a seat by an empty desk, and he took the desk chair. There were three other desks crammed into the old room, and they were empty. "I was the officer at your accident," he said, motioning for me to sit. "I just need to ask you a few questions so I can finish my report."

The chair was as hard as the pew in the waiting room. It was one of those old, straight-back office chairs with a padded seat – except the seat on this chair was long gone, leaving only a few tacks left to assure a thorough interrogation. "They tell me at the hospital that you rescued my dog. I can't tell you how much I appreciate that."

"No problem. I had a Golden myself when I was a kid. Best dogs in the world," he smiled. It was the first sign that he might be human after all. "I would have taken him home until you could pick him up. But it looked like he might have been hurt, so I dropped him off at the vet's. Doctor said it's just a few bruises, and he should recover in a couple days."

"I still can't thank you enough, Sergeant. The old guy means a lot to me."

"By the way, you might want this back," he said as he opened his desk drawer and removed my wallet. "I took it from the scene of your accident, so I could identify you. It was empty except for a couple credit cards and your driver's license. You should be able to pay Doctor Alton with one of those."

I could see my money had been removed even before I picked it up. "I had over a thousand in cash, Sergeant. It looks like I've been robbed."

"That's a lot of money to be carrying around. Only people I know with that much cash are drug dealers and pimps." He paused long enough to study my reaction. It made me very uncomfortable. He had piercing-blue eyes that seemed to be reading my mind.

"I cashed in a CD before leaving Colorado."

"Strange they didn't take everything. Are all your credit cards there?"

One of my credit cards was missing. Ironically, it was a card I couldn't use because I had maxed out my credit limit on it. "It looks like my VISA card is missing."

The sergeant opened a filing drawer in his desk and pulled out a piece of paper. "I'm supposed to do this on the computer, but that's not why I asked you to come in. You can fill this out and give it to the girl at the front desk when you have time, and if I was you, I'd cancel that card." Then he slid the form across his uncluttered desk without taking his eyes off me. I would never be able to do that at my desk back home. I usually had every square inch covered with notes, bills, or various papers. I envied this guy's tidiness. It was either a sign of organization or a person with something to hide.

I glanced at the form he gave me. It was an accident report with boxes for all the information he must have already had in his computer. "Don't you already have this information in your report?" I asked.

"More or less. But we need a signature to make it official. What we don't have are the details of the accident. How did you manage to wreck your van at that particular spot in the road? We know you weren't drinking, and there's no skid marks. Did you pull over at that spot to take a leak or something?"

"No. I swerved to avoid a deer. He jumped right in front of me, and the jerk behind me decided to pass at the same time. I missed the deer, but the passing car clipped the back of my van and sent me over the ditch."

Bennet's computer beeped at him, and he glanced at his monitor. "Quite a coincidence when you think about it," he said while typing something on his keyboard. "You went off the road at almost the same spot as your brother-in-law. Lucky you hit that tree. Your sister's husband wasn't as fortunate."

I thought I saw a gleam in his eyes when he turned back toward me. "Tell me about the car that clipped your rear? Did you happen to notice the make or model?"

"No. It was too dark. You don't think it was the driver of the other car that robbed me, do you?"

"It wouldn't be the first time someone took advantage of an accident. It would help if you could describe the other vehicle. At the least, they committed a felony by leaving the scene of an accident." He was staring into my head again. He must have been with the Gestapo in a previous life. "Unless, of course, there never was another vehicle involved, and the cash in your wallet never existed."

His tone put me on the defensive again. "Call my bank if you don't believe me, Sergeant. They can verify that I cashed out a CD before I left Colorado."

He smiled the grin of a hunter with a big buck in his cross hairs. "I don't believe in coincidence, so I ran you through the system. You and your sister have quite a history of collecting from insurance companies. Two total wrecks in less than a year. You want to know what I think really happened." His voice had risen a few decibels, causing the clerk in the adjoining room to poke her head through the open door.

"I think your sister had you stop at the scene where she dumped her husband's body, maybe to retrieve some incriminating evidence. You must have lost control of your van trying to jump the ditch and crashed into the tree. Can we just cut to the chase and tell me what you were looking for, Mr. Martin?"

"This is crazy, Sergeant. Those wrecks were my ex-wife's. She's a terrible driver. And I had no idea that was where Mike went off the road. Honest."

Bennet was standing now. "And you still believe in the Tooth Fairy and Santa Claus, right?"

"Do I need a lawyer, Sergeant?"

"Okay, you win," he said as he sat back down. "I don't need your lawyer to make me look a fool to the DA again, but I promise, I will find out what is going on with you and your sister."

I had heard of the good-cop/bad-cop routine before, nearly every cop show had it. This was the first time I'd seen it played out by a single cop. I owed the man dearly for saving Fred from the local SPCA (which I assumed was a redneck with a twelve gauge), but I knew I better get out of Dodge ASAP before Bennet's evil twin found a way to hang me.

When I hit the street, the hot wet-air nearly floored me. There was no chance the perspiration from my interrogation would be drying out anytime soon. I looked around to see if Kevin had come back to give me a ride. It must have occurred to him by now that I had no idea what his cell number was. He was nowhere in sight, but I saw a bench in the town square under a big shady tree. It would do while I thought about what to do next. My cell started ringing the minute I sat down on the bench. The caller ID said Carver M.

"Megan! God, it's good to hear from you. How are you?"

"Hi, Porky, where are you?" she asked.

I hated that nickname. Only Megan called me Porky. It was a name she had given me because I stuttered all the time as I was learning to talk. How could I help but stutter? She never let me finish a sentence.

"Sitting under a tree in the town square, contemplating the ironies of life," I answered.

"What are you doing there?"

"Long story, Sis. I'll tell you when I get to Mom's, but first I need a ride to Doctor Alton's office. They took Fred there when I had my accident. Do you know where that's at?"

"Only one vet in this town," she said. "Meet us at the Rusted Kettle for lunch, and we can get Fred on the way home."

"Didn't you have enough to eat at Mike's reception? And how do I get to this Rusted Kettle?"

"Mom's neighbors catered the reception, and no one could eat the food. Everything was either pickled or sour. It was horrible.

The Kettle is on Main Street, right down the street from the square. We'll see you there in five minutes."

The 'us' turned out to be the whole family, sans Kevin. The Rusted Kettle was a busy little place, two blocks away, well within walking distance, even for an invalid. When I got there, everyone was just getting out of my father's van. After the obligatory hugs and cheek pecking, we all entered the restaurant.

We were greeted by a middle-aged waitress who reminded me of Oktoberfest. She had her hair in pigtails that fell half way down her back and were tied off with red and white ribbons. She wore a name tag on her tight fitting vest, proclaiming her name was Linda. I nearly missed the name because of the way the vest pushed up on her ample breasts. "Hi, Meg. We were just talking about you," she said, showing us to a long table in the middle of the room.

Father drove his scooter to the end of the table while the rest of us sat down. He was in the middle of the aisle, causing our waitress to nearly pop out of her bra as she squeezed around him to hand us our menus.

Megan didn't take her menu. "Oh?" she asked, looking straight at Linda.

"Nothing bad, I assure you," Linda added with a nervous smile, still holding the menu in midair. "Sally said you're the talk of the town the way your lawyer finally put that DA in her place. That DA has been making everyone's life miserable ever since they hired her."

Megan at last accepted the one-page, plastic-coated menu. "You can thank my little brother for that. He's the one who found me a lawyer." she answered.

Linda forced a smile, and then turned toward me. "And what's your name, Handsome."

"Jake, this is Linda Bukowski," Megan said before I could open my mouth. "She knew Mike since they were kids."

Father started coughing and rolled his eyes at our mother. "I'll have the special if you girls ever stop yakking."

Like most Mom-and-Pop restaurants, the daily specials were written on a whiteboard above the cash register. But unlike most, where the daily specials were written in all capital letters by either a first-grader or someone with advanced arthritis, this was written in beautiful cursive in mixed case lettering. The curvature of the letter m made me think of our waitress, and I wondered if she was married. I really needed to get my hormones under control. Lately, every time I saw a good looking woman, my mind would start to wander.

"How about you, big boy?" someone was asking. It seems everyone had ordered while I was playing the old Charlie Pride song of "Daydreaming of Night Things in the Middle of the Afternoon" in my head.

"Sure, I'll have the special," I answered, feeling like a kid who was just caught looking at his first Playboy magazine.

Father brought me up to date on all the events of the last twenty-four hours. The crowd in the restaurant, it seemed, had lost interest in us when there was no new gossip to be heard, and went back to their own conversations. "You couldn't have found a better lawyer, Jake," he said, lighting a cigarette without asking if anyone cared.

"Simons, he's the judge around here, bought the argument that Mike's suicide note was real, and the young DA was too eager to make a name for herself."

I tried to dodge the cloud coming my way by waving the smoke from my face. "Suicide note?" I asked.

Megan spoke when our father started coughing again. "Looks like someone needs to bring you up to date," she said, fanning the smoke back into my face so she wouldn't have to breathe it. "The autopsy showed Mike had high levels of carbon monoxide in his body. Bennet had jumped to the conclusion that I had slipped Mike something to knock him out, and then put him in the garage with the car running. He said that I must have realized the insurance wouldn't pay off on a suicide, so I faked Mike's accident."

"But if there was a suicide note, why would they suspect you?" I asked.

Megan paused long enough to take a drink of her coffee. It was our mother's chance to add her two-cents. "Because it was written by a woman." Mom crossed her arms and didn't try to make it four-cents.

When Megan saw Mother had no more to add, she continued. "Bennet thought I wrote it to cover my ass after the coroner said Mike was dead long before he hit the water. Mr. Rosenblum got the judge to throw the note out as evidence after he found out the sheriff never did a handwriting analysis to see if it was real."

I started to ask about the note when Father's hacking got worse.

"Daddy, are you okay?" Megan asked.

My mother spoke for him. "Take your father out for some fresh air, Jacob. Can't you see there's too much smoke in here?"

Megan followed us outside, leaving our mother in the restaurant. "Do you need your oxygen, Daddy?" she asked. "Jake, would you get his tank from the van, please?"

Several people had stopped to watch the commotion. Our mother must have noticed from her seat because she joined us before I could fetch the oxygen tank. "Jacob, would you mind going back to pay the bill? We need to get your father in the van before the whole town sees us."

Father spoke before I could tell anyone about my empty wallet. "Jesus H Christ. I'm not dying. I just had something caught in my throat. Here, Jake, take this. I heard about your wallet, so consider this a loan until you get back on your feet. And don't forget to leave that cutie a big tip."

When I took the bills he handed me, Mother gave me a look to kill, so I tried to give them back. "Thanks, Dad. But I can pay with my credit card." He refused to take the money back, so I put it in my pocket. I could see the disgust on my mother's face, but ignored it and went back to settle the bill.

After I had paid the bill and went back outside, I was surprised to see Kevin's Tempo at the curb, waiting for me. My mother and father were nowhere in sight, and then I noticed Meg behind the wheel. "Hop in, Porky," she said. "What took you so long in there?"

I limped over to the passenger door and reached inside the window to open it. "I decided to pay with my credit card and hold on to the money Father gave me. Linda accidently ran my card twice, and I had to wait for the manager to fix it. How'd you end up with Kevin's car?" I said while pretending to buckle up. Like the door and the window, Kevin's seat belt didn't work either.

Megan forced a smile. "Sure, Porky. Did you get a date while you were at it, too?" Then she pulled away from the curb without looking for oncoming traffic.

"I thought you had a new Jeep," I answered while tying my belt in a knot.

Her smile faded to a frown. "Kevin came by while you were dally-gagging with Linda. He needed gas money, which I didn't have. Mom and Daddy already left, not that I dared to ask after the looks she gave you, so we traded cars."

I could sense I needed to change the subject before I felt obliged to split the loan with her. "How far to the vet?" I asked.

"About a mile down the street, but it's going to be all day if that fool doesn't get out of my way." She was evidently upset that the driver in front was going at the posted speed limit.

"It does get a little warm in here without the wind. I can't tell you how happy I'll be to get Fred and be on my way back to the mountains."

She seemed to forget she was behind the wheel of a moving vehicle and turned toward me. "Are you leaving?" She didn't see the brake lights in front of us.

"Megan!" I shouted. "He's stopping!"

She slammed on the brakes and swerved toward the curb, just in time to avoid hitting the other car. "Well, at least the brakes work," she said, grinning. The car in front of us swerved too, but for a different reason. There was a turtle crossing in front of him.

Megan didn't seem the least upset and waited for the turtle to cross the street before pulling out again. "First a deer, and now a turtle," I said. "What's next? A surfeit of skunks?"

She took her eyes off the road to look at me. "A what?"

"A group of skunks is called a surfeit. Please watch where you're going, Megan."

"Whatever, Mister College graduate. Don't you want to go in and get your dog?" she asked as she pulled up to a two-story century-old house that had been converted into an animal hospital.

I could hear Fred barking in the back-room kennels when we entered the building. When I walked in, the girl at the front desk lit up with a big smile. "You must be Jacob Martin," she said.

I had not called ahead, so I was surprised she knew who I was. Just when I was beginning to think her powers of clairvoyance where up there with Nostradamus, she turned to my sister. "Hi, Meg. Sorry to hear about Mike. We'll all miss him."

"Thanks, Katelyn, how's your mom doing?"

Luckily I didn't have to listen to the girls' chit-chat for too long. A middle-aged man, perhaps ten years older than me, came into the room with my best friend. He could barely restrain Fred. "Mr. Martin?" he asked.

Not another psychic, I thought. "How'd you know?" I asked.

"I'm Doctor Miller," he said without offering his hand. It took both of them to hold Fred back. "Your dog has barely moved since the sheriff brought him in. Five minutes ago, he raised his head like he hears something. First it was tail wagging, and then the barking. I swear these animals have a sixth sense." And then he let Fred loose.

When I bent down to hug him, Fred stood on his hind legs and tried to put his paws on my shoulder, so he could lick me to death. "Whoa, boy. Are you happy to see me, big Fella?" I asked before falling flat on my back.

"And to think I was starting to worry about him," the vet said. "Looks like he just needed his dad."

Megan and Katelyn stopped talking to watch the commotion, and then they both broke out laughing.

I managed to push Fred away from my face and get off the floor. "Anything broken, Doctor?"

"No. Just a few bruises. He should be his old self in a few more days. No need for a follow up unless he passes blood."

I was a little surprised when Doctor Miller gave me some free pain pills, and even more surprised when I paid the bill. The total bill, including two days board, was only one hundred dollars. And Katelyn only ran my card once.

Although the bill had been a fraction of what it would have been in Denver, I had decided to check my credit-card balance with my smart phone after we left the vet's. That turned out to be impossible when Megan slowed down at an intersection long enough to glance my way. "I wish you'd reconsider leaving so soon, Porky," she said, just before she stomped on the throttle to cross the intersection, right before a car on the cross-street could pass. I tried to remember the words to the Hail Mary as the other car kept on coming without slowing down.

"What an asshole," I said after we cleared the intersection by inches. "I think he tried to hit us."

"How are you going to get home anyway? Have you forgotten you totaled your car?" she asked, oblivious to our near-fatal wreck. "They won't let you on an airplane or a bus with a dog."

"My insurance should let me rent a car until they pay off my van," I answered, checking the knot on my seat belt. I had tried it that way to keep the warning buzzer from going off. The buzzer seemed to be the only thing in Kevin's car that worked as it should.

She glanced at the belt for a second then put her eyes back on the road. "Speaking of insurance, do you think Ira will take my case now that I'm no longer considered a black widow?"

"Ira?" I asked a little confused. "Oh. The lawyer. No, Meg. And I doubt that your insurance will pay a penny either way. Suicide or murder, either one is all they need to stop payment." I said while playing with the passenger air-vent. Because the rear windows were held in place with duct tape and couldn't be opened, I tried to direct the vent toward Fred, who was panting like a rabid hound

"Not if he was murdered by someone else," she said. "And I know how to find that someone, but I need your help to catch him, Jake."

"Jake? What happened to Porky? You wouldn't be buttering me up? Would you?"

Her cell phone started playing a punk-rock tune. "It's Kevin," she said without looking at the caller ID. "He programmed it for me to play that when he calls."

Kevin must have sent her a text message; I could see Megan trying to read the screen while passing a slower car in front of us. "He's spending the night at Taylor's," she said. "I can't understand why he just doesn't call instead of texting all the time."

I held back on asking about her Jeep. I knew from experience that she would defend him to the end if I said anything critical. "You were about to tell me how to find Mike's murderer?"

"Well, it's just a theory. That's why I need my smart brother. You know all about computers, so I thought you might break into his and get the goods on him."

"Who, Meg? Get the goods on who?"

"Don't you mean whom, Mister Writer?" she asked, while fixing her mascara in the visor mirror, without slowing down for a yellow light. The hot air blowing in from the window had made the mascara start to melt.

I glanced over at her to see if she showed any sign of seeing the light. "I stand corrected, Miss Grammar." There was no recognition in her face that she just broke the law, but I did notice she had aged considerably since I'd seen her. Although she was nearly three years older than me, she looked a lot older. As she had since high school, she was still dying her hair blond. I assumed at forty-eight that the red hair she had been so ashamed of was gray by now. She had gained a few pounds since the last time I saw her, and her eyes were not quite as blue as I remembered. But most disturbing was the loss of girlish innocence she used to exude. All the makeup in the Ozarks wouldn't bring that back.

Fred was still trying to get some air, so he stuck his head out the driver's window, knocking Megan's mascara brush out of her hand. Then he drooled over her when the air hit his face. I couldn't help but break out in laughter. "I'm sorry, Megan," I said, trying to regain my composure. "He just needed some air is all."

Megan looked at herself in the mirror. The streaks on her face left her looking like a clown with war paint. Then she too began to laugh. "Now I'll never find another husband," she giggled. "Not unless he's blind."

Fred must not have thought it was so funny, and he withdrew to the back seat. "Aren't you going to apologize to your aunt, Freddie?" I asked. Then for some reason, we started to really crack up.

We were headed down Missouri Seven by the time we regained our senses. I think we both realized it had been a pressure valve type of release more than anything else that had made us laugh. "You were about to tell me who killed Mike," I reminded my sister.

"Mike left me with more than a worthless insurance policy. He had a fortune in gold coins, and I need you to help me get them back and put the bastard who killed him in the gas chamber."

"Oh?" I answered, not bothering to tell her the gas chamber was no longer in use.

Then she told me a story right out of a Louis Lamour novel.

CHAPTER 4

Every so often, I could see patches of the lake through the thick trees and brush. I was tempted to ask Megan to stop and let Fred out of the car, but as usual, there was no place to pull over. "I'm not sure how to begin," Megan said. "Everything was great when we moved here. I didn't want to move out here in the middle of nowhere, but Mike begged me to just come out and look. Once I saw the house, and the ridiculous low price they were asking, I agreed and gave him the money for the down payment."

"I always wondered why you left Colorado," I said. "But I will be eternally grateful that Mom followed you here. It must have been hell having her live with you until Dad found a place in town."

"Tell me about it. Mike and Mom were at each other's throat every day for months. If he hadn't been so busy losing all my money, he probably would have left me because of her. I already knew about Mike's business failure. He had asked me more than once to borrow money that I didn't have."

She turned down a back road that was paved better than the highway. There was a sign every hundred yards warning intruders that the area was off limits to outsiders and was patrolled by armed-guards. The association was either paranoid, or this place had some pretty wealthy residents. "Mike was a dreamer and a loser," she continued without slowing down, despite the fifteen-mile-per-hour speed limit. "He had gone into a dock-building business with an old highschool friend by the name of Bill Atkins. They built great docks, but neither one of them had any business sense. They were losing money right and left. They would bid a job only to see the price of steel double before they could finish the dock. When they managed to get a small business loan of fifty thousand, Atkins disappeared, taking the funds with him. The business folded soon after, and Mike was forced into finding real work.

"Well, here it is," she said, pulling into a driveway at the end of the road. "What do you think?"

The house was impressive to say the least. It was three levels built on top of a bluff, with a million dollar view overlooking Lake of the Ozarks. Megan had bought the house during the last downturn in the economy and had purchased it for half its original value of five-hundred thousand. The two hundred-fifty thousand was a steal, but the down payment took most of what was left of her last husband's life insurance. The same home in Colorado would have cost over a million – assuming you could find one. Lake of the Ozarks is one of the few large lakes in the country where one can still find lake-front property. And Meg had acres of it.

After giving me and Fred the nickel tour of her mini-mansion, Megan led us out onto the second level deck. We waited while she went back to the kitchen for some beer and wine. The beer was for me and Fred; Megan had classier tastes.

Ever since Fred was a puppy, I would give him some of my beer when we sat on our deck back in Colorado. I would pour a small puddle on the weathered-cedar boards, and he would lap it up, then pester me for more. He especially loved to bite the bubbles. He would sneeze when they went up his nose.

"Anyway," Meg continued. "Just when we were ready to put the house up for sale, Mike found a bunch of gold coins. He thought they were hidden there by Jesse James and his gang after the civil war."

I wondered if she saw my jaw drop to the deck boards. "That must be some pretty strong wine, Sis."

"Let me finish, Porky. It's true. Really."

I poured Fred the dregs of my beer, and opened another. "Sorry. You were saying."

She followed my lead and poured herself another glass of wine before continuing. "You can't see it from here, but there is a cave right below us. We couldn't get to it, not even from our lift, so we didn't think much about it. Only a billy goat could have reached that cave. Then Mike saw a show on TV about Jesse James and the Knights of the Golden Circle, and how they hid treasure in caves."

"I remember seeing that on the History Channel," I said. "Some believe Jesse and his gang hid money down in Texas and Oklahoma to fund a new civil war. But I don't recall them mentioning Missouri."

"I didn't see the show. You know how boring history is to me," she said as she poured Fred some of her wine. He ignored it and looked the other way. "Like father, like son," she said.

"So what happened after Mike saw the show?" I asked.

"He dug a path with nothing but a pick and shovel to get to the cave," she answered. "The steep terrain didn't allow for any machinery, so he did it the old fashioned way. He found the coins when he heard his pick break glass."

I wasn't surprised about the cave. Missouri was called the Cave State because it was built on ancient limestone bedrock. Over the eons, the surface water had seeped into the ground and carved out thousands of caves and caverns. The majority were found along the rivers and lakes.

"We decided to keep it a secret," Megan continued. "We didn't want people digging up our property looking for more treasure. Besides, we didn't know if the gold was ours to keep. Some states have laws about lost treasure belonging to the State."

"Like that billion dollar sunken treasure in Florida," I interjected. "Every government agency and half the people in Florida tried suing for that find. It was tied up in court for years."

"Exactly," she said. "Then Mike took a single coin to the local pawnbroker. The broker told him it was not worth much more than its gold content because of the condition and offered him fifteen-hundred for the coin. Mike thought the dealer was trying to rip him off and left after telling him where he could stick his fifteen-hundred."

"Didn't he get another appraisal?"

"I wouldn't let him. I wasn't happy when I found he went to the dealer. Someone might start asking questions."

"Good point," I replied. "If they were part of a James' stash, someone would probably claim them because Jesse must have robbed them from a train or something. How many coins did Mike find?"

"An even dozen," she said. "Mostly double eagles made after the war."

"That's a hard tale to swallow, Sis. Wouldn't someone have found them before now? I mean with all the people on this lake and after the show aired on TV, that cave would have been a magnet for every treasure hunter in the state."

"You can't see the cave from the water because of the trees. Besides, the gold wasn't in the cave. Maybe that's why no one found it sooner. Mike found it when he made the trail. The coins were in a couple glass jars buried at the base of a big rock." She stopped long enough to finish her glass of wine. She stared at her empty glass, "Not that it matters now."

"What do you mean?" I asked.

She seemed to lose interest in her empty glass and looked up at me. She had the faraway look of an absentminded daydreamer. "The coins were stolen," she answered when she came back from wherever her mind had been. "Whoever took them must have killed Mike. If you help me prove it, I can collect the insurance and save the house."

I suppressed an urge to laugh – not so much at the story of Jesse James and his gold, but at Megan's naivety to think I could solve a murder mystery. Even Fred must have thought it was funny; he started to bark at me. But all he really wanted was another sip of beer. "What do you think, Freddie?" I asked, pouring the last of my beer on the deck. "Should I grow a wax mustache so I can look like Hercule Poirot?"

Meg got up to leave, "I'm serious, Jake. Wait here and I'll show you."Fred saw Meg leave and followed her into the house. He must have thought she was going after more beer. I decided to follow the leader, too. I had seen a guest bathroom by the great-room on my earlier tour.

By the time I returned to the deck, Meg and Fred were waiting. She had a printout in her hands of a digital picture. Mike was grinning like a school boy who had won a spelling bee. "What do you say now, Hercule?" she said, handing me the printout.

"Is this from your printer?" I asked. The print was made by a defective printer. There was a line running through it exactly like the mysterious article someone had sent me.

She ignored my question. "So will you help me now? I need you to hack into Mike's computer and see who he was chatting with. He said he found a buyer for the coins online, and two days later, Mike is dead and the coins are gone. Whoever the buyer was must have killed him for the coins." She began to cry.

I never knew what to say or do when confronted with female emotions, so I didn't push for an answer to the printer and waited for her to regain her composure. It only took six beers and two bottles of wine later to hear the rest of the story.

After Bill took off with the business loan and the dock business went belly up, Mike began working on a demolition site to make a few bucks. The county had hired a firm from Kansas City to tear down the old museum after a wall had collapsed. It was the only job in town that paid anything because the construction firm was a union shop and paid union wages to any local help they hired. The wages didn't come close to making the mortgage, but it did put food on the table.

Mike started to come home later every night. He would hang out with the crew and its security guard at a local bar after work. Ron Nixon, the security guard, was an old friend of Mike's. Ron had been bad news back in high school and had been in and out of trouble ever since. It wasn't anything serious, at least he never got caught doing anything to put him in jail.

"That place they hung out at should have been named the Pig's Bed instead of the Pig's Roast," she said, opening another bottle of wine. "Almost every night, I could smell that pig Linda on him when he came home drunk."

"The waitress from the restaurant?" I asked.

"Yeah. She works at the restaurant part-time. Her real job is a barmaid, or should I say, a barfly. Mike had been so depressed about losing his partner and business; I thought he was going to leave me for her. But then the job ended; his buddy, Ron, took a job at Tyson's in Sedalia, and Mike went back to work on his path. That project kept his mind off his troubles and Linda.

"Mike found the coins not long after that. You could see him change overnight. He even quit drinking for a while. Then his drinking started again after taking the coins to the pawn shop, and he found out they would barely catch up the house payments," she said, pausing long enough to refill her drink.

She continued after downing half a glass. "Amy had mentioned to me once that Hal collected rare coins, so I thought this would be a great way to get a second opinion on what they were worth."

"The nurse?" I asked.

"Yeah. Amy and Hal are my neighbors, but I guess Mom must have told you that. She worships the ground Hal walks on. He makes me sick the way he's always hitting on me." Megan seemed to shudder in disgust. "I asked Amy if she thought Hal would mind taking a look at them. That same night Hal calls and asks Mike to read off the dates and mint marks, whatever that is."

"A mark on the coin that indicates where it's made," I answered. "Our mint back in Denver uses a D, San Francisco an S, etc." I didn't bother to go on; I could see she wasn't really listening. "Maybe Hal stole the coins and not some mysterious online buyer."

"When Mike called, Hal was on his way to California. Otherwise, Mike would have taken the coins over to him instead of describing them on the phone," she answered.

"What did Hal say? Did he think they were worth anything?"

"No. And he wasn't interested in buying them either."

"Sounds like they weren't collectable – like the pawn broker said. Even if Mike did find a buyer online, it doesn't look like they would be worth killing for."

"Will you at least see who Mike was chatting with online? Please, Porky."

"Only if you tell me why you sent me a copy of that article about the old couple."

Megan looked at me like I had spoken in an obscure dialect. "What the hell are you talking about?"

I explained how the copy had arrived the day before I left Colorado, and how it had the same defect as the picture she had just showed me.

"Well, I didn't send it," she said after I finished.

"That leaves Mike or Kevin," I said. "I can't fathom why Kevin would send me it, so I have to assume it was Mike. I wonder what he was trying to tell me."

My sister simply shrugged. "I think the beer is making you paranoid. I doubt I have the only defective printer in the world. Besides, what frigging difference does it make? Are you going to help me or not?"

"Guess I've got nothing better to do. What do you say, Fred? Do you want to go looking for treasure?" Fred looked at me when I mentioned his name. I swear he looked at me like I'd lost my mind.

Fred woke me early the next morning. He could be like an alarm clock with his morning ritual. At first I didn't want to get up; I had stayed out on the deck long after my sister had gone to bed. My mind wouldn't let me sleep. Her story of the coins and the discovery of the defective printer had erased the effects of the beer and kept me up most of the night. But I had a terrible itch to see the cave anyway, so this time it didn't bother me to get up at the crack of dawn to let Fred out.

Meg had said I shouldn't go down there alone in case I fell. Neither lack of backup, nor calamine lotion, was going to stop that itch. Access to her dock on the water was by a hillside tram or by stairs from the middle deck; I preferred the tram. The stairs were more for a younger man in better shape than me. I had only gone halfway down the hill when I saw the cave. It wasn't visible from the water or the top of the bluff.

Hidden behind several tall cedar and oak trees was an overhang in the limestone bluff. A huge piece of rock, the size of a barn, had broken off ages ago and slid down the steep slope resting halfway between the cliff and the water. The effect was such that the small cave was completely concealed from any passing boat on the water. Only a rock climber, or mountain goat, could have reached the cave before the tram had been built. I had the luxury of stopping the tram midway down the hill, walking to the cave on the path Mike had made shortly before his demise. How Jesse James and his cohorts could have made it here over a hundred years ago is a mystery.

Fred was waiting for me when I got off the tram. He had taken the stairs and beat me to the path. "Did your aunt send you down here to keep an eye on me, Freddie?" Fred answered with a bark. It could have been a yes or no – I still had a long way to go before I could understand dog language.

"What do you think, Boy? Did Jesse James really hide his coins here?" This time, Fred answered by running ahead to the cave.

It was conceivable that Jesse's gang had hidden some of their stolen loot along the river. Lake of the Ozarks had been created during the depression of the thirties by damming the Osage River nearly one hundred miles downstream from Truman. At the time, it was the largest man-made reservoir in the world. But before the dam, the Osage ran from Kansas to the Missouri River by Jefferson City. As the Osage was the superhighway of mid-Missouri, Truman had been a booming town.

Missouri was a Union state during the civil war, but someone forgot to tell the proud rebels of Truman and the rest of the Ozarks – including the James brothers. The brothers had been raised in Missouri and must have known the Osage River well. After the South lost the war, they returned to Missouri and continued their own private war against the local banks and trains. I figured the link to the James gang made the coins worth far more than the gold they were struck from. If the story could be verified, the coins would be worth a small fortune, maybe enough to kill for.

The cave itself looked more like an Anasazi cliff dwelling than the dark hole I had envisioned. It was simply a very large, deep depression in the limestone bluff. Fred had managed to make it to the cave before me – in fact, several times before me. He would run ahead, turn around, and look at me as if to say, "Are you coming slowpoke?" then come back to see what was taking me so long.

That's when I saw the footprints. A cold chill came over me and stopped me dead in my own tracks. We were not alone. The prints had to be fresh because they were as deep and visible as mine and Fred's. There were none of the telltale marks of boots or tennis shoes. The stranger must be wearing street or dress shoes; otherwise, the prints would have left grooves like my hiking boots.

Fred stood at my side, panting, while I tried to listen for the intruder. "Quiet, boy," I whispered. It did no good. I couldn't hear anything besides Fred. Whoever had been here before us was gone now.

I followed the footprints to the cave. Other than a still damp spot next to the wall of the cliff where someone had recently relieved himself, there wasn't much else to see. There were no signs of digging or anything – just the spot on the wall and the ground. I went up to the wall and made my own contribution; not so much to mark my territory, but to gauge the height of the intruder. I figured he had to be less than six feet tall; his spot was several inches below mine. Of course, he could have been much more endowed than me; in which case, all bets on height assessment were off.

When I made it to the top, Meg was standing at the deck-rail, petting Fred. Once again, he proved himself faster than the tram. "Looks like you've had visitors," I said to my sister.

Meg stopped petting Fred and looked back down toward her dock. Someone had started their boat. "What do you mean?" she asked.

I just managed to catch a glimpse of the boat and its solitary driver speeding off. "Do you know anyone with a Tracker boat?"

"Just about every fisherman on the lake," she replied. "They like to fish around the docks – it's where the crappie hide out."

"Something tells me whoever that was, they weren't fishing for crappie," I said, shaking my head back and forth. "Not unless you have a new species of walking crappie on this lake."

"What are you talking about, Porky?" she asked.

We were interrupted by Megan's phone. "I need to get that, Jake; it's probably Kevin. He never came home last night."

The smell of fresh-brewed coffee coming from the kitchen made me follow my sister back into the house. She went in search of the ringing phone, and I headed for the coffee pot. Wireless phones are a great invention, but they're a pain for someone like my sister, who leaves them in places where only a psychic could find them.

I could hear her raise her voice from wherever she had found the phone. It was none of my business, so I went back outside with my coffee to watch the boats on the lake.

"That was the mortgage company. I should have known Kevin would never call this early," Megan said when she joined me back on the deck. "Now what's this about walking crappies?"

The sun was high enough to hurt my eyes, so I took a seat under the deck umbrella across from her. Then I told her about the signs of the intruder, but left out the part on how I measured the intruder's height. "What's really weird is there was no evidence of digging. You would think if word had gotten out about the coins, people would be swarming all over your hillside."

"Maybe he wasn't looking for coins," she said. "Maybe he just had to relieve himself, too."

I checked my crotch to see if I had a wet spot. "Maybe you're right, but my money's on the coins," I said, realizing why Megan had made her remark. My jeans were indeed showing my age. That seemed to happen a lot lately when I drank too much the night before. I continued like nothing was wrong. "That's quite a climb from your dock to the cave. Whoever was down there must have heard us up here and got out of there before Fred went down, or Fred would have been all over him. He was probably hiding at your dock until we left. Who else knew about the coins besides Hal and the guy online?"

Megan seemed to be trying to replay a tape in her head. Her expression went blank for a moment before I could see her eyes return to mine. "Well, there's the pawn broker for starters, and I would think the half the town by now," she said. "God only knows who Hal and Amy have told."

"Did Mike tell the pawn broker about all the coins or just the one he had appraised?"

"I told you, Porky," she answered, looking annoyed. "He only took the one. We didn't want anyone to know about the others."

"How about Kevin? Didn't you say he helped with the path? Do you think Kevin and Taylor might have taken them?"

I must have hit a nerve. Her voice raised a few decibels. "Kevin wouldn't steal from me, Jake. We all know how you feel about him. But he is my son, and I'll tell you right now, he would never take a dime without asking. You of all people should know better than to judge a book by its cover."

Like our mother, Megan always brought up my teenage exploits when she wanted to put me down. Before I could defend myself, we heard a vehicle coming down the driveway.

"That's Taylor's truck. You can hear that pile of junk a mile away," she said without getting up. "Kevin must be right behind him."

Fred started barking when he heard the front door open. The boys had let themselves in and joined us on the deck. I didn't think it was possible to find a kid freakier than Kevin, but I was wrong. Taylor made Kevin look angelic. His ear lobes were stretched to accommodate what looked like wind turbines, and they actually spun when the wind caught them just right. *"Birds of a feather,"* I thought.

"Hi, Mom," Kevin said, bending down to give her a hug while his friend went over to Fred. "Sorry I didn't go to the jail to see you. That place gives me the creeps the way they stare at me."

"Hey, Uncle Martin, this is Taylor," he said without waiting for his mother to respond to his lame excuse. But the hug was all Megan needed. Her mood changed instantly. It was good to see her smile again.

"Hi," Taylor said. He was giving Fred an ear massage, and Fred loved it. Fred started thumping his tail against the table so hard I thought he would knock it over. Maybe the kid wasn't half bad after all.

While I had been watching Taylor and Fred, Kevin had produced a cigarette from somewhere. "What the cops want, Uncle Martin?" he asked while lighting it.

"Jake tells me that I'm still their prime suspect, and they think he's my accomplice," Meg answered for me, still beaming.

"No shit," Kevin replied while expelling a cloud of smoke at the same time. I expected him to ask why, but he quickly changed the subject. "Hey, Mom. Can I use the Jeep tonight? Me and Taylor want to drive over to Party Cove, and we need some cool wheels."

Megan's smile faded. "Don't you want to spend some time with us? I've barely seen you all week."

"Please, Mom. Becky's only gonna be there tonight then she has to go back to school."

Megan sighed and got up from the table. "You'll need gas. I suppose I'll have to let you use my credit card."

After Kevin and Taylor left, we spent the rest of the day catching up. Meg wanted to know why I hadn't tried harder to keep my marriage together. She and Natalie had been good friends at one time, and they still kept in touch. I learned more about how Allison, my daughter, was getting by in a few hours than I had since the divorce. From there, we talked about our parents. She didn't want to discuss what would happen to our mother once Father passed. She acted like as long as we didn't broach the subject he would never die. Eventually, we got back to Mike and the coins. By that time, we all had too much to drink, and we called it a night.

Unlike Fred, who fell asleep at the foot of our hide-a-bed in Mike's office, sleep eluded me. Mike's computer was sitting on his desk at the end of the bed, staring at me with its Cyclops eyeball. I had thought CRT monitors were extinct. I wondered if his computer was a relic as well. "Could I be that lucky," I said to Fred, who woke from his slumber at the mention of his name, then laid back down just as quickly.

I knew I'd never rest unless I checked out Mike's computer, so I got up and went over to his desk. His computer was turned on its side with the monitor on top. It was running a version of Windows almost as old as the one-eyed monster it resembled. I simply booted it in Safe mode and logged into the Administrator account and changed his password. I was so engrossed in my hacking, I failed to notice Megan.

"I was getting a nightcap when I heard talking," she said, standing outside the open door. I could feel the blood drain from my face. I felt like I'd been caught watching porn. "I thought you might have been talking to Kevin. I need to get my card back before he uses it for more than gas. Is he home?"

Fred was wide awake by now and thumping his tail on the bedcovers. Either he was happy to see Megan or thought the spread needed an old-fashioned cleaning. "Some watchdog you turned out to be," I said to him. Then turning to my sister, I said, "No. I was talking to Fred. It beats talking to myself when I'm thinking out loud."

Megan came into the room and took a seat next to my fierce guard-dog, so she could see the monitor clearly. She took one look at what I was doing then turned back to me with a look of shock. "You got into Mike's account?"

"Piece of cake," I answered while raising my head to adjust my reading glasses. "Good thing he wasn't one for updating."

Her initial shock morphed into admiration. It was the look I used to give my father when he would fix my bicycle. "Kevin and me tried for days to get into that computer."

"It would have been a lot harder if he was current. These older versions of Windows are a hacker's dream. His email is set up to insert the username and password from a cookie. I'm reading his mail now. Shall we see what he was up to?"

"Born2fish," she said pointing to the last inbox entry. "I wonder who that is."

"I can try a reverse email lookup, but don't hold your breath."

"You might as well be talking to the wall, Porky," she said with a frown. "Skip the jargon and get on with it."

"Sorry. Hey look at this message." I opened the email from born2fish.

Megan read the message out loud. "I'll have your money tomorrow. Meet me at my house after six." She turned away from the monitor and shifted in her chair. "Do you think it's about the coins?"

"Sounds like it. Check the date."

"June third. The day before Mike was killed. I told you he was murdered for those coins."

We spent another hour reading through emails, but didn't find any more correspondence with born2fish. Megan went to bed shortly after. She had lost interest once I started reading files that only a hacker could understand.

Mike had made several web searches, trying to find the value of the coins. I couldn't discover any searches with specific dates or mint marks, which left me clueless as to how much they were worth. I too had become bored after a few hours, and I was ready to turn in when I ran across a web page in one of his history files that had the URL of the local newspaper. I copied the link to a browser and waited for it to load. "Damn thing's slower than you chasing a rabbit, Fred." Once again, I woke my sentry from his dreams.

CHAPTER 5

I probably would have slept until noon if not for the smell of fresh brewed coffee. I woke more confused than usual. As I suspected, the link for the local paper was the article about the murdered coin dealer and his wife. Even Fred could see the connection. Mike must have printed it on his defective printer and sent it to me. I really needed coffee if I was ever going to solve that puzzle.

"Good afternoon, sleepy head," Megan said when Fred and I joined her in the kitchen. She was sitting at a small table. The table rested in an eating nook with a large bay window. "What time did you go to bed? You look terrible."

"Must have been around two this morning," I answered while letting Fred out the door leading to her deck. Then I went to the counter and poured myself some coffee. "Wow what a view." Her kitchen looked out on the lake through a twin of the nook's. I was tempted to take my coffee out on the deck despite a warning from a thermometer nailed to a post. It read ninety-six with equal humidity. *Thank God for air conditioning,* I thought.

"So what do we do now? Do you think born2fish is the guy sneaking around in that Bass Tracker?" she asked. I returned to the table and took a seat where I could enjoy the view without going out to the sauna.

I started to turn toward her when I saw a Great Blue Heron land on the deck. Fred had already gone down the stairs and wasn't around to scare it off. "My thought too," I answered while watching the bird poop on her railing. "I got nowhere with tracking him down after you went to bed. Not unless you believe Mickey Mouse did it. Oh, and by the way, I found the clipping about the murdered couple. It looks like Mike must have been the one who sent it to me."

"What? Why would Mike do that?"

"Exactly what I wanted to ask you."

Meg got up from the table and headed toward the coffee pot. "Maybe I bragged about you too much. I once told him how you always guessed who did it when we used to watch Murder She Wrote when we were kids." She took her coffee pot from its burner and pushed the off button. "Just enough for two more cups. You want a refill?"

I held up my empty cup, nodding yes. "Why would he want me to solve the murder of a couple of strangers? They are strangers? Aren't they?"

"Far as I know," she said, filling my cup. "He never mentioned them to me. But what is this about Mickey Mouse? Sometimes your comments don't make any sense at all."

"Nothing I did seemed to work, so I broke down and spent the money on a reverse lookup of born2fish's email address. It's registered to Mickey Mouse who lives at 123 Main Street, Disneyland, CA."

Meg walked back to her kitchen counter with the empty pot. "There must be some way to find him," she said, looking over her shoulder.

"Of course there is. All you need to do is subpoena the records of the ISP that born2fish sent the email from. Do you have any friends at the FBI?"

She turned toward me looking defeated. "So it's a dead-end then?"

"Maybe, Meg, it's time to bring in a professional who has connections."

Megan turned away from me and placed her coffee pot back in its machine. She had her back to me when she answered, so I couldn't tell for sure, but it sounded like she was crying. "I don't have the money to hire a private detective. You're all I've got, Jake. Please, don't quit now."

Fred was back at the sliding door wanting in. He must have gone for a swim to cool off; he was dripping wet. "I better go out there with him before he starts scratching at your screen." His timing was perfect. I never knew how to respond to female emotions. "And don't worry. We'll find a way to prove Mike didn't kill himself."

"Oh, Porky. You're the best brother in the world," she said while wiping away a tear. I was out the door before she could ask me how I planned to turn into a male version of Jessica Fletcher.

Fred gave me plenty of time to think while I waited for him to dry off. Ironically, the drier he got the wetter I became. Because of the humidity, I was soaking with perspiration. Fred didn't have that problem. Dogs don't sweat, nor do they worry about how to prove an in-law didn't kill himself.

Once Fred had dried off sufficiently enough to not ruin my sister's imported hardwood floors, Megan was nowhere in sight, but I could hear her on the phone in Mike's office. I gave her a wave as I passed, heading for the guest bathroom to take a shower. Fred went to the kitchen where she had put out a water bowl for him. She had had the sense to put it on a large throw rug.

Megan was back in the kitchen when I finished my shower. I could hear her talking to Fred, so I wrapped myself in a bath towel and went back to Mike's office to change into some dry clothes. I spent the rest of the afternoon on the phone with my insurance company. Contrary to their television ads, getting them to help in a fast and friendly manner was simply BS. They finally agreed to pay twenty-five dollars a day for a rental until the adjuster could estimate the damage to my car.

Next, I searched Truman's twenty page phone book for a car rental. There wasn't any, so I tried the Sedalia book. A quick call to the first listing got me a car for only thirty-five dollars a day on a weekly basis. So much for insurance.

Megan and Fred were on the deck when I finished. Fred had his head in her lap getting an ear massage while Meg talked on her phone. She had it on speaker mode – evidently so her hands would be free to work on Fred. "Okay. I'll see you later then," she said, then reached over and pushed the off button.

"Was that Kevin?" I asked.

"No. Just an old girlfriend. Kevin never came home last night," she answered without making eye contact. Her tone sounded worried.

"Is something wrong? Is he okay?"

She quit giving Fred his massage and looked up at me. "Yeah. He's okay. He left me a text saying he spent the night at Taylor's house."

"My damn luck," I said and sat down. "I was hoping you would give us a ride to Sedalia."

She sort of tilted her head when she looked at me. Then she must have seen why I was upset. "Oh. You thought we'd have to take the Tempo. Kevin can be considerate you know. They came back to get Taylor's truck and left my Jeep."

Twenty minutes later, we were stuck in a traffic jam. At first she hesitated on taking Fred, but relented after he laid down in front of her and given her his sad puppy look. "I haven't seen traffic like this since they redid I-25," I said.

"It's either an accident, or they must be blasting today. I'll be so glad when they finish with the road work. It seems like it's been going... What the hell!" She stopped in mid-sentence when we saw the roadblock up ahead and a sign that read 'Drug Check'.

We were waved on when we approached the checkpoint. We must not have fit the profile of world class drug smugglers. Either that or my fierce guard dog scared them off when he started barking at the drug sniffing German Shepherd one of the cops had tethered to a leash.

It was past noon when we finally go to the rental lot. Having skipped breakfast, I was famished. I could see mine and Fred's favorite fast-food restaurant across the street. I swear he knew that those golden arches meant lunch; he barked in their direction when I let him out of the Jeep. "Are you hungry, Meg? How about some lunch first? I can get the rental anytime. I'll buy."

"Can I have a rain check? I'm meeting an old friend, and we're going over to Big Lots and then check out the clothes at Goody's. You know - girl stuff." She didn't wait for me to answer and took off going east on Broadway.

"Now, I wonder why your Aunt lied to us, Freddie?" I asked. I didn't need the eyesight of a canine to see Penny's a block down the street in the other direction. McDonalds would have to wait. Fred wouldn't pass as a seeing-eye dog, so I needed a vehicle before I bought us lunch.

The rental agent had no recollection of the thirty-five dollars a day he had quoted me. Maybe he had changed his mind because of Fred. But once I agreed to pay a non-refundable pet deposit and accept an 'older' car, his Alzheimer's vanished, and Fred and I were headed for lunch in a car that would have made Kevin proud. But at least the air conditioner worked.

As it turned out, we didn't need the air once we left the rental lot. A storm front had come in while we were negotiating with the rental agent, and the temperature had dropped considerably. I drove across the street to McDonald's and parked under a giant-oak tree, then let Fred out to water it. That's when I realized I needed to go as well. After putting Fred back into the car with all the windows down, I headed into McDonald's and straight to the men's room. I figured it was better than reliving myself at the oak tree, considering someone might object.

I was on my way back to the car with a bag of McDoubles when I passed by a large screen television and happened to catch the tail end of the newscast. I froze in place. The announcer was talking about the recent drug busts around Lake of the Ozarks. A film crew out of Kansas City was reporting on the drug check Meg and I had seen earlier. I sat down at the nearest table to watch.

"If you ask me," said the old man next to me, "it's the Mexicans."

"What did they find?" I asked, regretting it almost before the words were out of my mouth. Experience dictated one should never get started in a conversation with old men unless one had nothing but time on his hands.

"Found a whole bunch of prescription drugs hidden in the door panels of a truck. I done seen this special on CNN where they are smuggling counterfeit drugs now because it's more profitable than marijuana. You can't even..."

He was interrupted by a woman who had lipstick on her teeth. "Raymond. Let the man eat in peace. I'm sure he don't want to hear your right-wing views." By the tone she used on him, I guessed the woman was his wife.

"I'm sorry," I said to her and quickly got up to leave. "I must be in your seat."

"I can't leave him alone for five minutes while I go to the little girls' room," she said. "I hope he didn't offend you with his views."

"It was a pleasure talking to him, Mam," I said and made my escape, but not before looking back at the old man. "You take care now, Raymond."

Megan's lie about meeting her girlfriend was still bothering me. I needed time to think, so I took the long way and drove around the lake. The road to Bagnel dam wasn't bad; however, I had expected to see the lake, but it didn't materialize until I got to the dam. It was a pretty drive, just the same, and it gave me time to reflect on my life and the events of the last week.

I was getting nowhere as an over-the-hill programmer back in Colorado, and the pittance I made writing and doing handyman work was getting me there fast; maybe, I needed a new career. My degree in math and computer science had been little help in a state with one of the highest percentages of college graduates. Maybe I would have a better chance where the competition wasn't so fierce. I could always teach, couldn't I? Then I thought of my nephew and his friends, before washing that thought from my mind. I'd rather drive a septic truck than babysit kids like that.

Then there was my love life – or lack of one - that reminded me of the nurse back at the hospital. Was it really possible to fall in love at first sight or had it been the anesthesia? She was beautiful. Her dark hair and violet eyes reminded me of Allison's mother. I was a sucker for the Cleopatra look played by Elizabeth Taylor in the movie. But Amy already had her Julius Caesar. Although some people told me I wasn't bad looking, I knew I was no Marc Anthony.

"How about that sexy waitress at the restaurant?" I asked Fred. "What was her name? Linda? Forget about love. That one was more like lust at first sight." Fred didn't bother to answer. But now that he was awake, I had his undivided attention.

Once I passed the dam, I could finally see the water and was brought back to the present. This end of the lake was huge. And unlike sleepy Truman, it was quite crowded. There were large expensive houses and condos everywhere, and the boats weren't the little fishing boats and pontoons of Truman – they were yachts. Just one of those monsters must have cost more than I'd make in a lifetime. "What did these people do to make that kind of money, Fred?"

There were outlet malls, every major fast-food restaurant on almost every corner, and several high-class restaurants that would cost me a week's wages for a meal. There were shopping centers, banks, and even a couple small theme parks. But what was most impressive were the boat dealers. I never saw so many expensive boats in one place in my entire life. I drove through Osage Beach and Camdenton traffic jams, then headed west on Highway Seven, thinking my sister was one lucky gal to live at the other end of the lake. I would have traded this entire part of the lake for the solitude of her backwoods retreat.

If the road to Truman had been a roller coaster, this part of Highway Seven was a bob sled on steroids. When I pulled into her driveway some four hours after I had left her in Sedalia, my sister's house was a welcome sight. I got there just in time to see her crying, and Kevin leaving in the back of a sheriff's car. Almost as surprising, Taylor's mother, my nurse from the hospital, was standing next to Megan. I could tell she had been crying too. She wasn't surprised to see me, so I guessed someone had told her by now who I was.

Fred went straight to Megan and seemed to smile at her as he gently put a paw on her thigh. She reached down to pet him, but before I could ask what was going on, a black Mercedes SUV pulled up behind my rental. It was Amy's husband, Hal.

"What's so important that I had to leave the clinic before seeing Dr. Arnold?" His question was directed toward Amy. Fred's smile turned into a growl. I guess he didn't like the tone of Hal's voice.

"I thought your son might be more important than trying to make another sale," she answered with a look of disdain. "They arrested Taylor on some bullshit drug charge."

CHAPTER 6

We all went into the house to sort things out. I had to put Fred on the deck; even though Fred was no longer growling, it was obvious Hal was uncomfortable around the big dog. In the meantime, Meg had opened a bottle of her favorite Merlot. I settled for a Keystone Light. It was the closest I was going to get to Colorado for some time.

"Now can someone tell me what happened?" I asked.

Amy gave Hal a sour look then turned toward me. She was wearing her nurse's uniform, so I reasoned she must have been on her way to work when she got the call. "The boys were on their way back from Sedalia when they saw that drug check. Taylor did a quick U-turn, but the cops saw him and gave chase. He stopped at a turn in the road where the cops couldn't see the truck until they came around the corner. By that time, Kevin had bolted and was hiding in the bushes. Can you finish, Meg? I need another glass."

Amy got up to leave, then turned toward me. "Can I get you another beer, Jake?"

I hesitated before answering. I had never known anyone so beautiful. "Sure," I answered once I woke from my trance. "How about you, Hal? Do you need anything?" I asked.

"He can get his own," she answered and left the room.

My sister took over where Amy had left off. "Taylor acted like he never saw the road block, but they didn't buy his story and brought in the dog who found drugs in the door panels."

"Then Kevin made it back to the house," I said. It was more of a statement than a question. "Didn't he think this would be the first place they would look?"

"He didn't think they were looking for him," Megan answered. "He said the cops thought Taylor was alone because they never got a good look at who was in the truck when it first turned around."

"Taylor turned him in?" I asked.

Amy had returned to the room and handed me my beer. "Taylor wouldn't do that," she said adamantly.

"I think I need a refill," Hal said, reaching for the bottle of Merlot.

"And I need to get rid of some of this beer. It seems to go right through me lately." I headed toward the bathroom. "Wait 'till I get back before you finish, will you?"

When I returned, they were all watching the six o'clock news on a big flat screen television. There was one of those annoying banners at the bottom of the screen that read, 'Ozark Drug Bust'. The room was quiet as the news anchor was talking.

"One suspect had been arrested at the scene, and the other was apprehended several hours later at his home at Lake of the Ozarks," he said. "An alert pawn broker led to the arrest of the second suspect. The suspects had tried to sell an old twenty-dollar gold coin at his shop in Sedalia only an hour earlier."

Megan spilled some of her wine on the table then nervously wiped it up with a doily. No one else seemed to notice. They were glued to the television.

The scene shifted to an interview with the pawnbroker. "I recognized the piece of junk they were driving when I saw the twelve o'clock news. That's when I called the police to let them know about the other boy. They both looked like something from a vampire movie. I hope they put those two creeps away before they hurt someone."

Hal shifted his body so he was facing his wife. It was the kind of movement only an obese man could make. A thinner person would have just turned his head. "I told you that damn bastard took it. I'll be lucky if I ever get that coin back from those cops. Do you have any idea how much it was worth?"

Amy stared at her husband with a look that could turn Medusa to stone. "You're the bastard! Always cutting him down just because he's not your son!"

"Not now, Amy. You can tell me later what a bad step-father I've been. I'm sure our neighbors don't want to hear us fight in their house."

"If you cared the least bit for him, he wouldn't act the way he does. He only does it to get your attention, you bastard." She stood up and ran out of the house.

We heard Amy's car start up and peel out of the driveway. Hal didn't follow her. "You have anything stronger than this, Jake?" He asked as he held up his wine glass.

"The liquor is in the cabinet next to the wine cooler, Jake," Megan said when I stood up. "Mike had some cheap stuff in there somewhere."

I poured Hal a tall glass then returned to the great room. Megan had left to join Fred on the deck.

Hal downed the drink faster than a bum at a free wine tasting party. "Maybe it was this scotch that killed Mike," he said.

Megan had returned with an empty glass in her hand. It was just in time to hear Hal's remark. She gave him a dirty look and snatched her bottle of Merlot off the coffee table.

Hal didn't miss a beat, "I guess it doesn't matter much now that she let the cat out of the bag, so to speak," he said. "Amy was already pregnant when we met. I was crazy about her, and I thought I was the luckiest guy alive to reel in a catch like that – pregnant or not. I mean look at me. I'm not exactly George Clooney."

More like George Costanza with a fat suit, I was thinking as he went on.

"I was lucky to get any woman, but a gal like her? It was like winning the lottery. Anyway, it was over before all this happened," he said, pointing to the television screen.

I wanted to ask if he meant the boys being arrested or Amy leaving in a huff, but I let him continue.

"I've known for some time she's been screwing around on me. Never marry a good looking younger woman, Jake. They will break your heart."

"So Taylor's not your son?" I asked.

"Taylor is six-one and good looking. Does Taylor look anything like me?" He said.

His remark conjured up a vision of the movie *Twins* with Arnold Schwarzenegger and Danny De Vito.

"I've got to agree with Amy," Megan cut in. "You raised that poor boy as your own, and now you won't stick up for him? What kind of man is that?" And then Megan stormed out to the deck to join Fred.

"See what I mean, Jake? I really have a way with women, don't I?"

"She's just upset about Kevin. I'm sure she'll get over it." I said.

Hal finished the rest of his drink and then got up to leave. "Well, looks like I wore out my welcome here. I better see if I can make amends at home."

I joined Megan on the deck as soon as I let Hal out. It was the first chance since my trip around the lake to confront her about the lie she told me in Sedalia.

"We know they didn't do it. Don't we, Boy?" She was asking Fred. Fred might not have understood what she was saying, but he acted like he knew she was upset. He sat there listening to every word while wagging his tail.

"Guess he's not talking," she said when she saw me. "What about you, Jake? You believe them, don't you?"

"What is it I'm supposed to believe?" I asked, losing the opportunity to ask about her lie.

"The drugs of course," she said with a tone usually reserved for young children or senile seniors.

"Oh. I thought you were asking if they stole the coin from Mike."

"How could you even think Kevin would steal from me?" she nearly shouted. "If you didn't dislike him so much, you could put two and two together. It's pretty obvious who stole from who."

My first thought was to correct her grammar the way she had corrected me at the vet's, but then I thought better of it. I could see she was on the verge of walking out on me, too. "I didn't mean it that way. Sure Kevin dresses a little strange, but I don't hold it against him. I'm sorry if I insinuated he stole the coin from you."

Megan's anger faded, and she started to cry. "What's going to happen to him? He's never been in jail."

"Why don't we call Rosenblum in the morning? I'm sure he can arrange bail. I don't see how they can prove Kevin had anything to do with the drugs in the truck. It's all circumstantial, but we need a good lawyer to prove otherwise. In the meantime, I need to find a way to hack into Hal's computer. As you said, it is obvious he stole the coin from Mike."

Megan didn't wait until morning. I could hear her leaving a message with Rosenblum's answering service while I was making the office couch into a bed. She had promised to clean out the guest room for me but had not got around to it with all the commotion, so I was within earshot of her kitchen phone.

She woke me the next morning even before Fred could. "Sorry to get you up so early, Jake, but I have to go into town and thought you might want to know."

"My God, Megan, what time is it?"
"Six o'clock. I've got to see Dad for a loan, so I can make bail for Kevin and pay Rosenblum. Do you really think he can get the drug charges dropped?" She stood in the doorway, holding onto the jamb. I had a brief vision of the Three Stooges' episode where one of them was leaning against a wall and asked if he was holding it up. Of course, it fell down when he let go. I must have been smiling. "This is serious, Jake. Kevin will never get a decent job with a felony on his record."

"Do you know it's only five o'clock back in Colorado? Even Fred isn't up yet?" I asked, trying to act serious. "And yes, I think Rosenblum can do it. He's good, but good lawyers cost, so let's hope Father has the money to lend you."

"Sorry I woke you, Grumpy." she answered. "Coffee's still hot if you decide to get out of bed. I'll call you later," she said and started to leave.

Fred was up by now, so going back to sleep was no longer an option. "Wait for me to get dressed, and I'll go with you."

"Sorry, I'm meeting Ira for breakfast. That's why I got up so early. I'll be late if I wait for you. Besides, I need you to work your magic and check out Hal." She didn't wait for me to respond, and before I could get out of bed, she was headed toward the front door.

I threw on the clothes I had worn the day before and headed for the kitchen. Then I let Fred out on the deck and poured myself a cup of coffee. The sun was coming up over the lake when I joined him. There were just enough clouds to hide the rising giant, so all I could see was its red and orange fingers touching the lake.

Fred wasn't the least impressed with the sunrise and had gone down the stairs to find a place to do his morning chore. That reminded me of the cave and the story of lost gold. The fastest way to find those coins, if they existed, was with a good metal detector. Hal's computer would have to wait.

"What do you think, Freddie?" I asked loud enough for him to hear. "Should we see if there are any more coins down there?" Fred gave me that attentive look dogs have when they pretend they understand.

"Well, just don't sit there. Help me figure this out, you lazy mutt." Fred barked and ran down the stairs. I watched as he sniffed the ground like he was tracking a fugitive, then he seemed to find what he was searching for. He picked up a ball-sized rock and ran back up the stairs, dropping it at my feet. So much for the canine ability to understand human speech; he was more interested in playing keep-away than being a sounding board. I managed to pull the slimy rock from his mouth and throw it over the side of the deck. I figured the time it took him to run down the stairs and retrieve the rock would give me some time to think.

Where did the boys get that coin, and what were those drugs doing in the truck? Was Kevin suckered into all of this by his freakish friend? If so, where did Taylor get the drugs? Nothing made sense. And what about Mike, was he involved in a drug deal and murdered for it?

The autopsy said Mike died of carbon monoxide poisoning, not by drowning. That sure sounds like suicide. But then how did he manage to drive the car off the cliff and into the lake if he was already dead? Could someone have found him dead then made it look like an accident, and if so, why?

I didn't like where this train of thought was leading. The only motive I could think of to make a suicide look like an accident was for someone to collect the insurance. That someone would have to be my sister. I was still trying to sort out how Megan could have gotten from the accident scene back to the house when Fred returned. Fred wasn't carrying his rock. He had what looked like a man's white cotton sock, or what was left of one.

"Where did you get this, Fred?" I asked as I tried to take the sock from him. As usual, Fred thought any piece of clothing was made for a game of tug-of-war. Socks were his favorite. I'm sure he thought the victor had the right, if not the honor, to rip it to shreds.

The sock wasn't too badly torn, but when I finally wrestled it from his mouth, it was wet with Fred's saliva. I guess I'd seen too many CSI episodes; all I could think of was how Fred had just destroyed any DNA evidence there might have been to identify who owned the sock. My imagination could see a buried body with a missing foot. But reason told me it was more likely lost by a boater and washed up on the shore.

The mystery of the sock and its owner would have to wait. Not that I believed there was a body down there. But if there was, I didn't want every cop in the county digging up the hillside before I had a chance to search for more of the treasure. "Come on Fred," I said. "Let's go get a metal detector and some breakfast."

My first stop, after satisfying our hunger with three sausage McMuffins, one for me and two for Fred, was the only store in town where I might purchase a metal detector. Though the local SuperMart claimed to be a superstore, I came up empty handed. My next stop was back to McDonald's. Not that I thought I'd find metal detectors on the dollar-menu. They had free wireless access so I could look for something online with my laptop.

I found several sporting-goods stores within driving distance in the online directories and started calling them. I soon found their prices would have put my last available credit card over its limit. Then I tried craigslist, and I found a private party who had what I needed for only fifty dollars.

The guy I called was in Lincoln, which was only ten miles north. He said the metal detector was like new, but he had no use for it since his wife had passed. Twenty minutes later, I was in his backyard getting my first lesson on how to find lost treasure. He was a dead ringer for Jackie Gleason. Or he would have been if Gleason had ever worn bib overalls without an undershirt.

"Marge and me used to go everywhere looking for coins and jewelry. You'd never guess where the best places was," he said, sweeping the wand back and forth.

I was tempted to ask if Marge had a sister by the name of Alice. The more he talked, the more I thought of the old TV show

The Honeymooners. All he needed to convince me that I was talking to Ralph Kramden, who had been played by Gleason, was a bus driver's uniform instead of his farmer's overalls. "Under the coaster at amusement parks?" I answered.

"Yep. Them and old farm houses. How'd you know?"

"ESP," I lied. Then I thought better of being a wise guy with the old man. "Guess I must have seen it somewhere on TV."

"Would you like to give it a try?" he asked as he handed me the detector.

"Sure," I answered while trying not to stare at his boobs hanging out the sides of his bib. "Old farm houses? I never heard that one. What did you find there?"

"It used to be our secret, Marge and me, but if you're going to buy it, I'll tell you."

"Consider it sold," I said while adjusting the grip on the shaft to fit my longer arms. He seemed to be considering if I could be trusted with his secret. I must have looked trustworthy. "Mostly money. Old gold and silver coins and some paper money. Once in a while some jewelry, but mostly money. Them old folks didn't trust banks after the big depression, so they hid their money in mason jars and buried it under the old oak tree."

His theory made a lot of sense. I wondered why the television show I had seen didn't mention it. "Gold coins?" Maybe this guy knew what a double eagle was worth. "I hear they can be worth a lot of money if you find the right one."

"Paid for my motor home over there," he said. The motor home was a beauty at one time. But like most RV's, time had been its enemy. Several tires were flat and weather-checked. It must have been sitting there for several years.

"No kidding," I said. "Bet that took quite a few coins to pay for. Did you buy it new?"

"Brand spankin' new in eighty-nine. We put fifty thousand miles on her before Marge couldn't travel no more. Been sittin' ever since. If you're interested, I'd let it go real cheap. Ain't doing me no good just rustin' out sittin' there. Come on, I'll show it to you."

Ralph's face seemed to light up. I imagined he was overjoyed to tell his stories to someone who hadn't heard them a hundred times. He reminded me of my own father. I didn't have the heart not to look at the old RV.

The interior of the motor home looked like the day it came off the showroom floor. Marge must have been a very neat housekeeper. Most RVs I'd ever seen sit out in the weather for over twenty years had so much water damage they weren't worth the metal holding them together. A person would have to pay to get rid of them. This old lady was the exception.

"We kept her in the barn most of the time we wasn't usin' her. She's been sittin' here since we sold the farm before Marge died. Would you like to hear her run?" He didn't wait for me to reply, and to my surprise, it started after a few seconds cranking on the starter.

"What you think?" he asked. "I'd let you have her for five hundred if you buy the metal detector."

What was I thinking? I needed a motor home like I needed a lobotomy. And what would my customers think when I pulled up to fix a toilet or roof? Assuming, that is, I could drive it on any of Colorado's back roads. It wasn't huge by RV standards, but I knew it would be too wide and too low in the back for most of the roads I had to drive. But then visions of sitting by a mountain stream with Fred and a fishing pole drifted through my mind. "Five hundred is way too cheap. I'd be willing to give you a couple grand once my insurance company pays off my car. But I'm sure you'll sell it by then if you put it on craigslist." I must have had my own senior moment to even consider buying a motor home.

Ralph gave me the look one gives a slow child. "Ain't never heard of nobody offering more than I wanted. She's all yours. Pay me whenever you can."

I gave the old man what cash I had in my wallet – the huge sum of one hundred and fifty dollars – and promised to pick up the motor home in a few days. I would need to replace a few tires before I could drive it away, and he had to find the title. I told him to hold the title until I could pay him in full, but he insisted he sign it over in case he kicked the bucket.

I was on my way back to the house, and the treasure hunt, now that I had high-tech on my side. That's when I passed the pawn shop Meg had told me about earlier. It was too much to resist. I had to check out the guy who had low-balled Mike. *What if he stole the coins*, I thought.

The pawn shop was in a mini-shopping center on East Main Street. I only noticed it because the road crew had shut down a stretch of Highway Sixty-five and detoured traffic to the next onramp. It was the middle store in a single-story building that housed half a dozen businesses. These stores were newer than the ones I'd seen downtown. It looked like they had been constructed in the mid-fifties. They were built plain and low, with flat roofs and plate glass fronts. Only two of the stores were occupied: the pawn shop and a junk store claiming to be Grandma's Attic. When I entered the pawn shop, I felt like I was playing the lead role in a Twilight Zone episode from the same era as the building. A brass bell over the door dinged when I crossed the threshold. A short, balding, beady-eyed man popped his head out of the back room. He had a poker dealer's visor and a jeweler's loupe hanging from a gold chain around his neck. "What can I do you out of?" he asked when I closed the door behind me.

He moved from the back-room to a glass case that displayed jewelry, coins, handguns, and late-model electronics. Behind him was a rack of rifles and shotguns. "Hi," I answered. "Just passing through town and saw your shop. My stock broker's been bugging me to buy gold lately. Said it's a good hedge against inflation. Just wondering if you had any gold coins to sell. I would really like to get my hands on some double eagles. He says they make the best investment."

"I'd get a new broker if I was you," he said.

"Why do you say that?"

I noticed he was looking past me to my car. Maybe he thought I was the front-man for a holdup, and Fred was driving the getaway car. "Double eagles are for coin collectors," he answered, now looking at me straight on. "Pain in the ass to sell, and the price fluctuates all over the place. If you want to buy gold, get the modern gold eagle. Their price is determined by the spot price of gold, and they're easier to sell than condoms to a whore."

"Really?" My ignorance was about to blow my subterfuge. "Maybe I misunderstood him."

"Where you're from, Son? We ain't got many people around here lookin' to buy gold – they only want to sell it. And then they gets all upset when they find out their grandma's heirloom jewelry ain't worth what they thought it was."

"Denver. Well actually, twenty-five miles west – a little town called Evergreen."

"What you do there?"

"Freelance writer. I write articles then try to sell them to the weeklies and other magazines." I thought twice about mentioning my handyman business. He might not think a handyman could afford to buy gold.

"Really? Anything I've read?"

"Probably not. I've only had a few How-To articles so far. Local stuff." I wondered where that came from. The more I talked, the more I amazed myself. I had no idea I could lie like a politician. That's when I decided to try a different tactic. "I'm thinking of doing a freelance piece on the James' gang and some of their robberies. From what I've been able to gather, they came away with a lot of double eagles. I was wondering how much those coins would be worth today."

He pushed back his visor then started rubbing the stubble on his chin. "I didn't think you were here to buy anything. People who buy gold don't drive around in cars like that," he said, pointing to my sad-looking rental. "If you got something to say, Boy, say it. Don't go sneaking around the bush."

"Sorry. Most dealers in Denver wouldn't give me the time of day unless they thought I was going to buy something."

"Well, you should of come right out and said so. But like I said, double eagles are for coin collectors. I don't deal in them because I got burnt too many times buying coins that I thought were one grade only to have PSGC grade them lower. Now, I won't pay more for a double eagle than what the gold's worth."

"PSGC, what's that?"

"It's the number one coin grading service. Don't even think about buying a rare coin unless it's been graded."

"So if someone came in to sell a coin, it's possible it would be worth more than what you would be willing to pay?"

"Could be. Had a guy last week bring in a double eagle that could have been worth a lot more than its gold content, but I haven't kept up on collector prices lately. They change too much, but I remember the early Liberties were pretty common. So I didn't offer more than the gold was worth. I felt bad cause he's been a regular for as long as I can remember, been coming in since he was a kid. It really pissed him off. I tried to tell him that I knew someone who might be willing to pay more, but he told me to stick my offer where the sun don't shine. I knew something was bothering him, and then a couple days later, he goes and kills himself."

He stopped long enough for me to write down what he had just said, and then he continued. "Don't write this down, okay? He used to be a good kid, but ever since he married that big spender from Denver, he ain't been the same. Sure as shit and shinola, she had something to do with it. I hear she's some kind of black widow. Like I said, I knowed the guy since he was a boy, so I told my collector to give Mike a call anyway. Guess it was too little too late."

"Not a problem," I said, tearing out the page I had written on and crumbling it up. "Those words will never be repeated. You wouldn't happen to have the number of your collector, would you? Maybe he can tell me how much Jesse's coins could be worth."

"I could look it up, but he's in the book under Harold Morgan."

I nearly dropped the crumpled ball of paper in my hand.

"You know, Hal?" he asked.

"No. Never heard of him."

"I make my living reading people's faces, Son. You ain't lying to me again are you?"

"Guess I got a little excited knowing I was on to a real collector who could help me with my story. The James' gang is really hot right now, and the sooner I get my story to the editors the better. Thanks for the information. I'll be sure to send you a copy of the article when it's printed," I said and left the store.

Fred was sitting in the driver's seat, drooling all over my dash and steering wheel. There was no way I could scold him – it was my own fault for overstaying my welcome in the pawn shop. I'd left him too long in the ninety-degree heat and should have been arrested for animal cruelty. He didn't seem to hold it against me. He started wagging his tail and barking when he saw me, moving over to the passenger seat when I opened the door and slid into my seat. I started the car and immediately turned the air to high, but I left the windows down to purge the hot air. Then before I could tell him I was sorry, my phone started to ring. "Hi, Meg. How's Kevin? Did Rosenblum get him out?" I asked after seeing her name on caller ID. I noticed the pawn broker watching at the window when I looked up. I waved and turned my head to back up.

"No. Not yet," she said. I was still holding my phone in my free hand. "The judge set bail at ten-thousand. Mom said she'd put up the house, so all I need is another grand. I thought I'd ask you to lend it to me, so I didn't have to listen to any more lectures on how to handle money and raise kids."

By now, I was back on Main Street, heading south. A police cruiser passed me in the opposite lane. "Hey, is it illegal to use a cell in this state while you're driving?"

"I don't know, Jake. Don't you hear me? Can you lend me the money or not?"

I watched the cruiser in my rear-view mirror. He kept on going. He had probably been watching Fred imitate an airplane. Fred had his head out the window, his long ears flapping in the wind. The cop must not have noticed the cell phone. "Sure, Meg. I still have a couple thousand from a CD I cashed before I left. Will they take a check?"

"Shit! That will take at least a week to clear. I can't leave Kevin in that long."

"I can ask Mom for the money if you want. Speaking of which, why is she putting up her house. What's wrong with yours?"

"Long story, Porky. And thanks for the offer, but I'll bypass her for now and ask Daddy. By the way, where are you anyway?"

"Just leaving the pawn shop. Why not meet me at McDonald's? I'll buy you lunch, so you don't have to face them on an empty stomach."

I pulled over to the side of the road and searched for the police cruiser, then did a U-turn when I saw the coast was clear. I made it to McDonald's before my sister, so I let Fred out and stood by while he searched for the perfect spot. He was finished and back in the car when Meg drove up. I got in for a second, started the car, then closed the windows. "Don't go driving off on me, Freddie," I said while getting out again. "Be a good boy and I'll bring you back a couple McDoubles."

"You can't leave him there with the car running, Jake," Megan said when she caught up with me.

"I can't leave him out in this heat again. It nearly killed him while I was talking to the pawn broker."

"That's what I thought you said on the phone. What were you doing there?"

I started for the door. "Let's go inside, and I'll tell you all about it."

***

"Wow, you two have been busy boys," she said, removing a pickle from her burger. "They could save a fortune on these if they just left them off. I don't know anyone who likes pickles on their burgers." She tossed her pickle on the tray and then got back to our conversation. "And you didn't check out the sock? What if someone really is buried down there?"

"I'm sure the sock wasn't attached to a body, or Fred would have brought me back a foot rather than just a sock. I asked him where he got it, but he wasn't talking. Maybe if I bribed him with a Big Mac instead of a dollar burger, he would tell us."

"Mom's right. You are a smartass," she said. "So are you buying the crap about the coins not being worth more than the gold they're made from?"

"Here, see for yourself." I had taken advantage of the free wireless and searched the web on my smart-phone for double eagles. The articles neither confirmed nor disputed the broker's evaluation.

"Typical web information," Megan said. "I'd have a better idea if I'd asked a fortune teller."

Prices on the double eagles, according to the pages I'd pulled up, went from $800 to over seven million. Ironically, the seven million dollar coin was one of the last, a 1933 coin that wasn't supposed to be released because of the end of the gold standard. The Mint was supposed to destroy the new twenty-dollar coins when Franklin Roosevelt set the price of gold at thirty-five dollars an ounce and outlawed the ownership of gold. Someone at the Mint decided to keep a few coins for himself, and they started showing up years later. At first, the Secret Service would confiscate any coins they found until only two were known to exist: one that sold for millions and the other in the Smithsonian.

"Mike showed the dealer a common Liberty Head coin," I said. "They were minted up until 1907 when they were replaced with the Walking Liberty. That definitely fits the timeline for Jesse James to have buried them."

Megan put her burger down. "God this is awful. How can you eat these all the time?" She had barely taken a bite.

"Where else are you going to get a meal for a buck?" I asked, reaching for her discarded burger without taking my eyes off my internet search. "Can I give this to Fred? He doesn't seem to mind the taste."

Before she could answer, I found a web page that stopped my search cold. "Wow, look at this one from Carson City – it's going for over one hundred grand."

She reached over and took a fry from my pack. She had already eaten all of hers. "I wonder if Mike had one of those. That would go a long way toward keeping the wolves off my back."

"Wouldn't it be easier to just sell the house? It might be easier than trying to find a buyer for the coins – assuming you ever find them."

"I already thought about that, Genius. I'm upside down on the mortgage. Mike used what equity we had as collateral for his stupid dock business. I don't have a single thing to sell or hock that will give me the kind of money I need."

"What about your car? Isn't Missouri one of those states where you can get title loans?" I asked and pushed the rest of my fries toward her.

She laughed without smiling, before shrugging and reaching for another fry. "These aren't bad. A lot better than their burgers. I might have to get used to this food if I can't get my insurance company to pay up."

"You'll get to like the burgers after a while. I hear they are going to quit using the pink slime, so maybe they'll taste better."

Instead of getting her to laugh, she started to cry. "I hocked the title yesterday and used the money to catch up on my payments."

"Yesterday?" I asked. "So that's what all the secrecy was about. You made up the story about meeting your girlfriend because you didn't want me to know?"

"I'm sorry, Jake," she answered, regaining her composure. "They wouldn't leave me alone, and I didn't want you or Mom to know how bad off I am. They were going to take the car back. How was I to know I'd need money to bail out Kevin?"

"Let me ask Mom for the money, Meg. You know Dad can't do it without her okay. We'll save a lot of time if we skip him and just ask her for it."

After giving Fred his lunch of two double cheeseburgers, plus Megan's partially eaten meal, we all went knocking at our parents' door for help. Within an hour, the four of us were sitting in Rosenblum's office.

The lawyer sat behind his desk chewing on the end of an unlit cigar. "I did a little research after we got off the phone, Mrs. Martin. If you and your husband are willing to put your house up, like you said, nobody will need to come up with a penny." He then slid a formal looking document across his desk.

"Will we lose it if Kevin runs away?" my father asked.

"Marvin! What a terrible thing to say," Mother cut in. "Where do we sign, Mister Rosenblum?"

"Right here on the X," he answered. "I'll have my secretary take them over to the court annex immediately. We should have Kevin out in a few hours."

Father started to fumble for his walker, but he was stopped short by the lawyer. "Please don't get up, Mister Martin," he said as he put down his cigar and walked around his desk with the papers.

Mother intercepted the lawyer before he could hand the papers to Father. She signed first then gave them to Father, showing him where to sign. "I can't thank you enough," she said to Rosenblum. "He really is a good boy, and I'm sure you will see he had nothing to do with those drugs when all this is over."

After a little more chit-chat, we all thanked the lawyer and started for the door. Rosenblum waited for Mom and Dad to leave then called out to Meg. "Megan, I need to talk to you about my retainer."

"Sure, Ira," she answered. "I'll meet you guys at the restaurant in a few minutes." I swear I saw her loosen a couple of buttons on her blouse as I followed my parents out the door.

Father was on his second cigarette, and we had finished our coffee when Megan joined us at the Rusted Kettle. The handwritten menu on the wall reminded me of the sexy waitress who had served us the previous day. I was still wondering what time her shift would start when Megan came in smiling.

"What Rosenblum want?" Father asked her.

"Ira said I could sign a promissory note for the balance." Then, turning toward me with a huge grin, she said. "We should be able to pick Kevin up within the hour, so lunch is on me."

"What about that friend of his?" Mother asked. "I hope no one bails him out."

"Hal has already bailed him out, Mother. He put up a cash bond of twenty thousand. Taylor's bond was twice that of Kevin's because of a trumped-up charge of driving a vehicle with contraband. They also took his driver's license," she answered. "I wonder if the kid knows how lucky he is to have parents with that kind of money."

Mother slammed her cup on the table. Everyone stopped talking. "Talk about ungrateful," she said. "Your father and I could be out in the streets tomorrow if Kevin doesn't show up for court. And all you can say is how lucky Taylor is to have rich parents. I bet they wouldn't put up their chicken coop for that kid."

Now I remembered why I lived in Colorado. "Hey guys, I hate to be a party pooper, but I've got an online interview at three. I need to get going." I surprised myself when I came up with that white lie. But I was still determined to solve the riddle of the coins, and there was plenty of daylight left to search for Jesse's treasure. Megan stayed behind, waiting for Kevin to be released, while Fred and I went treasure hunting. I'm sure Mother would feed her an ample serving of crow while she waited for the call from the jail.

Once back at the house, I let Fred out on the deck and headed straight to the bathroom. McDonald's had great coffee, but, like my beer, it seemed to go straight through me. Before I could finish, I heard Fred barking like he was going to kill someone or something. I knew Fred's barks and growls better than I knew my ex-wife's nagging. He was telling me to get my butt out there.

I quickly zipped my pants and ran to see what all the commotion was about. There must have been at least a dozen boats in Meg's cove and around her dock. Two of them were from the Missouri Water Patrol. The other boats weren't marked, but it was obvious they weren't fisherman – not unless it was legal to fish with guns in Missouri. Luckily for Fred, the gate to the stairs was closed. If Fred had had a chance to get close to them, one of the deputies may have shot him for trying to protect Megan's property.

CHAPTER 7

Though the nearest boat was at least a hundred yards away, I could make out the wiry figure of my favorite Fremont County deputy. Except for two men in wet suits, everyone else had uniforms. When Bennet saw me on the deck, he started his boat and drove it to the dock. I figured I had just enough time to go back into the house and hide my metal detector and call Megan.

I was waiting for Meg to answer when I heard the lift motor engage. "We have company," I told my sister when she finally answered.

"I was just getting ready to call you, Jake. I already got a call from the nosy bitch on the other side of the cove. She spends her day listening to police scanners. She heard that some fisherman found a body in the lake by my dock, and now the cove is swarming with cops."

"Tell me about it. You better get back here quick. Bennet is on the way up." I left Fred in the house and went out to greet the deputy as he emerged from the lift.

Bennet served me with a search warrant before Megan made it back to the house. When she and Kevin arrived twenty minutes later, he and his deputies were already combing the hillside. My fantasy of finding Jesse's treasure with my new metal detector would soon be shattered by Fremont County's finest, assuming, that is, there was a cache left down there by the infamous outlaw in the first place.

Kevin was two steps ahead of his mother and headed for the deck railing without saying anything to me. He looked different. I guess a night in jail will do that to a person, and then I realized why. He wasn't wearing any of his rings or piercings. "How you doing, Kev?" I asked.

"Hope the bastards get covered with ticks," he answered without bothering to turn around.

By now, Megan had joined us. It had only been a couple hours since I last saw her. Was it possible to age several years in so short of time? I wondered what our parents said to her after I left. "The little twerp say who it was?" she asked.

"Bennet said a fisherman snagged the body when he pulled up his trot line. He wouldn't say who the corpse was. He was too pissed off about the sock."

The look she gave me reminded me of the time I had tattled on her for kissing her first boyfriend. "The one Fred found?" she asked. "You told him about the sock?"

"I didn't see how it would hurt. But then he said he should make an arrest for tampering with evidence. When I pointed out Fred would plead the fifth, he called me a smartass and went back to his search."

She finally smiled and turned toward the house. "I need a glass of wine. How about you, Jake? Can I get you a beer?"

Kevin broke in before I could say yes. He was wiping a drop of blood from his nose where a ring had been, and I realized why Megan had been so upset. I wouldn't be surprised if she wasn't considering filing charges for police brutality. "Looks like the pigs are giving up, Uncle Martin. Do you think they found the coins?"

Megan turned and looked toward the dock. We all watched while Bennet and his cohorts walked back to their boats. One of them was carrying a yellow bag. "Hard to tell what's in that bag from here," I answered.

Megan shrugged and went back into the house. Fred escaped when she opened the door and went over to the railing, so he could tell them goodbye with a loud bark. They had combed every square inch of my sister's hillside, including the path Mike had made and the cave it led to. If there had been any James' treasure, they would have found it, so I was probably going to waste my time when I got around to using my new metal detector.

Kevin must have lost interest in watching the boats depart and went back into the house, leaving me and Fred to see the mini-armada off. I began to join my sister and nephew, and then stopped dead. One of the boats was a Bass Tracker. I swear it was the same boat I'd seen snooping around a few days earlier. I waited until it was out of sight before going back inside.

"Talk about letting the fox guard the chickens," I said when we were all seated at Megan's kitchen table. Well, not all of us were at the table. Fred had gone over to his water bowl and proceeded to wash Meg's floor.

Megan took a long sip of her Chardonnay then looked at me. The wine had already brought back some of her color. "What's that supposed to mean, Jake?"

"I swear I saw that Bass Tracker leave in the flotilla. He must have been on the other side of the dock before then."

"Can I have a beer too, Mom?" Kevin asked. The kid was starting to annoy me the way he interrupted when someone else was talking.

Megan got up and went to the refrigerator. "You ready for another, Jake?"

"So, Kev, how was jail food? I hear it can be pretty bad." I couldn't think of much else to say to the kid, so I said the first thing that came to mind.

"F-in gross. The slop tastes like shit."

"Kevin!" Megan said when she returned to the table. "Don't talk like that in my house."

"Geez, Mom. Don't be such an old fart. Everyone uses the F word."

"Not everyone, Kevin," she answered. "Only low-life's talk that way. Have you ever heard Jake cuss?"

Kevin grabbed his beer and got up. "I'm gonna go over to Taylor's. At least his mom ain't always telling us how to talk."

We watched while Kevin made a show of leaving, scraping his chair across the floor and slamming the door on his way out. "Sorry I asked," I said. "I really wanted to ask about the drugs in the truck, but I didn't want to hit him with that first thing."

"Kevin says they didn't know anything about the drugs."

"Who? The cops?"

"No, Silly. Him and Taylor. He said they must have been in there when Hal bought the truck."

"Kevin and Taylor were in the truck when Hal bought it?"

"Quit being such a smartass. You know I meant the drugs."

"Sorry. Just trying to make you smile. So what do you think? Mothers are pretty good at spotting a lie. Is he telling the truth?"

"Rosenblum had the boys take a lie detector test. That guy is good, Jake. I would have never thought of that."

"And?"

"Came out negative. But the DA still wouldn't drop the charges, so now I've got to find a way to pay Ira when we go to trial."

"I thought you said he took a promissory note for his retainer?" I asked.

"That was to cover what I owed. If we go to court, I'm going to owe him big time."

"Well, there's always the slim chance we can find more coins. I bought a metal detector today. If you're up to it, we can go on a treasure hunt tomorrow morning."

Megan forced a shocked look. "You're not going to church with us?"

"Church? You still go to church on Sunday?"

"I had to promise Mother I'd go. There's always a price to pay for her help you know."

***

The morning treasure hunt turned out to be in the afternoon. I found some ticks on Fred the night before and called the vet in the morning. They had an emergency number that they actually answered. I think I became the laugh of the week. People in Missouri didn't waste money on professional tick removal – not unless their name was Gates. But as I tried to explain, we didn't have ticks back where I came from, or at least I never saw one, so I listened over the phone on how to remove ticks without leaving the head buried in the flesh. Contrary to the old-wives tale of burning it out with a match, I was instructed to pull it out slowly with a pair of tweezers. They said I could come by during regular office hours, pick up some Frontline, and settle up then. I didn't know where Meg kept her tweezers, so I simply used my fingernails. Other than a little blood under the nails, it worked quite well.

Megan returned from church in time to watch me remove the last of the ticks. I hadn't heard her scream like that since we were kids, and I came home with a garden snake. "That is so gross, Jake," she said, downing a glass of wine to calm her nerves.

She had gone back into the house, or should I say ran back, after seeing me pull a tick from Fred. But now she was back on the deck with wine and beer. "At least you had the decency to do it outside," she said, still shaking. "Why didn't you warn me?"

I didn't usually drink so early, but I decided to make an exception and took the beer. "It's only a tick, Megan. It's not like I was cutting him open. Look. He's not the least upset." Fred was at my feet waiting for his beer.

Then Fred heard something and went to the sliding door, wagging his tail and prancing back and forth. "Must be Kevin,"

Megan said. "Why don't you ask him to go on that treasure hunt? You know he thinks the world of you. "

She no sooner finished when Kevin came out to join us. Fred was all over him in an instant. "What's for breakfast, Mom?" he asked while he bent down to scratch Fred's ears.

So much for an early start. By the time we finished breakfast, it was after noon.

"Did Mike really find a treasure down here?" I asked while waving the detector back and forth, the way the old man in Lincoln had shown me.

"I guess," Kevin answered. "He never said nuthin' to me about it. Give it to me, Fred." Kevin had lost interest in our treasure hunt, and he was playing catch with Fred. Except with Fred, it was more of a game of keep-away.

"So tell me about the coin you and Taylor tried to sell. Was it made of gold? Do you remember what date it had on it?"

He was engrossed in trying to wrestle a slimy stick from Fred's mouth. "Yeah. Taylor said it was gold."

"And the date?" I was beginning to wonder if I'd ever get the kid to talk.

"Hell, I don't know, Uncle Martin. Taylor took it from his dad's collection. Why don't you ask him?"

"Try to think what it looked like, Kevin. I'm trying to help your mother, and the date is very important."

"Shit. I don't know. Just an old coin with a sexy bitch on it. You could almost see her boobs," he said. He threw the stick toward the water and smiled. It was the kind of smile teenage boys make when thinking of girls.

Kevin told me all I really needed to know. I wasn't going to have to interrogate his friend, the walking wind farm, after all. "You've given me an idea, Kevin," I said. "Let's go back to the house and look at that picture your mom showed me the other night."

It took Megan a while to find the picture, so I grabbed a beer from the fridge and went out on the deck to wait. Fred and Kevin were still playing keep-away when she joined me. "I still don't understand what you hope to find in this," she said, handing me the photo.

Even though I couldn't quite read the dates on the coins, the picture confirmed my suspicions "Do you still have the JPEG this was printed from?" I asked.

"The what?" she answered.

"It's not digital, Uncle Martin. Mike used an old thirty-five millimeter with a timer to take it."

I nearly jumped out of my seat and managed to spill my beer on my crotch. I had been engrossed in the picture; I hadn't noticed Kevin and Fred return. Fred was holding a stick in his mouth which must have been why I didn't hear his usual panting. "Even better," I said, feeling a little embarrassed. "I'll get the negative blown up so we can see the dates on these."

"Did you wet your pants again, Jake?" Megan asked, trying her best not to laugh.

Fred had dropped his stick when he saw my spilt beer and started licking the spots on the deck. I had expected Kevin to say something too, but his cellphone beeped with a text message; he went back into the house.

"Okay, but you won't be laughing for long." I poured Fred the last of my beer and then pushed the picture toward Megan. "It looks like Mike sent everyone on a wild goose chase. There is no way those coins were put there by Jesse James."

Megan surprised me when she fished out a pair of reading glasses from her blouse. I hadn't seen her in glasses before. "And how did you come to that deduction, Sherlock?" she said, studying the picture.

"Look at the coins. Several of them are Saint Gaudens. They weren't minted until 1907. That's long after Jesse and his brother could have buried them." It astonished me that I remembered this fact after perusing the web page back at McDonald's.

She put down the photograph and removed her glasses. "I never did believe that crap about Jesse James," she said as she rubbed her eyes.

I continued now that I had her attention. "I never mentioned this before because it was, well, it was weird, and until now, I didn't think it had anything to do with Mike." Then Fred raised his head and started to wag his tail.

Kevin came out on the deck and cut me off in mid-sentence. "Hey, Mom, I need the car to go over to Taylor's." He already had the keys in his hands and started toward the front door. Fred was right behind him.

Megan jumped out of her chair to run after Kevin. "Hold that thought. I need to talk to him before he takes off."

While waiting for Megan, and my dog, I went back into the kitchen and took two more beers from the refrigerator. I could see her and Fred in the foyer talking to Kevin. Actually, Megan was doing all the talking. Fred just sat there listening.

I thought about calling my dog but thought better of interrupting, so I went back to the deck, where I put one beer on the table and opened the other for myself. Then, while sipping at my beer, I went over to the rail to watch the boats. The view was fantastic; you could see boats a mile in either direction. I was watching a Cuddy Cabin go by with a couple of girls in bikinis when Megan and Fred returned.

She picked up her beer and walked over toward me. "A little young aren't they." Her tone was more of a statement than a question.

"Who's a little young?" I pretended to see the girls for the first time, "Oh. Them. I didn't even notice. I was checking out the motors on that boat: two, two-hundred outboards. That's some setup."

"Sure you were, you old pervert. Like you can see that far," she said and smiled before sitting back down in her deck-chair. "Now where were we? Weren't you about to tell me a weird story about Mike?"

I returned to my own chair and opened my beer. Fred was pacing back and forth, so I poured him some of the brew before I continued. "We've determined the story about Jesse James hiding a stash down there was just that – a story. So where did Mike get those coins in the first place?"

Her smile disappeared faster than the boat with the girls. "I've been asking myself the same question," she answered.

I unconsciously straightened my back before I continued. "Do you remember that news clipping I told you about?" Megan put her beer down and looked at me. Even Fred sensed that I had something important to say; he stopped licking the deck and sat up, too. "You know, the bad copy about a coin dealer and his wife who had killed themselves," I said, pouring Fred more beer.

This time she spilled the beer. "You think that's where Mike got the coins?" she demanded without even looking at the spill.

"I'm only thinking out loud, Meg. Don't bite my head off," I answered. "Isn't it strange that he comes into a fortune of gold coins shortly after the Fergusons meet their maker?"

Megan didn't speak for several seconds. Then before she could say anything, her phone began to ring. "I better get that. It may be Kevin," she said as she left the deck.

Fred must have felt the tension. He laid down by my feet, his head in his paws, staring at me. I'm sure he was trying to tell me not to make Megan cry.

"It's Rosenblum," she said when she returned a few minutes later. "The body was Bill Atkins, and now Bennet wants to charge us for his murder."

CHAPTER 8

Forty-five minutes after the phone call, Megan and I were sitting in Rosenblum's office. It would have been fifteen minutes sooner, but my sister insisted on changing into something less casual. The low-cut slinky dress she chose wasn't exactly a Sunday-school outfit. We left Fred at the house to sleep off his hangover.

"Why does Bennet think the body is Bill, and where does he get the idea that we killed him?" she asked the lawyer after he showed us to a pair of chairs facing his desk.

Rosenblum tried not to look directly at my sister, but he couldn't keep his eyes off her chest. "The coroner will need the DNA report from Jefferson City to confirm his identification. The fish had eaten the flesh on his face down to the bone, so visual ID was impossible. But the driver's license they found says it was Bill Atkins."

"But how in God's name did he come to the conclusion that we killed him?" I asked raising my voice before Megan had a chance to say anything. "I was in Colorado when all this went down."

Rosenblum must have felt embarrassed for staring at my sister. His face was bright red when he turned toward me to answer my question. "Let's all calm down, please. Bennet believes you helped your sister cover up the murder. He's charging you with accessory after the fact." Then Rosenblum regained his composure, suddenly grinning like a kid who just won a spelling bee. "But he isn't going to arrest either of you. I was able to stop him from getting the warrant."

Megan's attitude changed instantly. "How did you manage that, Ira?" she asked, leaning forward to put her elbows on his desk so she could rest her chin in her hands and return the smile. I was afraid her breasts would pop out of her dress.

"Well, Bennet doesn't even know for sure the body is Atkins. All he has is that driver's license, and it could have been planted by anyone. I was able to get George to see reason, and he agreed not to issue the warrant until Bennet can come up with a positive ID and more than a hunch that you killed him."

"Who's George?" Megan asked, sitting back in her chair.

He snuck another look at her cleavage. Then averting her eyes, he answered her question. "Sorry. I assumed your brother had told you the judge is an old friend of mine."

I had completely forgotten that Rosenblum had mentioned George during our initial phone conversation back in Kansas. I was about to make some excuse for my lapse of memory, but he spoke first.

"I'll get to Bennet's misguided murder theory in a minute, but first I need someone to tell me what happened out there to get Bennet so mad?"

"Maybe it was the ticks," I answered, trying to add a little humor to show I wasn't upset.

"Ticks? What are you talking about?" He asked while thumbing through some papers he had on his desk.

"Well, after fishing the body out of the lake, Bennet and his deputies did their forensic search. They made the mistake of leaving the path and going into the brush, so I assume they got covered in ticks the way Fred did," I answered.

Rosenblum put down the papers he had been scanning. "I don't see any mention of anyone named Fred in this report. Who the hell is he?"

"My brother can be a little obtuse sometimes, Ira." Megan answered while adjusting her skirt. "Fred is his golden retriever. He's the one who found the sock."

Rosenblum just stared at us, and then picked up the report again. "I give up. There's no mention of any socks either. Would one of you mind bringing me up to date? And please don't leave out any details."

Megan was still making a show of playing with her skirt, so I jumped in to tell the story. It took over half an hour to relate the events of Bennet's search. Megan only interrupted once. That was when I mentioned Kevin's claim that he and Taylor knew nothing about the drugs.

"Except for the sock, it's all old news." Then he turned toward Megan.

"And don't worry too much about the drug charge, Mrs. Carver. I ran a carfax on that truck just to see its history. Taylor's father bought it at a police auction after it was seized in a drug bust. I doubt if the DA will even take the case to trial. But if she does, I'll make the Fremont County Sheriff's Department look like school crossing guards."

"Thank God," Megan said, slowly crossing her legs. "But why does the creep think I murdered Bill?"

He started to answer her, but his voice failed him; all he could do was cough.

"Are you okay, Ira?" Megan asked.

"Just need a drink," he answered in a whisper and reached for a coffee cup that had been sitting on his desk before we arrived.

He shifted his attention to the coffee and made a sour face. "I need to ask you something personal about this, Megan," he said, still studying his coffee. "Do you want your brother to leave?"

"No problem. I was ready to leave anyway," I said. It was the first time I heard him call her anything other than Mrs. Carver. It sounded like the personal question might really be personal and have nothing to do with the case.

"Stay put, Jake," she said before I could get out of my chair.

Now I was really confused. All this time she had been hitting on the lawyer, and now that he wanted to get her alone, she wanted me to stay? I sat down like a good little brother and shut my mouth.

"Okay, but stop me if there's something that gets too personal." Rosenblum put his coffee cup down and looked directly at Megan. "Were you having an affair with Bill?"

She nearly knocked over her chair when she stood up. "Bill Atkins! You've got to be kidding. I'd rather sleep with Pee Wee Herman!"

Then she placed both her hands on his desk and lowered her voice. "I loved my husband, Ira. It's no secret that we hadn't been getting along. But I swear, I wasn't screwing anyone. Who would even think I was messing around behind Mike's back?"

"Sorry, but I had to ask." This time his eyes never wavered from hers. "Bennet thinks you were having an affair with Bill, so you could get him to kill Mike."

"Go on," she said without taking her eyes from his. It made me think of one of the staring matches Fred and I would get into when he wanted something.

Rosenblum lowered his eyes and continued. "Bennet couldn't get his first murder charge to stick because of his handling of the suicide note and lack of any real evidence. But now he thinks Atkins is all the proof he needs to connect you to Mike's murder."

"That doesn't make sense, Ira." I cut in without getting out of my chair. "Bill Atkins must have been dumped in the lake long before Mike was killed. And besides, you said the new warrant was for Atkins' murder."

"I was thinking the same thing, Jake," Megan said and sat back down.

The lawyer adjusted his glasses and leaned back in his own chair. "An anonymous witness called the sheriff's office when he heard about Atkins on the news. He claims Bill was bragging about getting you into bed by playing along with a murder plot. Supposedly, you would split Mike's insurance if Bill would make it look like an accident."

I could see Megan turn red. "What? That's an f-in lie. Why would someone make up such a lie?"

The lawyer didn't seem surprised with Meg's sudden foul mouth as I was. "But unless they can find the witness and get him to testify in court, they don't have a case. George wouldn't issue the warrant on hearsay."

I jumped in before Megan could show us any more of her new vocabulary. "He called the sheriff's office. Wouldn't they be able to trace his call?"

"You've been watching too much television, Jake. That kind of equipment is way beyond the budget of Fremont County. But they do know the call came from a phone at the Pig's Roast. The caller never turned off caller ID."

Megan rose from her seat without trying to act sexy. "Thank you for all you've done, Ira. I would appreciate it if you keep us in the loop on any news. I'd really like to have a talk with this anonymous witness." She then headed for the door.

Rosenblum rose to say goodbye, but Megan was already gone.

"It's been a tough week for her, Ira. And we do appreciate all you've done," I said and then ran after my sister.

"What was that all about, Meg," I said when we were back on the road to her house.

She had been staring out her window in a daze, the way she use to do when we were kids on a road trip. "What do you mean?" she asked, turning her head toward me.

"Hey, none of my business," I answered without looking at her. "I mean it was kind of obvious you were upset when Rosenblum brought up the witness."

She went back to her window. "I need a drink, Jake. Pull in over there would you?" The sign on the tavern read, "Pig's Roast."

I pulled close to the front entrance into an empty parking space between two pickup trucks. The only other car in the lot was parked several yards from the front door, toward the side of the building. Before I had a chance to set the parking brake, Megan was headed for the door. It didn't take me more than a millisecond to realize this was the infamous bar from where the anonymous witness had called in his false report, or so Bennet claimed. I didn't say so at the time, but I had wondered if the deputy had made it all up. Maybe that was just paranoia on my part, for surely all incoming calls at the station must be recorded.

"Hold up, Meg," I called out. "I'm sure they won't sell all the beer before we get inside."

She stopped short of going in and pointed at the other car in the lot. "That's Linda's piece of crap. Looks like you're in luck, Porky." Her pause gave me the time I needed to catch up with her.

I had visions of walking into a dingy bar with Linda serving drinks in a skimpy uniform. I couldn't have been more mistaken. The place was as bright as a solarium, and the bartender was a bald guy who looked to be in his forties – not exactly my type. Megan spotted Amy, sitting alone at a table by a window that overlooked the lake. The entire lakeside wall was mostly windows allowing the sun to light up the bar. She must have been crying. Her eyes were slightly swollen, and her mascara was in streaks.

"Jake, would you get me a double anything?" Megan said and headed toward her friend.

"And ask Sam for another of whatever Amy is drinking."

I assumed my sister was referring to the bartender. He was wiping down the bar with a dish cloth as he watched me approach. On closer inspection, I could see the telltale marks of a shaved scalp and an earring in his left ear. "You're Megan's brother, aren't you?" he asked.

"That's what our mother says. So, you must be Sam."

He put his towel aside and offered his hand. He seemed to have a worried look about him. "Glad to meet you, Jake. I'm the owner of this sorry place."

"Glad to meet you too, Sam. Although, I was hoping Linda would be in. Isn't that her car out in the parking lot?" I asked and returned the handshake.

"Yeah. You just missed her. She couldn't get her car started and got a ride with one of our regulars." Sam let go of my hand and went back to wiping the counter. "Speaking of which, I hope Meg's okay with all the shit that's been coming down on her. Her and Mike were some of my best customers."

"Thanks. Nice to know someone who isn't out to get her because she's not from around here." All this patronizing was starting to get to me. I couldn't help but imagine what he really thought of my sister and her late husband.

"I can empathize. I'm from the big city myself. My dad bought this place after he retired, and I came to work after losing my job in Saint Louis when the economy tanked. It keeps me busy until the market comes back, and I can go back to selling mortgages instead of beer." He picked up his towel and began wiping some glasses that had been sitting in a rack next to a sink under the bar. "Well I doubt you want to hear my troubles. What can I get you?"

"How about a couple of Bud Lights. I'd really prefer a Coors, but when in Rome…" I thought better of ordering Megan a mixed drink after seeing how the glasses were cleaned. "And let me have another of whatever Amy is drinking."

He smiled and said, "Two Coors and a Jack Daniels on ice. Anything else? The grill's not open for another hour, but I can serve some snack food if you're hungry." Then he pointed to a hot dog machine at the end of the bar. The hot dogs looked like they had been cooking since last Christmas.

"I'll pass on the snacks. We just came from McDonalds," I answered while watching him mix Amy's drink.

Sam opened two bottles of Coors and wiped off the condensation before placing them on a tray alongside Amy's. "That doesn't sound like the Meg I know. Mike used to say she wouldn't go within fifty yards of there."

I made a mental note to re-wipe the top of the bottles with a clean napkin. "Sounds like you knew Mike pretty well."

"He used to stop by almost every afternoon with his buddies Bill and Ron. Everyone got to calling them the three amigos. Hard to believe both Mike and Bill are gone."

The mention of Bill triggered a memory about the anonymous phone call made from here, and I looked around for a phone. There wasn't one I could see. "Speaking of Bill, did you know Bennet tried to arrest Meg and me for his murder?"

"News travels faster than a rabbit at a greyhound track in these small towns, Jake. The whole town knows that, but I didn't feel I knew you well enough to mention it."

"Do you know why Bennet thought we did it?"

Sam looked around the place before answering. The only other customers were a couple of guys in their fifties at the far end playing pool. Then he reached under the bar and brought out a half-filled glass of what looked like whiskey and took a sip. "Bennet sort of told me already. He came by this morning and said someone called in a tip from here. Asked me if I had let someone use the phone yesterday."

I was afraid to say anything. The wrong response and he might remember that bartenders are supposed to keep gossip to themselves. He was acting like someone who was revealing top-secret plans on the B-2 bomber to the Russians. I waited for him to continue.

"I told the sorry SOB it could have been anyone. The phone is right here under the counter. And besides, Monday's are slow, and I let Linda run the place herself on Mondays. I wasn't even here."

I picked up my Coors and took a drink, forgetting about the thousands of germs that had jumped off his bar-rag. "Do you think it was Linda?"

He bent closer and spoke in a near whisper as though the pool players might be listening. "My thought too. So I checked the call list. I've got one of those newer models that store the last twenty calls coming in and going out. I don't know who made the call, but I know who didn't."

Sam grinned like he just lost his virginity. "There was a call from Hal and another call to Ron Nixon only minutes before the call to the sheriff. So, we know it wasn't Ron or Hal."

"Hey, Sam, how about a couple more beers?" It was the pool players.

"Thanks for your help, Sam," I said, handing him my last twenty. "I better let you get back to work. And keep the change."

Amy was doing better when I joined the girls at their table. She must have made a trip to the restroom when I wasn't looking. She had washed away the black streaks, but she hadn't replaced her makeup. She was more beautiful without it. "What took so long, Porky?" We were about to get our own drinks." Megan said.

I winked at my sister and said, "Went on a fishing trip and caught a big one."

Megan gave me her blank look. "What does that mean?"

"A stupid metaphor," I answered. I realized this wasn't the time to tell her it looked like Linda was our anonymous tipster.

She rolled her eyes and looked at the tray. "Where's my drink?"

I slid Amy's drink over the table and proceeded to wipe the necks of the beer bottles with a napkin from the dispenser in the middle of the table. "I'm sorry, Meg. I thought you were kidding about the double. I got you a beer instead."

"Whatever," she answered. "Amy needs a ride home. That bastard just left her here and drove off."

Amy took her drink and downed half of it, then she looked at me. "Do you mind giving me a ride, Jake? It doesn't look like Hal is coming back to get me."

"Sure, no problem." Other than asking her to run away back to Colorado with me, it was all I could think of to say. I kept the vision of her in Daisy Mae shorts and a halter top at my cabin to myself.

I spent the next hour listening to my sister and Amy talk about men as though I wasn't one. I guess brothers are invisible, or eunuchs, in the world of female gossip. Sam didn't give me an excuse to leave the table. My tip had insured table service whenever he saw an empty glass. When it finally came time to pay up and leave, I tried using my credit card. It didn't clear. Amy jumped in with a hundred-dollar bill before I could try my debit card.

I was too embarrassed to say much on the short drive home, and I just let the two girls talk. I had tuned out most of what they were saying until Megan offered her friend my room. "You can't go home tonight. That creep might beat you again. You can have the guest room. Kevin's staying the night at your house, so Jake can take his room."

I ended up sleeping on the couch in the family room. Kevin and Taylor were at the house; Hal had started in on Taylor about cleaning up his act. Amy took the guest room, slash office, where I'd been sleeping, and Fred and I got the couch. It wasn't supposed to be that way, but somehow he had managed to squeeze in at my feet.

***

Fred woke me around two in the morning having to go. It was a ritual he started about a year ago, and I attributed it to a shrinking bladder as he got older. I should know. I was wide awake anyway, so I let him out on the back deck where he could use the stairs to get to his bathroom. I fetched a beer from the refrigerator and, while enjoying the full moon reflecting off the water, waited for him on the deck.

"Can I join you?" It was Amy wearing only a bathrobe.

"Sha shure," I muttered after getting a glimpse of her naked breasts. "Can I get you something to drink?"

She realized it was open, and she quickly closed the robe before sitting down. "Sorry about that. I just took a shower, and Meg's robe seems to be missing a few buttons. One of those beers would be great," she answered with a smile.

While I was getting up to fetch the beer, she let her hair fall from the bun it was in and flung it behind her. The moonlight bounced off her wet hair and lit her face.

When I returned a few minutes later, I found Fred was getting a massage I could only dream of. He must have heard her on the deck and cut his tree watering short to join her.

"I've been meaning to ask how your headache is. You must think I'm pretty self-centered not to have asked sooner," she said.

"Thought never crossed my mind," I lied.

Amy stopped massaging Fred and reached for one of the beers. Her eyes locked onto mine, and she smiled. "You are so different from Hal. He would not only agree, but gone on to call me a narcissistic gold-digger."

"Hal didn't strike me as a man who knew any ten dollar words," I tried to joke, all the while gazing into her eyes. Her pupils were large in the dim light of the moon and hid the beautiful violet I remembered.

She laughed at my remark nonetheless. "You got that right. He probably thinks a narcissist is one of those drugs he pushes."

I didn't let on the fact that I wasn't too sure of the meaning either. I was already feeling embarrassed for getting caught looking past her open robe. I didn't want to look stupid, too, so I quickly changed the subject. "Meg mentioned you might be staying awhile. You're more than welcome to keep the guest room, and Fred and I will move downstairs."

"But that room's unfinished, Jake. I couldn't ask you to do that," she answered, no longer smiling. "God only knows how long I'll have to stay before he goes on another sales trip."

"No problemo, my Lady. Meg has a hide-a-bed in storage I can fetch, and there's a bath down there; it will be just like a suite."

"Wish I'd met you sooner, Lancelot. That is so sweet of you," she said. Then she stood up and walked over to the deck railing. "I'm going to miss this view. The lake is so beautiful this time of the year."

"Are you planning on going somewhere?" I asked.

She half turned toward me to answer, and I realized why she had left the table. I could see the reflection of the moon in her damp eyes. "That's the trouble with alcohol. It always makes me talk too much or do something stupid," she put down her empty bottle on the deck rail.

"No way. You could never do anything stupid."

"Leaving Hal would be. You have no idea how close I came to asking you to take me back to Colorado with you."

I nearly dropped my beer. *Can this woman read minds,* I thought. Then she blew my fantasy. "I was thinking of hitching a ride with you as far as Denver. I've got an aunt who lives there that I could stay with for a while."

"I'd love to have the company. Fred doesn't say much when we're traveling. But it may be some time before I can leave Meg and head home."

"Thanks, Jake. But it was a stupid idea. Taylor wouldn't leave his friends, and I doubt if Megan would want him moving in permanently. Besides, I'm not about to let Hal have everything."

I couldn't think of a quick comeback. Not that I needed one. Someone inside the house turned on the deck light, and we both looked toward the sliding door. "I'm not interrupting anything, am I?" Megan asked.

Amy quickly checked to make sure her robe was closed. "No. I heard Jake talking to Fred out here, so I thought I'd join them. We didn't wake you did we?"

"Yeah," she answered, looking at Amy. "My room is right above you guys, and I like to sleep with the windows open. But I couldn't sleep anyway. I keep thinking about what Jake said back at the Pig's Roast." Then she looked over at me. "What did Sam tell you anyway?"

Amy picked up her empty beer bottle and started to leave. "Thank you for the beer and the company, Jake. I've got a double shift at the hospital tomorrow, and I really need to get some sleep." Fred woke up just as she was leaving. She bent down and patted him on the head. "Take care of your master, Boy. He's a real gentleman."

I watched her go back into the house and wanted to shoot my sister for scaring her away. "Thanks a lot, Sis," I said after Amy closed the door.

"Forget her, Porky. You can't afford her, believe me," Megan said, sitting down across the table from me. She leaned back in her chair and looked me straight in the eyes. "Now you want to tell me what Sam said?"

***

Fred was the first one up a few hours later, and he wanted out again. I can usually buy a few more minutes of sleep by petting him on the head and telling him to lie down, but just like the snooze button on an alarm clock, he will start in again within ten minutes. "Okay, Fred, I didn't need to sleep anyway," I told him and got out of bed.

When I opened the door to let Fred out, I saw the boat down by the dock again. Fred saw it too. He started barking at it and ran down the stairs. I'm sure it was the same boat I had seen the first day I came here. With all that had happened since, it seemed like a long time ago, but it had only been a couple of days.

Meg's deck was nearly two hundred feet from the dock. My eyes were no longer what they used to be, and I couldn't make out the driver. I quickly rushed over to the spotting scope Meg had on the deck to get a better look. The boat had been slowly pulling away from the dock, but when he heard Fred, he pushed the throttle full forward and was gone before I could focus the scope.

Fred made it to the water by then, but it was too late for him to get a good look at the intruder, not that he would tell me what the guy looked like in this lifetime anyway. I yelled down to Fred to quiet down before he woke everyone in the house.

"What's all the commotion?" Meg asked. I could also see Amy through the glass doors as she went into the bathroom.

"Earth to Porky," Megan said. "Are you with us or did your circuits disconnect."

"Sorry, Sis, just thinking."

"I can see that, Rodin. What's Fred barking at?" she asked as she went over to the spotting scope.

"It's that boat again, and this time I know it wasn't a fisherman." I said, watching her adjusting the focus. "Don't waste your time. He's gone"

"And how do you know it's not a fisherman, Sherlock?" she said, still trying to find something in the scope.

"Since when do fishermen carry picks and shovels?" I asked.

She stopped fiddling with the scope and turned toward me. "He had a shovel?"

"And a pick. By the time I managed to focus that thing, the pick and the name on the side of the boat were all I caught," I answered and leaned back in my chair to prop my feet on the table.

Her pupils seemed to get larger when she asked, "Was it the Bass Tracker?"

I tried to act smug with my answer, but my feet slipped off the table just as I said, "Yep." The chair fell backwards throwing me on the deck.

"Are you okay, Jake?" she asked as she started to crack up.

She came over to help me up, but I was already to my feet. "I'll live," I answered.

"How about I make some fresh coffee and throw together some breakfast," she said in-between laughs. Then she went back into the house, holding her hand to her mouth.

It was just the four of us for breakfast, if you want to call coffee and burned bagels a breakfast. No matter how much Fred barked, the boys wouldn't be up for hours. It would take a direct hit by an asteroid to get those two out of bed before noon. It was just Megan, Amy, and me, sitting around Meg's glass-top deck table with Fred standing next to me waiting for someone to feed him. I threw him another one of the burned bagels then turned toward Amy. "Can I give you a ride to work this morning?" I asked.

She smiled when she saw Fred devour the bagel in a single gulp. "Well thank you, Jake, but I really need my own car. Meg said she'd take me home to get it."

"Won't Hal be there?" I asked, watching my traitor go beg from Amy now that my food was gone.

"He's gone already. I'll be OK," she answered and gave Fred her un-touched bagel.

"How do you know that?" I asked, trying not to show my disappointment at not being her chauffeur.

"I have an app on my phone that tells me when the security alarm is armed, and another that can pinpoint the location of his Mercedes," she answered while picking through the plate of bagels. "No one can be in the house when the motion detectors are on, and the GPS shows his car headed toward Springfield."

My sister didn't act surprised, so I guessed Amy had already said the same to her. Then she threw Fred her half-eaten bagel. "These are really bad," she said, and got up to leave. "Looks like you'll have to make yourself a real breakfast, Porky. Amy and I need to get going, or she'll be late."

Amy was already out of her chair, but she stopped and looked at my sister. "Why do you call him Porky, Meg? He's got a body most women would kill for." She said with a wink in my direction.

I wanted to say something clever in return, but my mind went blank. Then Megan spoke before I could recover. "Is there something going on here I don't know about?" she asked with a big smile on her face.

"No. I'm afraid your brother is too much of a gentleman to take advantage of a damsel in distress," Amy answered my sister but was now looking at me. She winked again and went inside.

Fred ended up with most of the so-called breakfast, and I was trying to think of an excuse to run into town and get a couple of Sausage McMuffins, but I had better things to do now that the girls had left.

"Come on, Freddie Boy, let's go see what our fisherman was fishing for." Fred and I got on the tram, and I pushed the down button. We took the tram all the way to the dock instead of stopping off at the path. I was assuming that our intruder had been searching for treasure, and I'd be able to track him back toward the cave. I was also hoping the trail wouldn't be through the brush where I would surely be joined by my bloodsucking friends, the ticks. My luck failed on both accounts.

The army of deputies from the other day had trampled every weed and bush growing on the hillside. They would have done the same to the tick-infested cedar trees had the trees been short enough to walk on. Without crumpled grass and weeds, it was impossible to see where our fisherman had been. I was going to have to backtrack under those damn trees if I had any hope of finding a freshly-dug hole. I was wondering if I should have brought the metal detector when nature supplied me with one that didn't use batteries. This detector was running on burnt bagels.

Fred jumped off the short bank to the rocks below. The water level of the lake was constantly changing depending on the electrical demands in Saint Louis. This part of the shore had been under water when the deputies had searched the area two days ago, but the summer air conditioners two hundred miles away had drawn the lake down at least three feet, exposing the rocky shore.

Fred led me straight to where our fisherman had been digging.

CHAPTER 9

Several boulders had been set aside and a small hole dug in the muddy soil. As soon as the demand for electricity in Saint Louis eased, the water would reclaim and cover the hole. Whatever had been in the hole was gone now – supposedly taken by my mysterious fisherman, without a fishing pole. Even his footprints would be washed away with the rising water. I wished I had brought my cell phone, so I could get a picture of them.

One print stood out in particular. I could barely read the muddy imprint of '2 3 T'. There were more numbers or letters to it, but they quickly dissolved before me.

When Fred and I got off the lift, Kevin was leaning over the deck railing, a cigarette in one hand and a can of soda in the other. "What you doin' down there, Uncle Martin?"

"Fred and me were fishing," I answered, trying my best not to nag him about cigarettes and wild fires.

He took another drag, and then dropped the cigarette in his soda can. "Without a pole?" he asked. "Were you noodling catfish?"

"Not that kind of fishing, Kevin. We were fishing for clues."

He picked at the infected hole in his nose where there had been a diamond stud. "That's good. My friend got busted for noodling. Don't let no water cops catch you doin' that."

I was beginning to think about a vasectomy. The thought that we swam in the same gene pool made me want to avoid more children at all costs. I got lucky with Ally, but she probably had her mother's genes. Fortunately, Taylor was just getting up, and Kevin went to join him. I'd much rather talk to Fred, who never once, that I could remember, made a stupid remark. And it seemed he always understood my metaphors, no matter how obtuse they could be. But, alas, I needed to ask Taylor a question that had been bothering me for some time.

"Morning, Taylor," I said after joining the boys in the kitchen, where they were sharing the last energy drink. Fred elected to stay outside and catch up on his sleep. "I've been thinking about that truck of yours ever since Meg and I saw the lawyer yesterday. Rosenblum said your father bought it at a police auction. Is that right?"

Taylor passed the drink over to Kevin before answering. "Sure is, Mister Martin. Dad thought it would be a great way to save some money. He had promised me a truck for my eighteenth birthday, so he took me to the auction. I really had my eye on a cool four-by-four Chevy, but he insisted I buy that piece of crap — said it was all he could afford. He makes over two hundred thousand a year and couldn't spend more than a couple thousand on my graduation present."

I was afraid Taylor would keep talking all morning. He was the complete opposite of my taciturn nephew. Luckily, Megan had returned from dropping off Amy, and Taylor stopped long enough to greet her. "Good morning, Mrs. Carver," he said when she joined us in the kitchen.

She went straight to the coffee pot and poured herself a cup of cold coffee before answering. "Good morning to you too, Taylor. I hope you slept okay on that trundle of Kevin's," she answered as she sat down at the table.

Kevin ignored his mother. It was plain to see she was waiting for him to greet her too, but he just stared at the label on his energy drink. I could see the disappointment in Megan's face.

"Taylor was just telling us how Hal bought his truck, Meg," I said before she had a chance to say anything to Kevin. "You didn't miss much. It's basically what Rosenblum told us yesterday."

Fred barked at the sliding door to come in just as the phone began to ring. When Megan got up to answer the ring, Kevin must have seen his chance to escape. He was out of his chair and heading for the front door before she could reach the phone. "Hi, Ira," she said, glancing at the caller ID. "Hold on a sec." Then, holding her hand over the receiver, she yelled, "Kevin, where are you going?"

Kevin didn't stop to answer. Taylor looked over at Megan, shrugged his shoulders, and went out the door too. I, in the meantime, had been standing at the sliding door, watching it all until Fred got impatient barking and started scratching the door to be let in.

Megan acted like nothing had happened, removed her hand from the phone, and gestured for me to leave by pointing toward the sliding door. "Sorry, Ira. Kevin was just leaving. What's up?" After a short pause, she said, "Sure he's right here," and held out the phone for me to grab.

"What's up, Ira?" I asked. "Don't tell me the DA changed his mind, and we need to head for Mexico."

Now it was Megan's turn to try and follow a one-sided conversation. She tried to get close enough to hear Rosenblum, but when he said it was about a motor home, I waved her off. I could see her expression change from curiosity to concern in response to my short answers. As I hung up the phone, she went over to the sink and tore off a paper towel from the dispenser hanging nearby. "Is that a tear I see?" she asked, handing me the towel.

"Must have got a bug in my eyes while letting Fred in," I answered. Then I turned away from her and walked over to put the phone in its cradle. It was more a move to avoid looking at her than to put the phone back where it belonged.

"It's the guy I bought the motor home from. He died and left it to me, free and clear, along with some prospecting tools. Ira said to drop by his office, and he would give me the title and fill me in on what I need to put it in my name."

"Why would he do that?" she asked as she tore off another paper towel. "Here, you missed a bug."

"I guess he felt sorry for me – I don't know," I answered while trying to avoid direct eye contact. "He was terribly lonely after his wife died. But I know he's happy now that he's with her. Damn, Sis, he was such a nice old guy. It sure makes you realize how short life can be." I sat back down at the table and began telling her about my encounter with the old man. Fred wanted out about halfway through the story, so we grabbed a couple of beers and went out to the deck. It was quite early for our afternoon libations, but the beer was necessary now that I had Megan on the verge of tears, too.

I stopped off at the Pig's Roast on the way to see Rosenblum. Not that I needed another beer; I was hoping Linda would be working the bar. There was always the chance I could charm her into telling me why she made the call to the sheriff. Considering how charismatic I can be, I guessed my chances were about the same as winning Powerball.

"Hi, handsome," she said when I took a seat at the bar. She was wearing shorts at least two sizes too small and a halter top made for a teenager. Maybe her skimpy outfit was because the air conditioning wasn't working, but I wasn't complaining on either account.

I turned on my barstool, pretending to see who she was talking to, then came back full circle. Except for an overweight cat sleeping in one of the booths, the place was empty. "Hi, Linda. Did you lose a contact, or are you talking to your cat?" I answered.

She giggled then continued wiping down the already spotless bar in front of me. It gave me a great view of her ample cleavage. "Sorry to hear about your nephew," she said. "What can I get you, Sweetheart?"

I almost forgot why I had stopped by. "Can I have a Coors?" I said, quickly raising my eyes from her chest.

She reached for a bottle from under the bar and wiped it off the same way Sam had the day before. "Here you are, Sweetie," she said as she placed a small napkin on the counter for the beer. "Sure has been a lot of shit goin' on at Meg's lately. First, they find

Bill's body; then, they arrest Kevin, and now I hear Amy's moved in with you."

I tried to look her in the face, but my eyes wouldn't cooperate. When she had bent down to fetch my Coors, her right boob had popped out of her halter-top. "Wow, word gets out fast around here," I said as I re-wiped the bottle with the napkin she had put under the beer.

"Faster than a tick can jump on a dog," she answered while she put her breast back like it happened all the time.

I took a quick swallow to regain my composure. "I doubt that Amy will stay long, but did you know that bastard deputy tried to pin Atkins' murder on Meg?"

She quit playing with her halter top and went back to wiping down the bar. "Really?" she answered without looking in my direction.

"Seems someone made a call from here saying they saw her dump the body at her dock. Whoever it was tried to block the caller ID, but that doesn't work when you call 911." The part about blocking the call came to me out of the blue. I was hoping she might be dumb enough to say she didn't try to block the call.

"Must have another customer," she said, looking at the cat. "Tonto hears them before anyone."

I could hear several voices coming through the front door. "Tonto?" I asked, following her gaze. "That's a funny name."

"He was named after the movie." She went to greet her new customers while I sat wondering what movie she was talking about.

When they took a booth next to his, Tonto decided he didn't care much for the newcomers, so he came over to me and started to rub against my leg. I reached down to pet him, and before I knew it, he was up in my lap, purring like the kitten he once was.

"Well if that ain't the cat's meow," Linda said when she returned to the bar. "He don't usually take to no strangers."

I smiled and continued petting him. "You were telling me something about a movie?" I asked.

"*Harry and Tonto.* The old man who used to own the place was named Harry," she answered while mixing some drinks. "Said it was his favorite movie, so when that old Tom kept coming around, he decided to call him Tonto."

I made a mental note to rent the movie someday, but decided to get back to the reason why I had come here in the first place. I just had to figure out a clever way to pick her brain.

She handed me another beer before I could say anything. "On the house, Catnip. Hey why don't you come back after six when my shift is over? You could get us some Chinese takeout and a six pack. I've got a tape of that old movie, and we could watch it together at my place." Then, before I could answer, she was off with the tray of drinks.

Linda didn't return before I finished my beer. It seems she knew the people at the booth and wouldn't stop talking to them. "Sorry, Tonto," I said to my new friend while putting him gently on the floor. "It looks like I need to get going." I glanced once more at Linda and headed for the door.

It was only three o'clock, and I had three hours to kill before picking up Linda. I decided I'd stop by and see Rosenblum to take care of my motor home. Before I managed to make it two blocks down the road, I saw the flashing red and blue lights in my mirror. It was a sheriff's car, and I didn't have to guess who.

"Please pull over now," said a voice from the loudspeaker in the sheriff's car. Luckily, there was a turnout on the shoulder ahead, and I pulled into it. I watched in my rear-view mirrors as the deputy got out of his car and headed my way. Sure enough, it was Sergeant Bennet.

Bennet stood just behind me on the driver's side, so I couldn't face him without breaking my neck. "What did I do, Sergeant?" I asked.

"Can I see your license and proof of insurance, please?"

He had to move forward in order to take the documents. He must have smelled my breath. "Have you been drinking, Mister Martin?"

"Just a couple beers, but that was a while ago."

It was all he needed. The breath test was close to the legal limit for Missouri, so he decided I needed a blood test. Refusal would be akin to admitting guilt, so he put me in his cruiser and hauled me off to jail – in cuffs. It wasn't an arrest; but it was several hours by the time he did the blood test, and they released me. Once outside the jail, I called the Pig's Roast from my cell phone.

Sam, the bartender from the other night, answered. "Hi, Jake, where are you?" he asked.

"I got tied up at Rosenblum's office," I lied. I had chosen to make my call from a bench in the city-center across from the jail. An older couple, in a bench across from me, stopped talking when I mentioned my lawyer. I lowered my voice then continued. "Is Linda still there? We, sort of, had a date."

"Sorry, Jake. She left with Ron Nixon over an hour ago," he answered. "Get off that stool, Tonto, and let a paying customer sit down."

"Ron Nixon? Mike's friend, the security guard?" I asked, forgetting to lower my voice.

"That's him. Sorry, Jake, but I'm really busy. Stop by sometime, and I'll fill you in." Then he hung up.

Next, I tried to call Meg but got her voice mail instead. I left her a message anyway. "Hey, Meg. I got shanghaied by your favorite cop, and I need a ride back to my car. Call me if you get this, or I will have to ask Mom for a ride."

The gray-hair lady across from me said something to the old guy sitting next to her. Then he got up and approached me. "Jake Martin?" he asked.

"Yes," I answered, shocked that he knew me. "Have we met?"

"I'm sorry," he answered back. "My name's Harley Maguire. We saw you with your family the other day at the Rusted Kettle. I don't mean to intrude, but Sharon, she's my wife over there, insists I offer you a ride."

Had this been Denver, or any other big city, I would have refused the couple on the spot. But this was Truman, Missouri. Unless this was Bonnie and Clyde grown old, I didn't think I had to worry about being robbed. "Well thank you, Harley," I said. "I could use a ride back to my car. My mother has her hands full with my father. I'm glad I don't have to ask them."

Sharon had joined us by now. "That's what I was telling Harley. Your parents go to our church, and I know what she goes through just to get him there. So I told Harley here to give you a ride. I knew it was you because you look so much like Marvin. Especially in ..."

Harley cut off his wife in mid-sentence. "We don't have all day to stand here and chatter, Woman. Let's get this boy to his car sometime this year," he said. Then he pointed toward an old Ford Crown Victoria. "Our car is right over there, Jake."

The ride back to my car was what I expected. They insisted I ride 'shotgun,' and Harley drove along at twenty-five miles an hour. Sharon never stopped talking. I had blocked her out almost completely, until she mentioned Nixon. "Bad news he is, Jake" she said. "I couldn't help but hear you mention his name. You take my advice and stay away from him. He's been nothing but trouble since he was a kid. He and that Bill Atkins were always getting into one scrape or another."

My car was in view when she woke me from my trance. "That's my car over there, Harley," I said and then turned around to answer Sharon. "Thank you, Sharon. I never met the guy, so I'll be extra careful if I ever do."

Harley pulled in behind my car, and I was out the door before the car came to a complete stop. "I can't thank you guys enough. I'll be sure to tell my parents how helpful you were." My phone rang before Sharon could reply.

I reached for my phone and waved goodbye. "Hello," I said without having time to see who it was. It was Megan, and she was crying. "Jake, Daddy's dead."

CHAPTER 10

Megan and Mother were a mess until after the funeral. Even Kevin surprised me when he broke down at the service. I held up fairly well, until the eulogy. Being the only son, I had the honor of summarizing my father's life in fifteen minutes. Luckily for me, Amy was in the church with Hal and Taylor, and I didn't want her to see a grown man cry. She had gone back home, and back to Hal, the same day my father died. Once my mother took over the guest room that had been vacated by Amy, Taylor followed shortly thereafter.

My father was buried the following Thursday morning in a cemetery overlooking the Osage branch of Lake of the Ozarks. The local chapter of the VFW gave him a twenty-one gun salute and presented my mother with a military flag for his service during the Vietnam War. I had been searching the crowd for Amy when I noticed the footprints left by two of the honor guards. They were nearly identical to the print Fred had found just a week earlier.

Because Meg's house was too far away, the reception was held at my mother's church; Mom wouldn't step foot in her own house yet. I noticed Amy and Taylor in the crowd and started to work my way toward her, but I stopped when I bumped into one of the VFW honor guards. It was Harley, the old guy who had given me a ride a few days earlier.

"I'm really sorry about your father, Jacob," he said while trying to balance a plate of food on top of his drink. "He will be missed at the meetings."

He was still dressed in his uniform from the funeral. "Thank you, Harley," I replied as I scanned the room for Amy. "I'll miss him too."

"Are you looking for someone?" he asked.

"Just checking on my mother," I answered, trying to focus on the old veteran. "I didn't mean to be rude. In fact, I wanted to ask you something. I'm glad I ran into you."

Harley put his food down on a nearby table and started to do the same with his drink. I could now see had hot coffee. It must have been burning his hand; it was starting to shake. "Let me get that for you, Harley," I said and reached out to steady his hand.

"Thank you, Jacob. The Parkinson's is acting up again," he said, letting me take the coffee before sitting down. "What is it you wanted to ask me?"

I saw Hal approach Amy out of the corner of my eye, but I didn't dare turn to look; I didn't want to offend Harley again. "It's those boots you're wearing," I answered. "What brand are they. I don't recall ever seeing those at Wal-Mart."

Harley grinned like I had just told a joke. "That'll be the day when Wal-Mart sells these," he said, lifting a foot a few inches off the ground. "You have to special order Bates in these parts."

Then it hit me. I felt so stupid. I should have realized the print would be in reverse making the S and E in BATES look like a 2 and a 3. "Where can I get a pair, Harley? They look comfortable."

Before he could answer, his wife came over carrying two huge plates of food. "There you are. I've been looking all over for you," she said as she sat down across from us. "That was such a nice eulogy you gave your father, Jacob. He would have been so proud of you."

"Thank you, Sharon," I said, looking past her while watching Hal and Amy leave. I was trapped. I couldn't run after Amy without offending the good Samaritans who had given me a ride when I needed it.

Sharon took a spoonful of potato salad and had it half eaten it when she looked up. "Isn't that the judge?" she asked in a muted voice. I didn't know if it was the food or if she was trying to be discreet.

"Hope that lawyer don't break his nose," Harley answered. "Makes me sick the way he's always kissing up to him."

I looked over just in time to see Rosenblum leave his friend and head our way. "I think he wants to see me," I said to the couple. "Thank you for coming, and thank you, Harley, for telling me about those boots." Then I left them and headed toward Rosenblum.

"Jacob, I'm so sorry about your father," he said and held out his hand when I met him halfway.

"Thanks, Ira," I replied while accepting his handshake, and I led him out of earshot of the Maguires. "I'm glad you're here. I've been wanting to ask a favor of you."

Rosenblum's expression changed immediately. "If it's about the will, Jake, your father put it all on tape. Your mother has a copy and will show it to everyone later."

Now I was the one caught off guard. I didn't think my father had anything worth putting in a will. "No. I was wondering if you could run a DMV check for me. Someone with a Tracker boat has been up to no good, and it occurred to me you might have the connections to run a check on Tracker boats in the Truman area."

A smile started to return to his face. "That search shouldn't turn up more than a few hundred boats."

"You're probably right," I answered. "Seems the only good idea I had since I got here was buying that motor home. Which reminds me, I think I'll call the son and see when I can pick it up. My insurance company won't pay for my rental any longer."

Rosenblum told me to stop by his office for the motor home title when I had a chance and promised he would have a friend get me the DMV search if he could. I didn't tell him what I was going to do with the search results once I had them. I didn't want to implicate the lawyer in the crime I was about to commit. All I had to do to find Mike's murderer was cross reference that data with

Hal's email contact list. And that would require some shady hacking.

We didn't get a chance to see the tape until later that evening. My mother wanted to stay after the reception to help clean up, and I had to find a VCR. It was a pain, but eventually, I found one in a second-hand store just before they were ready to close.

It was weird watching him on the tape so soon after the funeral. He was sitting in his favorite chair with his feet resting on a worn-out footstool and talking into the camera. "Rosenblum suggested that your mom and me consider a reverse mortgage in case this should happen. The mortgage was finalized last week, and I used some of the funds to pay everyone's legal fees and get Megan's house out of foreclosure. The rest has been invested in a trust fund that will be used to pay the taxes and insurance on the house, as well as help cover some of my lost Social Security benefits."

All this was news to me, but my mother and sister didn't act the least bit surprised. Then my father cleared his throat and continued. "I'm sorry, Jake, if you feel left out. The house is all I had, and I had to make sure your mother wasn't evicted after I died. I hope you understand."

He finished with a plea for Kevin to quit smoking. Whoever was running the camcorder must have accidentally tipped it to turn it off. I got a close-up view of Dad's boots. They were made by Bates.

***

As we sat on the lower-level deck later that afternoon, Fred and I discussed my dilemma. We were once again relegated to the walkout basement until Mother went home. "Well, old boy, do we go home or stick around and help Megan?" Neither choice appealed to me, so I thought I'd ask Fred. I had nothing but bills to face back home, and after getting cut from the will, I was not in the mood to help my sister.

Fred barked twice. His answer could have been a yes or no, but I had a feeling he just wanted more beer. We spent the rest of the night drinking the last of the six-pack. I should have been thinking of how I was going to hack into the Hal's computer once Rosenblum got my Tracker list, but my mind kept drifting to the night I spent talking with Amy only ten feet above. I couldn't remember the last time I'd been so happy or talked so much.

Once the beer was gone, Fred tired of my conversation and fell asleep. I resisted the urge to pet him before going back into my room. His legs were twitching and his eyes were going back and forth. He must have been dreaming. How I envied his ability to fall asleep at a time like this. I spent the rest of the night in the kitchen, drinking coffee, trying to figure out how to get access to Hal's computer.

Mother was the first to rise, unless you consider not going to bed at all making me first. "Good morning, Jacob. Did you sleep well?"

"As well as could be, Mom. How are you doing?" I said as I poured us both a cup of coffee and popped some bagels in the toaster.

Tears were forming in her eyes. "It's so strange waking up without your father." She wiped her eyes with a napkin then fished through her purse for her compact. "Jacob?" she asked. "You're not upset are you?"

"You mean about the will? No. I understand." I lied. *How could it not bother me*, I wanted to ask, but I held it in and lowered my eyes to study my coffee cup.

Mother had finished fixing her face and reached for a bagel. "I know it sounds like Megan is our favorite," she said in a softer voice I rarely heard. "But it's not true. Your father loved you just as much. He only did it to keep her from losing everything until the insurance comes through. She has promised to give you your share then." She was holding her bagel dangerously close to Fred.

"It's okay, Mom. Really." Fred couldn't resist any longer and grabbed for her bagel; he swallowed it in one bite.

"Jacob! He nearly took my fingers!" she yelled as she stood up. "I don't know why you don't get rid of that mangy mutt." Fred gave her his best smile and waited for more.

Mother left in a huff before I had a chance to respond. I felt like running after her and telling her how I really felt about the will, but I just held on to Fred for fear that he should follow her for more bagels.

Megan must have heard us in the kitchen. She had been heading toward us when she saw Mother leave upset. "What's wrong, Mom?" I heard her say. Mother said something to her I couldn't hear and then went on her way.

Megan was smiling when she joined me at the kitchen table. She reached down and petted Fred. "I hear you've been a bad boy this morning, Freddie," she said with a huge grin on her face.

"Good morning, Sleeping Beauty," I said to her. "Can I get you some coffee?"

"Thank you, Porky. I'd like that very much." Her smile had vanished. "Then, we need to talk."

Could she have heard Mom and me talking? I wondered while I got up and fetched her coffee. "Care for a bagel?" I asked, trying to remember if I had said something to hurt Megan's feelings.

"Maybe later. I'm sorry we didn't tell you about the money," she answered. "But I only found out a couple days ago myself."

The coffee was barely warm. A light was blinking on the coffee pot. First it was blue, then red, and then blue again. "What's wrong with this thing, Meg?" I asked while putting her cup in the microwave.

She looked at me with an odd, blank look. "Is the microwave broken?" she asked.

"No. I meant the coffee pot. These lights have been going on all morning. It's starting to annoy me." I set the microwave for thirty seconds and pushed start.

"It wants to be cleaned," she answered. "Another example of irritating technology."

The microwave dinged, but I just stood there frozen. Some people would call it an epiphany or, at the least, a revelation. Whatever one called it, I suddenly realized who murdered Mike and Bill. "It's Bennet," I said.

Her blank look was back. "What are you talking about, Jake?"

"Well, I don't have all the details yet." I was interrupted by another ding of the microwave before I could finish. I removed the cup and joined her at the table. "Bennet is the guy in the Tracker. He must be the mysterious Born2fish that we found on Mike's computer. He was evidently looking for something down by your dock that could connect him to Atkins' murder. I think he must have dropped something down there when he dumped Bill's body."

Megan took a sip of her coffee then made a sour face and set it down. "Nothing worse than reheated coffee," she said. "I know Bennet isn't your favorite deputy, but how on earth did you come to that ridiculous conclusion?"

"The blinking lights and the boots," I answered. "That's why computers will never take over. Only the human brain has the gift to make such a far-out connection."

Megan's expression changed to condescendence. "Have you been drinking already, Jake?"

I sat down at the table and took a deep breath to collect my thoughts. "Mike and Bill knew something that got them killed. My guess is they were blackmailing Bennet, or should I say Born2fish, and it cost them their lives."

Megan got up and went over to the coffee pot. "Go on," she said, and started to make a fresh pot.

"At first, I thought Mike was just trying to sell coins to Hal. Now I realize it was the other way around. Hal gave Mike, or Bill, the coins to pay him off."

Megan finished with the coffee maker and returned to the table. I could see I finally had her interest. "It must have been Bill," she said. "Mike would never get involved in blackmail. He was a lot of things, but he was not a crook. But I thought you said Bennet killed them. Why did Hal pay them off?"

"Hal is Bennet's partner. Hal and Bennet are involved in drugs. When Bill, assuming Mike was an altar boy as you say, found out, he decided to get in on the deal. That's when Hal paid them off with his coin collection until Bennet could take care of business."

Megan just stared at me. It seemed like forever, but the stare only lasted a few seconds. "And you got all this from a pair of boots and a coffee pot?"

I had to laugh. "That and Taylor's truck. Then I had a little help from my new friends, the Maguires."

Megan looked at me with a smile of recognition. "Of course. The police auction. Bennet must have told Hal to buy the truck. That explains why he insisted on buying that piece of junk. But how did..." Her coffee maker cut her off. Brown liquid was pouring all over her counter.

Megan jumped out of her chair and rushed over to the pot. "Damn piece of junk," she said. "Just because I didn't put the pot all the way in, it has to punish me." She unplugged the pot and began wiping up the mess. "But how did this Chinese piece of crap and the Maguires help you solve the puzzle?"

Despite my sister's predicament at the moment, I felt like I just won Jeopardy and couldn't wait to tell the world. "The boots that Harley wore at the funeral are the same brand as those that made the prints by our mysterious fisherman. They are made by a company called Bates, a company that specializes in boots for military and law enforcement. It was the red and blue flashing lights of your irritating coffee pot that turned on my neurons to make the connection to Bennet."

"Sounds logical," Megan said after returning to the table. "Good thing you haven't been drinking."

Now it was my turn to second guess. "Why's that, Meg?"

"Because now all you have to do is prove it, and there's no more coffee to sober you up. That was the last of it," she said, pointing toward her hissing coffee maker.

CHAPTER 11

The first step in connecting Bennet to the murders was to get the DMV check from Rosenblum. I needed some proof that it was Bennet in the Tracker boat who had been sneaking around Meg's dock. Rosenblum still had the title to my motor home, so I decided to drive over to his office and kill the proverbial two birds.

By the time I pulled on to the highway toward town, I was beginning to wish I had kept my theory of the murders to myself. I was going to need a lot more than a boat and a pair of shoes to prove Bennet was the culprit. Then I saw the Pig's Roast up ahead and impulsively pulled into the parking lot. With any luck, Linda would be working her shift.

The bartender from the day before was serving, and Linda was nowhere in sight. "Look who the dog drug in," he said.

"Hi, Sam," I said while taking a seat at the bar. "Did Linda get my message?"

He already had an open Coors for me. "Sorry, Jake. Better luck next time," he said as he handed me my beer. "She took off with the roofer who's been hanging around here. Came by this morning for her paycheck, and said they were on their way to California. But she did leave you this note." He handed me a folded piece of paper with the same beautiful handwriting I had seen on the menu of the Rusted Kettle.

I looked around the bar to see who was listening then stuffed it in my back pocket and reached for my beer. "One more Dear John to add to my collection," I said for the benefit of a couple at a nearby table. There were several more people at the window tables, but I figured with the juke box blasting out an old Dolly Parton classic that they were too far away to catch our conversation.

"Yeah, me too," he answered with a sad voice. "My note said basically the same thing. I'm going to miss her big fat-ass bouncing around here."

I started to say something almost as crude when we were interrupted by one of the patrons at the window table waving for Sam's attention. Sam rolled his eyes, but not so the customer could see, and he headed over to their table. I put a five on the counter and headed out the door. "Catch you later, Sam. I've got an appointment with my lawyer," I said.

Despite the white-lie I told Sam, I didn't have an actual appointment with Rosenblum. His secretary acted upset when I barged into his office. I knew he had a secretary from the first time I had contacted him on my phone back at the Kansas rest-area, but this was the first time I actually met her. "I'm sorry. Mr. Rosenblum has a client right now. Was he expecting you?" she asked. She was flipping through what looked to be an appointment book.

She didn't look like the sexpot I'd imagined. I was beginning to wonder if she was his mother when the office door opened and a balding, gray-hair, distinguished gentleman walked out. Rosenblum was right behind him. I recognized his visitor as Judge Simons from my father's funeral reception.

Rosenblum acknowledged me with a nod of his head while walking his friend to the outer door. "Thank you, George. And don't forget our tee-time tomorrow," he said before shutting the door.

"Jake! Come on in to my office. I thought you'd be here an hour ago," he said and offered his hand. He turned to his secretary, who had given up on her appointment book and was just staring at me. "It's okay Shirley. This is Jake Martin. We won't take a minute."

He headed for his office without waiting for her to greet me. I followed like a kid being led to the principal's office, wondering how he knew I was coming. Rosenblum offered me a chair and went behind his desk. "I think this is what you came for," he said, picking up some papers off his desk. "Here's the title for your motor home and the carfax I ran on Taylor's truck. Sorry, but I couldn't get the DMV check you wanted."

I dropped the papers. "How did you know I was coming?" I asked.

He smiled and retrieved the papers from his desk a second time. "Megan told me you were on your way. I expected you before lunch, so I didn't tell my secretary. Now tell me why you think Bennet killed Mike and Bill."

My mind was racing, trying to guess how much he knew. I sat back down and told him my theory about the murders. Like most stories that get told and re-told, it took me much longer than when I first told Megan. I had to fill him in on details like the boot print and how I met the Maguires. We were only interrupted by his secretary twice.

He didn't seem to mind that it took more than a couple of minutes to explain my theory. "I'd be careful who you tell that to. Bennet has a lot of powerful friends around here," he said after I finished. "That's why I couldn't get the DMV check."

Rosenblum leaned back in his chair the way I'd seen him do several days ago when Meg and I had been here. "I have a feeling Bennet was on the list of Tracker owners, and my source must have got cold feet. But if you're so sure he did it, you don't really need the list anymore – just drive by his place. He lives next to the school on Elm."

"If the boat is there. He could have it in the water someplace or in storage," I answered, waiting for him to slip and fall from his chair. To my disappointment, it didn't happen.

Rosenblum rose from his chair. I assumed it was my cue to leave, so I rose too. "Thanks, Ira. I'll check out Bennet's house like you suggested, and this carfax will be a big help once I contact some of the previous owners to see if they knew Hal."

"That would be dangerous, Jake. If someone on that list is dealing drugs, you don't want them on your tail. Look at the service locations. Check to see if Hal has any customers in those locations, and you might have some real evidence."

I thanked the lawyer again and left his office with the title to my new motor home, and I headed toward the license bureau. I had gone into Rosenblum's office thinking I had all the answers to solving Mike's murder, and now I realized, I had nothing. Like he said, I needed real evidence; hunches would never prove anything in court.

Truman had the only license bureau for the entire county. Most states called it the Department of Motor Vehicles, but I could plainly see the sign down the street saying otherwise. It was in the same square as the courthouse and only a short walk from Rosenblum's office. A bell over the door announced my presence. When I walked in, two women in their mid to late forties looked up from their computer screens. The office wasn't much bigger than a one-room schoolhouse. It didn't look the least bit official. There were no long lines waiting for the next available clerk - only the two women and one haggard-looking gray-haired man at the counter. I must have entered the wrong building. I went back outside, took a second look at the sign, and then went back inside. The bell rang again.

"Is this where I get plates for a vehicle?" I asked while walking toward the counter.

Everyone stopped whatever they were doing and looked my way, all three of them. "Yes, Sir," one of the women replied. She was a dead ringer for the actress in the movie *Misery*. "What can we help you with?"

"I just bought a motor home and need to get plates for it." I said, handing her the title. "Are you related to Kathy Bates by any chance?"

"Who?" she asked.

"The actress. You could pass as her twin." The bell rang again, and we both turned our heads to watch a huge guy come through the door. His head nearly touched the top of the jamb, and there wasn't an inch left on either side.

"Hi, honey," she said to the Incredible Hulk. "Would you be a sweetheart and lock the door? I can leave after I finish here." Without saying a word, her sweetheart did as he was told. And I began to wonder if I could escape out the back before they had a chance to torture me. Visions of her swinging a sledge hammer against my ankles, like in the movie, filled my head.

Kathy turned back to me. "We will need proof of insurance, and your personal property tax receipts. I also need to see your inspection report."

"Property tax receipts?" I asked, deciding to drop the chit-chat before hubby, or whoever he was, took offense.

"I can call over to the collector's office, and she can confirm you paid your taxes if you want. Unless you're new here. Then you will have to get a new residence card from her."

"Won't do you no good." The old man next to me cut in. "Mary done left already. I just come from there."

I couldn't help but turn to the old guy, but I was distracted by what I saw on the computer screen his clerk was using. It looked like a vehicle history report like the one Rosenblum had given me. "So I can't leave Dodge until Monday?" I asked.

He looked at me blankly. "What's that supposed to mean?" he asked.

He wasn't alone. Even the Incredible Hulk was staring at me. "Sorry. It's another one of my bad jokes," I answered before turning back to the clerk. "Actually, I don't live here. I only wanted to get a temporary tag to get me by for a couple of weeks until I go back to Colorado."

Being from out of town had been all the explanation I needed. The Hulk went back to reading his Sports Illustrated, and the leathered sole next to me finished his business and left without looking my way. The clerk that reminded me of Kathy Bates gave me a thirty-day tag, and I left without offending the Hulk.

***

Later that night, while having our beer out on the deck, Fred once again pretended to listen to me. There was a slight westerly breeze coming off the water that made the humidity bearable and kept the bugs at bay. I was working on my fourth or fifth beer. Fred was still on his first. "What do you think, Freddie? Do you have any good ideas on how we get that list?" It beat talking to myself.

Fred pushed my hand holding the beer. He answered me with a sneeze after slopping up another puddle full of bubbles.

"What list is that?" asked a voice from behind me. I didn't turn to look. I could pick out my sister's voice in a choir.

"Hal's contact list," I answered without looking at her. "Did you bring us another beer?"

Megan put a cold Keystone on the table and looked down at Fred. "Aren't you afraid you'll fry his liver or something?" she asked.

"What about my liver? How am I ever going to hack into Hal's computer when I'm hooked to a dialysis machine?"

She took a chair across the table from me and sipped on her wine. "Why would you do that?

"Oh yeah, you're right. That's for kidneys isn't it?"

Megan started to get up. "Maybe we should talk in the morning. I can see you and Fred have had too much to drink. You know I meant Hal's computer."

"Sorry," I said, raising my hands in a gesture of surrender. "Rosenblum thinks I need to check Hal's customers against a list he gave me today."

She leaned forward to pet Fred and started rubbing his ears. "Yeah, I know. He told me all about your visit."

"He called you?"

"No. I called him." She stopped rubbing Fred's ears and sat back in her chair. Fred pushed up against her, wanting more. "I got another notice on the house today. They're threatening foreclosure already, so I called Ira for his advice."

I poured more beer on the deck. It was a sure way to get Fred to stop bothering her. "So soon? What happened to the money Dad left you?"

Megan got up from her chair again. Only this time, she was on the verge of tears. "I used it to pay bills and bought a few things for the house. Hell, I don't know. I never was very good with money. You know that," she said, then started to sob.

I spent the next hour nursing the last of my beer while trying to figure out how on earth she had managed to spend so much so soon. Fred wasn't much help. He had left with Megan, probably hoping for another ear rub. Eventually, I gave up trying to analyze women's spending habits and went to bed.

CHAPTER 12

It was well after ten on Saturday morning when Fred woke me up with his ritual. If I had still been sleeping on the couch and not moved down to the unfinished lower level, he would not have bothered. Someone else would have already let him out by now. When I didn't respond to his pacing and tail thumping, he tried licking me awake.

"Okay, Boy, you win," I said and let him out the door. I hadn't hooked up a toilet, so I took Fred's lead and let my bladder go off the side of the deck, too.

"Jacob Martin. I didn't raise you in a barn. Can't you use the bathroom?" My mother was on the upper deck.

"Morning, Mom. Coffee still hot?"

I zipped up and joined the family on the deck for a late breakfast. Fred didn't care if his privates were showing and beat me to the table. Megan was grinning from ear to ear. "I see you're in a good mood this morning," I said to her. "What happened? Did you win the lottery since last night?"

"She's finally come to her senses and is going to sell this albatross." Mother answered for her while giving Fred a piece of burnt bacon.

Megan's grin turned into a frown. "The realtor will be here this afternoon. Ira says I can still come out with enough to get by for a while. At least until I can find a job, or somebody gets off his butt and proves Mike didn't kill himself."

"Rosenblum said that?" I asked, feigning shock. "I wouldn't think he'd be so unprofessional."

Megan played with the scrambled eggs on her plate, picking through them like they might be infected with ants. "No, of course not. But you know there are no jobs around here. I really need that insurance, Jake."

"Are you going to eat that?" I asked. "If not, give it to me, and I'll tell you about the dream I had last night to get the proof you need."

Mother spoke as though she never heard a word of our conversation. "I think it's time I went home," she said out of the blue.

Megan stopped playing with her eggs and slid the plate toward me. "Today, Mom?" she asked.

Our mother looked at Fred instead of looking at Megan. "It's so strange going back without your father. Maybe I should get a dog to keep me company." Then she raised her head. I could see tears in her eyes. "No. Not today. Maybe tomorrow. Anita's been keeping an eye on the house, so I'm sure she won't mind another day or two."

I started to ask who Anita was when we heard the sliding door open. Kevin and Taylor were up before noon. Fred was the first to greet them.

Kevin bent down to pat Fred on the head, "Mornin' Freddie." He looked at the empty plates on the table, and said: "What's for breakfast, Mom. I'm starving."

"Can't you greet your grandmother and uncle, too?" Megan answered.

My mother was already out of her chair and on her way to the kitchen. "Scrambled okay?" she asked.

Taylor opened the door for her. "Can I help you, Mrs. Martin?" he asked while following her into the house. Kevin and Fred knew where the food would be and followed alongside.

Megan waited for everyone to leave. She cupped her hands together, holding her head with her elbows on the table. "Well?" she asked. "Are you going to tell me about your dream?"

"Well, Mrs. Freud, it's quite elementary."

Megan laughed and said, "Aren't you mixing metaphors there? Even I know the difference between Freud and Sherlock Holmes. Maybe you should forget about telling me your dream and cut to the chase."

I thought about that for a moment and realized she was right. My dream involved a lot more than a solution to hacking into Hal's computer – it would be best if I skipped over the part involving Linda smothering me with kisses. "I'll take your pontoon for a ride down the lake and park by Hal's house. I doubt his internet is secured, so I'll simply connect to his computer through his router. Then I'll search his webpage cache and cookies for usernames and passwords. I can pack it up and leave once I get his email ID and password."

Megan gave me her Fred impersonation: the dumb look he gives me when he doesn't understand me. "Right. Clear as mud. What good will his email ID do you?"

"I'll bet my next paycheck there's an email in there that will connect Bennet and the drug dealers. And if we're really lucky, something to prove Bennet killed Mike and Bill."

Megan laughed. Not the hiccup inducing laugh of something really funny, but the Doubting Thomas kind. "Ah, Porky. Did you forget? You don't have any paychecks?"

Fred and I went on our little boat ride later that day. Megan stayed behind with our mother, who wouldn't go; she never learned to swim and didn't trust boats. I didn't dare ask Taylor to tag along on my intrusion into his father's computer, and Kevin was attached to Taylor at the hip. That left Fred as my only passenger.

The boat had been sitting in the dock since before Mike's death. Its pontoons had a thick coat of algae at the water line, and I didn't know if it had any gas or if it would even start. I took the keys from under the seat. Meg said Mike hid them there because he was always losing them, and I tried to start the motor. Nothing happened, not even a click. "So much for a three-hour tour, Gilligan," I said to Fred.

Gilligan started barking. I looked in the direction he was focused on. The outboard motor had a little round squeeze-bulb that had to be pumped to get gas to the motor. Fred must have thought it was a ball and wanted me to throw it for him. "Not now, Freddie," I said. "And if you're trying to tell me to squeeze it, you're dumber than I thought. There's an electrical problem not a fuel problem."

Nonetheless, I went over and squeezed the bulb. Then I saw the cable next to the battery. It was disconnected. "Maybe you should be the skipper," I said and started the motor after connecting the battery and squeezing the gas bulb three times.

We cruised out of the cove and onto the main channel. Fred acted like a puppy trying to catch the spray coming over the bow. I guess he was just a dog after all. For a while there, I thought he had more sense than me. You couldn't pay me to drink this water. Unlike the clear blue lakes and rivers back home, where you could see trout ten feet down, this water was the color of sewer water with visibility no more than three inches. There could be a shark down there, and you would never know it until it bit you. Water quality aside, I did have to marvel at how peaceful this end of the lake was compared to the hustle at the dam. We barely saw another boat, and when we did, the people never failed to wave. I was beginning to wish Hal and Amy lived further away when I saw their dock up ahead.

Maybe bringing Fred along on my first felony wasn't such a good idea. We were getting ready to tie up to Hal's dock when I realized Fred might start barking. I knew Amy would be at work, but I wasn't so sure about Hal. Then I saw the sign on the dock and quickly pushed off. "THIS PROPERTY IS UNDER VIDEO SURVIELLANCE," the sign read. It could have been one of those fake warnings to scare away an intruder; I couldn't see any cameras or wiring, but I couldn't afford to take the chance. With state of the art technology, it was possible to hide a wireless camera almost anywhere.

"What now, Fred? I don't have a plan C." Fred responded with his usual bark, and we pulled away from the dock and headed down stream. Although it was hot and humid, the wind and spray of the water felt good. I decided to mix business with pleasure and do a little cruising. Maybe I'd get lucky and find the Tracker boat in someone's dock.

The lake had another thing going for it that Colorado waters didn't. There was a bar or waterfront restaurant every few miles. I pulled the boat into the dock of a lakeside restaurant and tied her off. Fred stayed on the boat while I went in for my afternoon libation.

The bartender was an older woman who was missing most of her teeth. "Afternoon, stranger. What can I get ya?"

On closer examination I decided she had to be at least ten years younger than I first thought. She wasn't all that bad looking either. Given a set of dentures, she would be considered attractive. "Coors Light, Please."

"So what do you think of your Broncos now?" she asked while reaching under the counter for my beer. "Looks like they forgot to show up yesterday." I forgot I was wearing my Broncos hat, and this was Chief's territory. A quick look around the bar assured me I was in no immediate danger. There was only one other customer, an old man with a cane leaning against the bar. I figured I could probably take him if I had to.

"Tell me about it," I answered. "They can't seem to do anything right since Elway retired."

She wiped off my bottle with a rag that looked like it had been used to clean the floor. It reminded me of the same hygiene I observed at the Pig's Roast. Maybe they used river water to clean their towels. "Two bucks, unless you want to run a tab," she said, handing me my beer.

"No tab, but can I get a couple of burgers and a six pack to go? I don't want to leave my dog down there too long. He's liable to go for a swim any minute."

"Sure thing, Sweetie. I'm also the cook today, so if you need another beer while I'm gone, just ask Clarence," she gestured toward the end of the bar.

The old guy who had been watching us got off his stool at the mention of his name, then limped over and took a stool next to me. "Saw you pull up in that pontoon down there. I had a friend with one just like it," he said. "Clarence is my name. Clarence Bukowski. I don't think I've seen you around much."

"Mine's Jake. Thanks, but the boat belongs to my sister. It was her husband's before he died. Maybe you know her. Megan Carver. She has a house less than a couple of miles from here, on the lake."

"I told Carrie you was Meg's brother. Didn't I, Carrie?" he called out to the barmaid. But she was already out of hearing range or had just decided to ignore him. "Me and your dad used to fish all over the lake in that boat before we both got too sick. That's when he gave it to Mike. Bet you didn't know there's a live well under the front seat. Course we never put no minners in there, just our beer. I'm sure gonna miss Marvin."

Then I made the connection. "Bukowski? Do you know a Linda Bukowski?"

"Fraid so. She's my granddaughter. Been one wild ride with that girl, I'll tell you. But deep down, she's really a good kid. Why you ask? She leave you with a broken heart?"

I looked at Clarence and could see a slight resemblance to Linda. He had the same short-stocky frame as his granddaughter and the same dark eyes. "No. Nothing like that. I only met her a couple of times is all." It didn't seem appropriate to tell Clarence I once had the hots for his granddaughter. "Heard she went to California. How's she doing out there?"

"Oh, she's on her way back already. Went out with some construction worker who left her for a hooker in Las Vegas. We had to send her the bus fare to get back home," he answered.

Before I had a chance to find out when Linda would be back, Carrie came over with a brown bag and a six-pack. "No charge, Jake," she said. "I'm sorry to hear about your father, and tell Meg that I'm praying for her."

I forgot about Linda instantly. Carrie's words put a lump in my throat. "Thank you, Carrie," I said. "Thank you very much." And I took my burgers and beer and headed toward the door.

I returned to the boat a little too late. Fred had jumped out and swam to shore. He was giving a fisherman a shower as he shook the water off. "Fred!" I yelled. "Get over here."

After apologizing to the fisherman and offering him one of my beers, I gave Fred his burger, and we got back on the boat. Once out and away from the docks, I gunned the motor and headed for home at the breakneck speed of fifteen miles an hour.

Fred was out on the front deck of the boat again, biting the spray as it came over the bow. I was wishing life could be so simple for us humans when I heard the siren behind me. A Missouri water patrol boat was flashing his blue light and signaling me to come to a stop.

"Something wrong, officer?" I asked after he tied up alongside.

"I stopped you because of the dog up front," he answered. "It's not legal to have a passenger outside the fence when the boat is in motion."

Fred started to growl, so I quickly opened the gate for him before he jumped in the water to attack the cop. "I'm sorry. I didn't know," I said, grabbing Fred by the collar.

The officer didn't try to board my boat. Either it was standard operating procedure for them to stay on their own vessel, or Fred had scared him off. "Can I see your registration and boating certificate?"

"Boating certificate? What's that?"

"Missouri requires a boating safety course for anyone born after January first nineteen eighty-four. Looks like you won't need that. Your driver's license will do," he answered.

Fred sat at the side rail watching our new visitor while I fumbled with my wallet. I gave the officer my license then went searching for the boat's registration. I couldn't find it. "It's my brother-in-law's boat, or was. He died last month, so now I guess it belongs to my sister. I have no idea where he put the registration."

He pointed to the key hanging from the shifter on the side of the boat. "Look in there," he said while keeping one eye on Fred. "That bobber holding the key is meant to keep the registration dry."

Sure enough, it was where he said it would be. "That's a clever idea," I said, handing him the folded piece of paper.

He removed his sunglasses and studied the document for a moment. Then, without putting his glasses back on, he looked at me. "I thought that boat looked familiar. I was at your sister's dock last week when the sheriff pulled that body out of the water."

"Then you know Sergeant Bennet?" I asked.

His eyes seemed to soften. "Chuck? He's a friend of yours too?"

I decided to press my luck a little further. "You could say we know each other. I found something by my dock that one of his deputies must have lost last week. Have you seen him out on his Tracker today by any chance?"

"No, but I can check when I run your registration." He left the side of his boat and picked up a microphone from the helm. I could hear him calling in a check on his radio. Then he started writing something on a pad he had under his dash. *Had he seen through my lie that easily?*

"I couldn't raise Chuck, and your boat checks out. So it looks like you're okay," he said when he came back to my side of his boat. "You and your family have been through enough, so I'll let you go with a warning."

He had me sign the warning then untied his boat. "I'll let Chuck know you're looking for him, and take care of that beautiful dog," he said over his shoulder while pulling away.

***

When I returned to the dock, Megan's realtor was putting the finishing touches on her 'For Sale' sign. "You must be Jake," she said after I stopped the motor and started tying the boat to the dock cleats. "I'm Janet. Megan didn't mention what a handsome brother she had."

She caught me off guard. It had been some time since a woman hit on me and not the other way around. She had to be at least ten years older than me, but she still had her looks and figure. Though, I could see they came at a price. Her choice of knee-high shorts and low-cut blouse may not have been professional, but they weren't cheap either. "Glad to meet you, Janet," I replied, wondering what she paid for tanning sessions and her silicone breasts.

"Megan says you talked her into listing the house. I hope you don't expect a finder's fee," she said with a laugh. "Well, maybe dinner. I'm told I cook a really good Boeuf en Daube."

"A what?" I asked.

She laughed again. This time it seemed genuine. "Pot roast," she answered.

"You sell the house, and I'll buy you dinner," I said. I didn't mention it would have to be from the dollar menu because of my finances.

Before she had a chance to accept my generous offer, Fred saw a stick float by and decided to show his retrieving ability. Naturally, he chose to do a belly flop and splash water all over us. Megan's new realtor didn't seem to mind, nor did she notice her hard-earned tan streaking down her legs. I guess I overestimated the cost of her youth. Even spray-on tans didn't wash off that easily. Fred came back with his stick, but we had beaten him to the lift before he could shake the water off. He would have to take the stairs, or my sister's new realtor would be a zebra before we reached the top.

"What's her chance of a quick sale?" I asked on the way up.

"Not good, I'm afraid. This market is tough on higher-end homes. I'll put it on the MLS of course, but our best bet is to run some ads in the Kansas City and St. Louis papers."

We reached the top, and Megan was there, waiting with her arms folded. My mother and the boys were sitting at the table eating lunch. "Where the hell have you been?" Megan said. "I've been trying to get you on your damn phone all afternoon."

"Sorry. The phone kept losing its signal, so I turned it off. Guess I forgot to turn it back on. Is something wrong?" I asked.

"Mom wants to go home. We need your help with the big rug in the great-room. I told her she could have it and anything else she wants."

Janet must have realized it was time to leave. "Well, Megan, I need to get back to the office and get started on this listing. I'll have someone come back for pictures." Then turning toward the lake, she said: "What a wonderful view you have from here, Megan. That picture alone should sell the house."

"Mike used to say it was a view to die for," Megan said, lowering her eyes. Then she noticed Janet's legs. "Did you fall in the water?" she asked.

"No. Jake's dog jumped in after a stick and splashed a little water on me. One of the hazards of my profession," she answered with a forced laugh.

"I'm sorry, Janet. He can be as big a pain as his master at times. Come with me, and I'll get you some dry clothes," she said as she led her realtor into the house.

Kevin put his hand over his mouth and kicked Taylor under the table while pointing at Janet's legs when she walked passed him. Pieces of Taylor's sandwich went flying from his mouth just as Megan and Janet closed the door.

"Are you alright, Taylor?" Mother asked.

"Sorry, Mrs. Martin. It must have gone down the wrong way."

CHAPTER 13

Since the rug wouldn't fit in Meg's Jeep, Taylor let us use his truck. He couldn't drive after losing his license, which meant I had the pleasure of listening to Mother complain all the way into Truman. She said it made her look like Grandma Clampet from the Beverly Hillbillies. She could have ridden with Megan and the boys in air-conditioned comfort, but she didn't want to wait for them to get ready.

The little house my parents had bought on Sycamore Street had been sitting empty since the funeral. Except for the overgrown grass, the house didn't look that bad. I pulled into the driveway and went around to the passenger side to help my mother when I saw a woman with hair the color of snow beat me to it. "You must be Jacob?" she said, blocking me from helping my Mother out of the truck. Taylor's truck had a lift-kit which made it impossible for my mother to get in or out without help.

"I'm Anita, your mother's next-door neighbor. I'm so sorry to hear about your father. He was such a dear man. And so helpful. He would always cut my lawn when he cut his, but now look at it. I'm going to miss him. Did you know...?"

"Are you going to help me out of this pile of junk, Jacob?"

Anita stopped talking and stepped aside. I quickly moved in and offered my mother my hand. "Thank you, Anita," I said, hoping she hadn't taken offense.

Anita ignored Mother's rudeness and kept on talking while I struggled to get my mother down from her perch. "How are you doing, Hazel? I hope you forgive me for missing Marvin's service. You know I adored him and wouldn't have missed it for anything; but my sister had come down with a terrible case of shingles, and I was in Kansas City. I do hope you understand – don't you? I feel so bad after all he did for me."

"I'll let you two catch up," I said and started for the house. "I'll go check out the air conditioner and get it going. It must be over a hundred in there with all the windows closed." It was my excuse to get away. I knew from experience not to get involved when my mother, or anyone her age, gets caught up in the disease of the week conversation.

I could feel something was wrong when I put the key in the door lock. It was one of those feelings that can't be explained, but all of a sudden, I had a terrible sense that someone had been here. My fear was confirmed when I opened the door. The house had been ransacked. From the doorway, I could see the couch cushions had been cut and stuffing was everywhere. "Mother, you better come and look at this!"

My mother turned toward me and asked, "What do you mean, Jake?" Anita kept on talking as though nothing was wrong. Mother left her in mid-sentence and walked briskly toward me.

"Oh my god! What happened?" she asked after she walked past me and into the house.

"It looks like you've been robbed, Hazel." Anita had come in behind us. "I better go home and call the police. Make sure you don't touch anything. My cousin in Springfield had a break-in, and the police were so upset with him when they found he cleaned up before they had a chance to get there. But they made him wait two days before they…"

"It's okay, Anita," I said. I'll call from my cell phone, but you better take my mother and go to your house while we wait for them."

My mother's phone line was cut, so I called 911 from my cell. The operator picked up immediately. I was surprised when she transferred me to the Truman police department when I told her the nature of my call. She must have deemed my call didn't qualify as an emergency. Truman police must have had the same thought. They told me someone would be out in a day or two to take a statement.

I'd seen enough shows on television to know not to disturb a crime scene, but it was obvious nobody was going to rush over with a CSI unit. So I decided to take some pictures of the damage with my phone before calling my mother back in.

Someone had been looking for something and didn't care what they destroyed to find it. Pictures had been ripped off the walls and holes punched in the drywall. They had smashed my grandmother's buffet and broke mirrors as though there might be something hidden between the glass and backing. There wasn't a piece of furniture, picture, or mirror that was still intact. They had even torn up the carpeting, where I assumed, they were looking for a floor safe.

I was taking my last picture when the front door opened. "My god. What happened in here?" It was my sister. Kevin and Taylor were right behind her with their mouths open, and I could see Mother and Anita coming up the walkway.

"Mom's been burglarized," I answered.

"No way," Kevin cut in. "Wait 'till I tell my friends. Do you think we'll get in the paper?" Then he pushed past his mother and walked into the living room.

"Don't touch anything, Kevin," Megan said. "We should wait for the police."

"It's okay," I said. "They're not coming."

"Too busy giving out tickets, I'll bet," Kevin said while heading for the kitchen. Taylor had taken his lead and followed right behind.

By now my mother and Anita had made their way into the house. "Not my mother's buffet," she cried. "That was our wedding gift." She must have missed it on her first inspection.

"Why would someone do this?" Megan asked. She had already gone over by the buffet and was picking through a pile of broken picture frames. "What could they possibly be looking for?"

It didn't take long for Mother to regain her composure. "This would have never happened, Jacob, if you had checked on the house more often."

That was more like the mother I knew. "We'll find the bastards, Mom. I promise. Can you tell if anything is missing? We should make a list for your insurance company and the police for when they do show up."

"Must you swear so much, Jacob? No, I have no idea if anything is missing. Thank the Lord I took all my jewelry over to Megan's."

Father had never owned any stocks or bonds, and any savings they had managed to put aside before he died would be in the bank – he didn't trust mattresses.

"I know what they was looking for, Uncle Martin." We all went silent and looked at Kevin.

"What is that?" Megan asked.

"The coins of course. I'll bet they thought Grandpa had them."

***

My plan to hack Hal's computer got put aside until the boys and I could get my mother's house repaired - that and the fact that I really didn't have a plan after my failed attempt at his dock. Megan had the good sense to get our mother out of the house so the boys and I could get to work. I assigned Kevin and Taylor to collecting trash while I worked on packing my mother's belongings for her to sort through later. Fred was assigned to guard duty, but he was constantly falling asleep on the job. We would have been dead-meat if the burglar came back.

We used up the few boxes and trash bags that Dad had in his garage, so I made a quick trip to the SuperMart for more supplies. When I got back, Amy's expensive SUV was parked in the driveway.

All kinds of thoughts went through my head: *What should I say when I see her? And why is she here? To see me? No. More likely Taylor.* I quickly combed my hair with my fingers in the truck mirror, grabbed the beer and soda I had picked up at the store, and started up the walkway. Hal came out of the house before I made it to the door.

"Long time no see, Stranger. How have you been?" he asked, offering his hand.

I tried to. look past him for his wife, but he seemed to have gained more weight since the last time I saw him at the funeral. I set down the six pack of soda in my right hand and took his hand. He had a very large ring I could feel as he squeezed my hand firmly. I squeezed back and he squeezed even harder. "Getting by," I answered and let go. I didn't feel like getting into a pissing contest, and I let him have his little victory. "How about you? Keeping out of trouble?"

"More like trying to keep my kid out of trouble. Amy wanted me to stop by and check on him. It seems like he spends more time at Meg's than at home lately."

I bent down to retrieve the soda. "Why don't you come in and have a cold beer if you're not in too big a hurry. I've been meaning to call you, so now you can save me a quarter." Inspiration strikes at odd moments. I had just realized how to hack his router – I was going to sneak up to his dock at night to avoid the cameras, and I needed to know when his next trip to California would be.

Hal's expression of forced joviality faded to concern. He looked at his watch before answering. "I'm on the wagon. But I could use one of those sodas."

Taylor looked down at his step-father when we came into the house. "What did I do now?" He was at least a foot taller than Hal, so he couldn't help but look down on him.

Hal ignored him. "I'll take one of those beers after all, Jake. Is there someplace we can sit?" he asked, looking around at all the overturned furniture. He didn't ask what had happened, so I assumed the boys had already told him.

I could feel the tension between him and Taylor. "Hey guys, the boxes and trash bags are in the back of the truck. Why don't you work on the kitchen while Hal and I go out on the patio." The patio had the only table and chairs that hadn't been broken.

Hal followed me out to the patio and then stepped back into the house when he saw Fred. Fred was lying in the shade under the patio table. The thieves had taken the air-compressor coils which made the house unbearably hot for his heavy coat. The copper coils seemed to be the only thing missing in the backyard. "It's okay," I said. "He won't bite you unless you bite him first."

Hal forced a smile at my joke. "At least he didn't growl at me this time. But I'll stay here in case he changes his mind." Hal popped open the beer I had given him and took a sip. With an eye on Fred, he leaned his massive weight against the patio door frame. "What was it you wanted to ask me, Jake?"

I could see the frame bend and was afraid the glass door would pop out. "I was wondering if I could hitch a ride to Denver with you next time you go to California. I'm still without a car," I said, taking a chair next to Fred and reaching out for his collar. "I'll hold him if you want to come out here where it's cooler. You'll roast if you don't get out of the house."

Hal left his perch and took a chair at the far side of the table. The chairs were those cheap plastic ones that don't seem to last the season. "What happened to your motor home?" he asked. "Amy said you were given a motor home by some old coot in Lincoln."

There was a glint in his eyes. The look my father used to give when he caught me in a lie. I took a drink of my beer and wondered what else Amy had said to him about the night we spent talking under the stars. "Oh it needs too much work to drive that far. Tires alone will cost more than I'll get from my insurance company – assuming they ever pay me for my car."

Hal looked down at Fred. "Are you leaving him here?" I still had Fred by the collar, and he wasn't a happy puppy. He was on all fours trying to pull off his collar.

I got up and led Fred to the door, then closed it behind him. "Yeah. I'll only be gone a couple of days for my daughter's birthday and will be coming back on a plane."

Hal seemed relieved and crushed his empty beer can. It wasn't the normal crush where one squeezes the flimsy sides. He crushed it from the ends, which takes a lot more pressure and hands the size of a gorilla. It made me thankful I didn't get into the handshaking contest with him earlier. "Not a problem, Buddy. I was going to ask a favor of you, but you won't have time now. I'm leaving in the morning. Can you be ready that soon?"

I wanted to ask when he planned on coming back, but I didn't want to press my luck. I figured I had at least a couple of days to do my dirty work. "No. Maybe next time. I've got to finish here before I can leave. My insurance should come through by then anyway." Then I remembered he said he wanted to ask a favor. "What was it you wanted me to do?"

Hal put down his squashed beer can and pulled out a pack of cigarettes. "Damn kid got some kind of virus on my computer. I'd ask the tech at the office to look at it; they can do that online now, but it's probably full of porn. You don't mind if I smoke do you?"

Of course I did, but I didn't want to mess up a golden opportunity. This was better than trying to hack his router – if I could get my hands on that computer. "No. This is where I make the boys smoke."

He leaned back in his chair and took a big drag on his cigarette, letting the smoke out slowly. I was waiting for the chair's cheap plastic legs to break. With only two of them supporting his weight, they had to give in. "I hear you're into computers, so I was wondering if you wouldn't mind taking a look at it?"

This was getting better by the minute. "No problem. Have Amy give me a call whenever it's convenient."

"Let's keep Amy out of it," he answered. "No sense in letting her know what the kid's been up to. I'll drop it off before I leave. Just remember any porn you find on that machine is between you and me."

"Amy who?" I answered, trying to make a joke. "Do I know her?"

Hal looked at his watch once more. I was beginning to think he was on medication or something. "I need to pick Amy up by five. I've already got her kid pissed off at me; I don't need her ragging on me too." He dropped his cigarette on the ground and got up to step on it. I was a little disappointed not to see the chair collapse from under him.

Hal left through the backyard gate without going through the house. Either he didn't want to confront Taylor or was afraid Fred would take a bite out of his dress pants. After he left, I went over to the sliding door and opened it. "Hey guys," I yelled. "The coast is clear. Come on out and take a break." Then I sat back down and opened another beer.

While waiting for Fred and the boys, I was trying to decide the best way to hack Hal's computer. When they didn't show, I decided to get off my butt and see what was taking them.

Mom's house was built in the style I like to call cracker box. It had been built right after the Second World War to meet a pent-up demand in housing: a basic one-thousand square-foot rectangle with two bedrooms, one bath, kitchen, and a dining room. Someone had added the garage in the sixties. Because of the simple design, it was nearly impossible not to hear someone anywhere in the house. I didn't hear a sound when I entered the kitchen from the patio door. Then I heard Fred barking in the front yard.

My first thoughts were that Fred had Hal cornered, or worse yet, he had a piece of Hal's expensive pants in his mouth. I crossed the sparse living room in five steps and ran out the front door. I expected to see Hal's hands squeezing Fred's neck, but his car wasn't even there. Kevin was throwing an old piece of garden hose in the back of Taylor's truck, and Fred was doing his duty as a retriever to bring it back. Then he would bark at Kevin to throw it again. Taylor was watching it all and roaring with laughter.

"Hey, Slackers," I shouted. "Let's get back to work and get this place cleaned up before the sun goes down."

Fred was exhausted when he came back in ahead of the boys. He still had the hose in his mouth and dropped it at my feet, then went straight for the water bowl I had put in the kitchen earlier. The boys went for the sodas in the refrigerator. I picked up the hose and tossed it in a pile of torn cushions. "You guys want to give me a hand with this couch," I said as they opened their drinks.

"You think we should finish the job on this in case they didn't find the coins, Uncle Martin?" Kevin asked while kicking the battered sofa.

"I still don't see why you think your grandfather was hiding coins. He would have told your grandmother long ago."

"Yeah, but what if he was, and we end up taking them to the dump?"

"You've got a point, Kev. Don't throw out anything else until I've had a chance to go through it." Fred came back, went to the front door, and started whining. "Looks like Fred wants to go home. I'll take him out where it's cooler. Why don't you guys lock up and meet me at the truck?" Then I opened the door to let him out.

Fred didn't head for the truck. Whoever said dogs were dumb didn't know Fred. He ran back into the house, grabbed the hose, and then ran outside. I ran after him and tried to take the hose, but now, he seemed to be in for a game of tug-a-war. When the boys joined me, I finally gave up and let him have his hose. Taylor opened the passenger door and pushed the seat forward, so Fred could hop in the back jump-seat. The truck had an extended cab with a small seat behind the main seat.

"I call shotgun," Kevin yelled out.

"No way, Kev. You rode in the front coming out here. It's my turn to ride up front," Taylor said, holding the seat forward for Kevin to get in. "Besides, it's my truck in case you've forgotten."

Without saying another word, Kevin gave his friend a sour look and got in the truck. Taylor was already in the passenger seat and buckled in by the time I rounded the truck and took the wheel. I started the truck and pulled out of the driveway. "Did your father mention he wanted me to look at his computer?" I asked.

"Yeah. Do you think you can fix it, Jake?" I could see a glimmer of hope in his face.

"Sure. Tell you what. Tomorrow is supposed to be hotter than today, so let's take a break from this cleanup and work on that computer."

Nobody gave me the slightest argument, and the boys went back to talking about girls and sports while I drove us home with the biggest grin on my face. Even Fred seemed to understand the reprieve. He finally dropped his hose and stuck his head out the open window while I daydreamed about all the information I would gather with the spyware program I was going to put on Hal's computer.

CHAPTER 14

True to his word, Hal dropped off his computer the next day. My plan to plant a spyware program became a little complicated when he politely insisted Taylor give me a hand, so 'The boy could learn something useful.' Hal had shown up late – evidently to assure Taylor would be up and awake.

Taylor wasn't the only one awake. Now I had Megan and Kevin looking over my shoulder, too. Thank god Fred couldn't read, or he would have been watching me as well.

"Can they really recover deleted files even after I empty the trash can?" Taylor asked. I could imagine where this was going.

"Sure can. As long as the sector hasn't been reused. You see a file isn't really deleted from the hard disk, just from the file allocation table..." I could see I had answered his question and was now putting everyone to sleep. "Sorry about that. Here, let me show you instead."

I inserted my Norton utility disk and started the file recovery program. I immediately spotted several large JPEG files in the temporary internet folder and selected one for recovery. Taylor became extremely embarrassed when I opened it.

"Cool picture, Taylor," Kevin said while staring at the screen of two women and a man in a comprising position. "Got any video of them?"

"Those aren't mine, honest," Taylor said.

Megan gave us a disgusting look when she saw the picture. "I've seen enough. I think I'll make us all some late breakfast while you boys enjoy yourselves." She left for the kitchen.

"No idea what you're talking about, Taylor," I said. "Let me show you how to defragment the disk which will get rid of all the file pointers. Of course, the only way to truly delete them is by overwriting the space with zeros, but defragging will get rid of ninety-nine percent of them."

Kevin looked like someone just stepped on his toes. "Can't we copy those to my flash-drive first?" he asked.

Now it was my turn to pretend to be appalled. "That wouldn't be ethical, Kevin. Hal trusts me to be discreet about this cleanup. Besides, this is going to take at least a half-hour. Why don't we all get something to eat in the meantime?" I hoped I had bored everyone enough to not return after breakfast. I needed time alone to do my dirty work and violate Hal's trust. The boys didn't have to be asked twice. I no sooner started the defrag program, and we were off to the kitchen.

When we came in, Mother was sitting at the table talking to Megan. "Did you boys have fun in there?" she asked. She wasn't smiling, but my sister had a grin a mile wide.

"Just cleaning up the trash, Mom," I said while taking a cup out of the dishwasher.

"Those are dirty," she nearly yelled. "You'll have to clean one yourself. Nobody bothered to start the dishwasher."

Megan had already left the table and was headed toward the fridge. "Scrambled okay for everyone?" she asked as she took out a large carton of eggs.

"Have you forgotten about my house, Jacob?" Mother asked before anyone could answer Megan. "Or are you going to watch those dirty pictures all day?"

Megan finished cracking open the eggs and started mixing them in a large yellow bowl. I recognized it from yesterday's cleanup. "That reminds me," she said. "Amy said she would stop by to pick up the computer on her way to work this morning. I'll wait for her, so you guys can get to work on the house. Is that okay with you, Jake?"

So much, I thought, for my hopes of being alone with Amy when I took the computer to her. "Sure. I'll check to make sure the defrag is finished, and it should be good to go," I answered and left everyone in the kitchen. I knew the boys wouldn't miss a meal, so I calculated that I had fifteen or twenty minutes to do my dirty work.

Once I finished planting my spyware, I shut down the computer and unplugged it. My timing was close. Just as I was leaving, Taylor and Kevin finished with breakfast and came into the office. "Is it fixed?" Taylor asked when he saw me unplug it.

"Clean as a whistle. Let me grab a bite and then we can head over to my mother's house."

There wasn't a whole lot I could do while waiting for Hal to return and use his computer, so working on the house would help me keep my mind off the computer. The spyware I planted would let me know which websites Hal visited along with any usernames and passwords he was using. But he had to actually use the computer to make that happen. This kind of program could get me in a lot of trouble whether I used it for gain or not. I had no intention of stealing from Hal; I just needed a list of his customers so I could cross-check them with any previous owners of Taylor's truck.

Mother insisted on coming along to supervise the cleanup. Unlike the day before, there was no getting her out of our hair. She wanted to insure that nothing important was thrown out. "I really think I should go through those trash bags you boys put in the truck yesterday," she said to me when we pulled up to her house. Kevin and Taylor were waiting for us when we got to Mother's house. Kevin drove Taylor's truck, and my mother and Fred rode with me in my rental. It would have been a lot easier for all of us to go in Taylor's truck, but Mother refused to ride in it again.

Mother's neighbor must have been watching from her window. She was out her door and coming toward us before I had a chance to help my mother out of the rental. She was wearing brand-new painter's overalls with a matching painter's cap. "Good afternoon, Hazel," she said to my mother. "I felt so bad about not helping everyone yesterday, but I just didn't have any work clothes. Have you ever tried to find the right clothes in this town? I'll tell you, it took me all morning to chase these down," she said, proudly giving us a mini-fashion show.

"I'll let you two catch-up," I cut in. "I better get in there and make sure the boys don't throw out anything important. Once more, I left my mother to deal with her friend.

Our first task was to try and save my grandmother's buffet. It was the only piece of furniture left in the house. Everything else had already been put in Taylor's truck, or if they hadn't been damaged too badly, put in the garage, until we could patch and paint the walls before moving them back into the house.

"It looks like firewood to me," Kevin said while standing over the antique.

"Nothing a little Elmer's glue can't fix. Take a look at these dovetails," I said and picked up one of the pieces. "This drawer just came apart. It's not really broken. The glue dried up eons ago."

"He's right, Kev," Taylor said. He had been checking out the oak frame that had been tossed on its back by the vandals. "We learned how to make those joints in shop class. It's not like the mass-produced junk they make today. I don't see a single nail or staple anywhere."

Before I could say anything else, Fred started to bark. We all turned toward the front door to see my sister and Amy coming in the house. Mother was still talking to Mrs. Whitehead at the truck.

Amy bent down to pet Fred on the head. "Have you forgotten me already, Freddie?" she asked. She had her hair in a ponytail and dressed in some worn-out cutoff-jeans. Her shirt must have come from Taylor's closet. When she stood up from petting Fred, I could see a small diamond stud in her navel. She gave me an impish smile and said, "Tell me what I can do to help, Captain." I fell in love all over again.

"Don't you have to work today?" I asked.

"I called in sick," she said with a huge grin. "When the cats away, the mice will play."

I was about to say *what*, and then realized she was referring to Hal. "Well, Mrs. Whitehead is all dressed to paint. How about the women start in the kitchen? There's a couple of gallons of semi-gloss in the garage that my father must have had left over from the last time he painted. The boys and I should have these walls patched and spackled by the time you finish in there."

Amy pretended to pout. "Please, Sir, can't I help you instead? I promise I won't be a bother, and you could teach me how to patch drywall." She didn't have to ask twice. We spent the rest of the afternoon working together while Megan kept the boys busy painting the kitchen. Luckily, Mother and her friend found the house too hot, and they spent the day next door in the comfort of Mrs. Whitehead's air conditioning.

Amy turned out to be a great apprentice. She was putting tape and mud on the walls faster than I could patch holes in the wall with new drywall; I never was one who could talk and work quickly at the same time. It seemed she had a thousand questions. She wanted to know all about my cabin back in Colorado and couldn't believe it when I told her I had built it myself. Then she asked about my novel and how it was coming along. It seems we spent more time talking than working. I was almost wishing the vandals had done more damage, for we finished the job way too soon.

It was another week before we completed repairing and painting the house. Because of her work, Amy didn't return after the first day. Then Hal cut his business trip short, and he didn't like her out of his sight. Mrs. Whitehead turned out to be a great help. She and my mother spent almost the entire time at her air conditioned house and out of our hair. Megan spent her time as our gofer, and Fred stayed out on the back porch, panting when he wasn't sleeping on the job.

We never did find any coins in the trash Mother made us sort through; going through all that junk took almost as long as sanding and staining the floors. I for one was relieved that Kevin was wrong. It would have raised far too many questions of what the coins were doing in my father's house in the first place. I was sure

Hal had taken them back after Bennet killed Mike, and I didn't need to complicate that theory by having the coins show up at my parent's house.

Hal started using his computer the first day of his return. My spyware program caught his email ID and password on his company's network the minute he logged into their site. I was smart enough not to try to connect to his work email, for that would have been pure stupidity. Fortune five-hundred companies watched everything their employees did – especially from remote locations. Besides, I didn't think Hal was dumb enough to send email to Bennet through his work account. He had to be using an online email service that my spyware had yet to detect. Then, I got lucky the same day we finished with my mother's house.

It was well after everyone had gone to bed. Even Fred was asleep at my feet. I was on my laptop, at the kitchen table with a now-stale pot of coffee, when I got the alert from my spyware. I had it set to send me a message whenever it collected anything with the keyword of 'mail.' I should have been sleeping after working all day on the house, but there was just too much on my mind. It had been weeks since I had seen any kind of income – the last being an electronic deposit of two hundred dollars for an article I had written over a year ago. That deposit showed up when I logged into my bank account. I was down to less than a thousand dollars, so I needed to do something soon. I was in the middle of sending out some queries for an article I had written before leaving home when the computer beeped with the alert from my spyware. The world would have to wait for my article on 'How to fix a Roof Without Breaking the Bank or Your Neck.'

Hal was using a Yahoo account to do his dirty work. My little program sent me his username and password the minute he logged off. It was designed to collect web addresses, and anything he typed into his web-browser by storing the data in a cookie. The cookie was deleted once the information was sent to me. The program was far from perfect; any serious security measures would have either discovered it or disallowed the cookie, but I had made sure those precautions were turned off when I installed my program. I was so engrossed in my results, I didn't hear my sister come up behind me.

"What are you doing, Porky?" Megan must have seen the lights on in the kitchen and come down to see who was up.

I nearly had a heart-attack. "My god, you scared the living shit out of me," I said, clutching my chest.

Megan pulled up a kitchen chair and sat next to me, looking at the computer screen. "Sorry. It must be pretty interesting for you not to notice me. What is it? A porn site?"

"Funny. You should go on American Idol." She wasn't that far from the truth, though. I had the cookie data open and most of the sites Hal visited were porn. Then I opened up a web-browser and logged into his Yahoo account.

She smiled then squinted at the text on the screen. "You got into Hal's private email. You really are a genius."

"You won't think that if I get caught. I'm committing a federal offense for which I could spend the next twenty years in Leavenworth," I answered.

"At least we will be able to visit you then," she said. "We're only a hundred miles from there."

"Great. Don't forget to bring a cake with a file in it."

"Can't they trace it back to you somehow?"

"You would be the one they caught. I'm sure you'd never pass the metal detector."

She quit looking at the computer and slapped me on the top of my head. "Don't be a smartass, Porky. You know I meant whatever it is you put on Hal's computer."

I feigned injury by grabbing for the spot she hit me. "Sorry. A sour look would have sufficed," I said with a fake frown. "You didn't have to give me a concussion."

She gave me a look used by a parent talking to a misbehaving child. "Well. Can they?"

"Of course they can," I answered, "If they wanted to. But I'm not stealing from him. As long as they don't suspect any foul play, they have no reason to do an IP trace. So keep this between us, or I'll have to shoot you and anyone you tell."

"Yeah, right." She laughed and leaned in closer to the computer screen. "Is that Taylor's truck?" I had searched for messages with the keyword of 'truck.' She had seen the subject header almost as soon as the results came back.

Her face was so close to the screen, I had a hard time seeing past her. "Well, let's find out." I said and clicked on the message. It was from a body shop owner in San Diego telling Hal to buy a 1985 F150 that was being auctioned off in Warrensburg. He was instructed to buy the truck and don't touch anything until it was time. "I hate to say 'I told you so,' but it does confirm my theory."

Megan got up and headed toward the kitchen. "Most of your theory," she said while rinsing out the coffee pot, "I don't see where it implicates Bennet."

I sent the email to Meg's printer and leaned back in my chair with my hands behind my head, watching her make the coffee. "Don't make any for me; that last pot I made was terrible."

"Did you use the bottled water?"

"No. Why? Should I?"

"Of course, Silly. Our tap water tastes like it's from the septic. Mike always said he thought our well must be getting lake water, but when we had it tested, they told us it was the limestone that made it taste so bad."

I watched as she reached under the counter and came back with a gallon jug of water. "Maybe that's what killed Mike," I said and went back to my email search. This time I tried searching for born2fish. "Oh shit!" I yelled.

She put the pot back down and looked at me. "What happened?"

"Someone cut me off," I answered. "I can't believe they caught me so soon."

I immediately tried logging back in, thinking it was a connection issue with the internet. My password was denied. "Someone changed the password already." I began to wonder what prison food tasted like.

I could hardly sleep the rest of the night for fear of the internet police knocking on our door. What the hell had I been thinking? My career as a software engineer would be over even if I didn't go to jail. Of course, I knew the internet police were as likely to come crashing in as the library police. They didn't exist. But this was an offense the FBI would pursue if someone reported it. Forget trying to save Megan's house, I thought. I had to save my own butt now. I had to get my hands on Hal's computer and remove all evidence of my snooping.

CHAPTER 15

Fred didn't lose any sleep over my predicament, and he made sure I couldn't sleep-in the next morning. He woke me at the break of dawn, so I would let him out to water the trees. I was still making coffee when Megan joined me in the kitchen. "Don't you ever sleep?" she asked.

"There will be plenty of time for that in Leavenworth," I answered.

"Why don't you sit down? I'll finish this." She took the coffee pot from me and tried to smile. "Do you really think it's that serious?"

"Maybe. At first I thought Hal had simply changed his password, but my spyware hasn't sent anymore alerts. Hal, or someone at his office, must have found my program and disabled or deleted it."

Megan finished with the coffee pot and pressed the on button. Then she pulled down one of her copper-bottom skillets hanging above the cook-top. "I don't get it. If it's been deleted, why are you so upset?"

"Nothing to worry about if it was Hal," I said. "He can't turn me in without exposing himself to all the porn he has been downloading. However, if it was a remote administrator from his workplace, I need to get the first plane to Mexico."

She absentmindedly inspected the skillet. It seemed to be easier than looking at me. "I'm sorry I got you into this, Jake. I didn't know." I thought she was going to cry.

"Hey, it's not that bad. I just need to find a way to get my hands on that computer and remove all the traces of my snooping."

She put the pan on the kitchen counter and sat down at the table. "How do you do that without being caught again?" she asked, while rubbing Fred's ears. He had been lying under the table between our chairs, ignoring us until Megan had reached for the skillet. I could tell he was disappointed when she returned to the table without breakfast, but the ear-rub must have helped. He was smiling like a dolphin being fed a fresh mackerel until he heard voices coming from the upper-level.

"The answer to that problem, Sister Dear, is just getting up. Better make more of whatever you were planning for breakfast."

"What's for breakfast, Mom?" Kevin asked. I smiled when Fred went over to Taylor. I now knew how to get back into Hal's computer.

"I didn't think you boys would ever get up," I said after they helped themselves to the last of the energy drinks from the refrigerator and sat down at the table. "We all need to be out of here before noon."

"What's up, Uncle Martin?" Kevin asked.

"The realtor wants to do a showing today. Your mom and I are going to go see your grandmother until we can get back into the house." I amazed myself at my new lie. "Why don't you guys spend the day at Taylor's. You can bring me your Dad's computer, Taylor. I've got an update I need to install for him."

Megan put her pan on the stove and looked over at us. For a moment, I thought she was going to expose my lie. Then her expression turned from bewilderment to insight.

"Can it wait until tomorrow?" Taylor asked. "He's still pissed about the coin we tried to sell. I don't want to go anywhere near that jerk. Mom says he's going to go on another trip to California tomorrow."

Megan went back to making scrambled eggs, but she couldn't keep her eyes and ears from the yarn I was spinning. "Well, you guys can't stay here during the showing. I suppose you could come with us, but I really need to install that update. There's a new virus out that can destroy his hard-drive if he gets it before I apply the update."

"You better tell Dad about it. The tech at his work should be able to take care of it." That's the trouble with lying. It seems even a little white lie can grow faster than a vine and kill its host before you know it.

"Damn it!" Meg yelled. "I hope you guys like your eggs black because I can't make any more. This is the last of the food unless someone comes up with some money to buy more." She had been so busy watching me dig myself into a hole that she had burned the eggs.

"I know how to make some quick cash," Kevin said.

"Oh?" Megan asked while she scooped the eggs into Fred's bowl.

"All that junk in Taylor's truck, we can take it to the recycle yard and take what they don't buy to the dump after that. Kill us two birds with one stick."

"Stone," I said automatically. Then I realized it was the perfect way to keep Taylor in my sights until I could get to his father's computer. "But that's an excellent idea, Kevin."

Megan played along with my ruse, and said she and Fred would go over to Mother's, so the realtor could show the house. My guess was she would double back once she saw the truck leave.

***

When we made it to the recycle yard in Sedalia, there was a line waiting to unload. Taylor didn't have air conditioning in his truck, and it was hot and humid. With the wind blowing through the open windows, the drive up from Truman had been tolerable, but now that we were only moving a car length every fifteen or twenty minutes, I was suffocating. I sure missed my mountain air.

"What's the hold up?" Kevin asked.

An obese, middle-aged man dressed in jeans that hung too low, was at the front of the line, arguing with an attendant. I couldn't hear what was being said; we were several pickup trucks away. He should have been arrested for indecent exposure. His butt crack was sticking out for all to see.

"Looks like some people have to sort out the stuff they won't take. See the sign over there?" I said. The sign read in twelve inch red letters: "NO REFRIGERATORS OR AIR CONDITIONERS WITHOUT CERTIFIED FREON REMOVAL CERTIFICATE." The fine print went on to list all the different appliances they would not accept.

The overweight man finally got back in his truck and pulled over with the other customers, who were trying to separate the metals in their trucks into piles the yardman would accept.

Our load was no exception. When we finally got our turn to unload, the yardman refused our refrigerator."Sorry, Boys," he said. "Read the sign. I can't take those. But if you want to come back with just the coils, we'd be happy to buy the copper from you."

Then it hit me. I remembered seeing on television how the theft of copper coils from air conditioners had reached such epidemic proportions that some counties had started tracking their sale. "You keep a record of those, don't you?" I asked.

"Yeah. We give that to the cops whenever they get a hair up their ass to crack down on copper theft," he answered.

"Any way I can get the list for last month? My mother had her outside unit stolen. It might help track down the culprits."

"Axe 'em in the office. Maybe they can help ya."

It took us twenty minutes to sort through the junk in the truck before we were able to go back through the scales and determine how much scrap metal we actually had to sell. The boys waited in the truck while I went in to collect our reward. I was surprised to see a thick glass plate separating me from the clerk. I had seen a setup like this at a few convenience stores in some of the less desirable neighborhoods back in Denver, but it was a shock to see it here.

The girl behind the counter was a female replica of my nephew. It must have hurt for her to speak with the rings in her lips. "Looks like twenty-three dollars and sixty cents," she said through the speaking disk built into the glass. "I just need a driver's license and a signature." She slipped an invoice in the tray on her side of the window then pushed it toward me.

I signed the invoice, returned it to the tray along with my Colorado driver's license, and pushed the tray back to her. "They told me in the yard that you might be able to get me a copy of copper sellers for the last few weeks. My mother had her air conditioner ripped off, and I was hoping the thief might have tried to sell the coils to you."

"You'll have to get that from the police. We only give that information to law enforcement," she answered, then after looking at my license, "Do you have a Missouri ID? I can't accept an out-of-state license."

"No. I'm just visiting."

She pushed the license back to me through her tray and nodded toward Taylor's truck. "How about one of them?"

"Sure. They both live here. Hold on, and I'll go get my nephew."

I returned a minute later with Kevin. "Phat lookin snake bites, Sharene," he said when he saw her.

"You guys know each other?" I asked, looking at her lip more closely. Then I saw the connection. The holes from the rings looked like a snake had bitten her.

"Yeah, Uncle Martin. Me and Sharene used to hang together." Then turning to his old girlfriend, he said "What you doin workin here? Who's watchin the kid?"

"My mom. Hey, hold on, and I'll see if I can get your uncle what he needs."

The twenty-three dollars and change didn't even pay the dump fees when we eventually made it to the landfill. The place seemed even hotter than the recycle yard. And the smell was a lot worse. They wouldn't take the refrigerator either. It was looking like we would be stuck with a white elephant until the gal in the office gave me a number of someone who would take appliances for a price. I saw a McDonald's soon after leaving the dump and offered to buy the boys lunch.

The cool air of the restaurant was a welcome relief. I ordered six McDoubles, three fries and three large cokes. It was cheap, but it nearly broke me. "I'm sorry, Uncle Martin. I really thought we could make some money doing this." Kevin said when we sat down at a table by an older couple with their grandkids.

"It's okay. I still have a little put aside. We'll stop off at an ATM before we get home. Just don't tell your mom. Let her think we got it selling junk." Then the couple and their grandkids got up and moved to the far table. Either we smelled worse than I thought, or they thought the boys were vampires seeking new recruits.

"Do you think the disk will help catch the guy who trashed your mother's house?" Taylor asked after scarfing down his two burgers faster than Fred ever did.

"With a little luck, I might be able to find him. But it might take a while. Kevin's girlfriend copied the last two months of copper sellers to a floppy disk. My computer doesn't have a floppy drive."

"Don't look at me," Kevin said with his mouth full of fries. "I ain't seen one of them in years."

"You could buy an old computer at the Goodwill," Taylor said. "It's right on our way home."

"Great idea. But first we need to hit that ATM and then get rid of the refrigerator," I answered as I reached for my cell. "Finish up while I get the address of the appliance store. We need to get home before it gets dark."

The boys had to use the restroom before we left, so I amused myself by people watching. Only the old couple with grandkids seemed to be interested in us. They were probably wondering about the hygiene of vampires and wondering why the boys didn't use the restroom before eating. Once the boys joined me to leave, I waved to the grandparents on the way out. I swear I saw the grandmother grab the nearest grandkid.

After dropping off the refrigerator at the appliance store, we stopped at the nearest ATM. I withdrew a couple hundred, and we headed for the Goodwill Taylor had mentioned. I struck out again. They didn't have any computers – new or old. They no longer accepted electronic donations because there was no market for the stuff, and it cost them money to get rid of it. They suggested I could try one of the many so-called flea markets that lined Highway sixty-five on the way home, but I didn't want to waste my time. I would order a floppy drive online and wait to read the disk until it came. I had more urgent tasks at hand. There was still the matter of getting my hands on Hal's computer.

It was nearly dark by the time we left the SuperMart in Truman. I had stopped to get some groceries. The bill would have cleaned out my wallet, so I paid with my debit card. A quick mental calculation said I better get some money in the bank soon. "Think your father has left town yet, Taylor?" I asked as we left the parking lot and headed toward Highway Sixty-Five.

Taylor took out his cell phone and touched a single icon. "I'll check with my mom. She's probably wondering where I am anyway."

I pretended not to listen while he got his mother on the line and answered her questions on how he was and if he had eaten lately. I couldn't actually hear her, but it was obvious from his responses what she had asked. Then he completely surprised me and handed me the phone. "She wants to talk to you, Jake."

"Hi, Amy," I said, hoping the boys didn't notice my red face. "What's up?"

"Hal wanted to call you. But he has to be in San Diego tomorrow, so he didn't have time. He was wondering if you could come over and take a look at his computer. He says it has slowed down to a crawl since you fixed it for him."

"Really? That's odd. Maybe he got a virus somewhere. I was just telling Taylor I needed to update his virus program, so I'd be happy to come over."

"Oh, thank you, Jake. I know it wasn't anything you did. It's more likely the fool downloaded it himself from some porn site."

I didn't know how to respond. Should I agree or try to defend him? "Jake? Are you still there, Jake?" she asked.

"Must have passed a dead zone," I answered. "What time should I come over?"

"Oh any time. I have to work, but Taylor can let you in. He knows how to turn off the alarm, so come on over whenever he gets out of bed."

We continued to chat for a few more minutes about how my sister and mother were doing before I returned the phone to Taylor. He held the phone to his ear and rolled his eyes while she talked. It wasn't lost on Kevin. He made a motion with his hand that imitates someone who won't stop talking. I wanted to say something in Amy's behalf, but I thought better of it.

Taylor finally spoke: "Love you too, Mom," he said and hung up.

CHAPTER 16

When I finally got into Hal's house, it was well past noon the next day. It wasn't Taylor's fault. He was up and ready to go before ten. We had waited for Kevin to get out of bed and finally gave up and went on without him.

Once in the house, Taylor hurried over to a very expensively framed mirror in the foyer, and to my amazement, he opened it like a medicine cabinet. Then he punched in a code on a keypad that was hidden behind the mirror to disarm the alarm. I tried to act uninterested by looking past the foyer into the great-room.

The house made my sister's look like a shanty. There must have been at least six thousand square feet, and it had been designed without regard for cost. The foyer was larger than my cabin back home. It had a marble floor with a mosaic medallion I would expect to see in a Roman palace. The foyer led into a great room with a window three stories tall that had been situated to catch the view of the lake. This was no tract house; it was designed as a one-of-a-kind work of art. The entire house smelled of money, and it made me wonder if I'd gone into the wrong profession. Then I noticed a small camera with a blinking light pointing at us.

"Is that thing on?" I asked, pointing toward the camera.

"Yeah. Dad had them all over the house until Mom made him take them out," he answered while leading me toward a set of ten-foot tall French doors off the foyer. "She said only a pervert would want to watch our every move."

I didn't comment. I was awestruck by the rich mahogany doors and trim. It must have cost more than I could make in six months.

"Here's where they installed the main system and DVR," Taylor said once we were in Hal's office.

"Where are all the wires, Taylor? You must have at least six different cameras outside, but I don't see any wires." I said, pointing to the large LCD monitor on the wall with six different camera angles, including the dock.

Taylor opened a hidden door in the massive wall unit surrounding the monitor. The door led to what must have been a large walk-in closet at one time, but it had been converted to house the electronic equipment and, I assumed, a hidden safe for Hal's coveted coin collection.

"This box here is for the burglar system," he said, pointing out a small unit on top of a file cabinet. "It's hooked to the security company by satellite. It also has a backup power supply over here, so if we lose power, it still works." I was impressed with Taylor's knowledge of the system.

"And I take it this is the video surveillance system in this rack." The box said Surveillance Net 1000.

"Yeah. Cost more than he paid for my truck." He said with a note of sarcasm. "Nothing is too good for my father. It has a terabyte hard drive and can record up to sixteen cameras. The damn thing is set to record only when the cameras detect motion, so it can store a couple months of data on the hard drive before overwriting it. It even has a DVD recorder to backup data."

I did a quick mental calculation. "That would take a truck load of DVDs. Even with double sided recording, it would take at least a hundred disks to back up a terabyte."

"It only backs up what you want. You know if Dad wants a permanent record of something, he can put it on a DVD or copy it to a flash drive with the USB port. He never even bothered until a few weeks ago."

In less than a second, I knew how to find Born2fish. I tried my best not to show Taylor my revelation by making small-talk. "So there's that bad boy," I said, tilting my head in the direction of the computer. I had brought my laptop along as part of the charade and placed it on Hal's desk, and then sat in his leather office chair. "Guess I better get to work and see what's slowing it down."

Taylor stood behind me, watching over my shoulder when I started to work. It was exactly what I thought he might do which is why Megan and I had cooked up a plan the night before to distract him. I looked at the time in the lower corner of the screen, and I wondered why she hadn't called. It was already fifteen after one. She was supposed to call fifteen minutes ago. I pressed the CTL, ALT, and Delete buttons at the same time to start the Task Manager.

"Won't that reboot the computer?" Taylor asked.

"It can, but it is also a shortcut to show me which processes are running and the resources they are using."

Taylor started to say something else when his cell finally rang. "Hello... Hi, Meg... Sure, I'll be right back."

I waited until I heard the truck leave the drive before I started going through Hal's desk. I didn't know how long Megan would be able to keep Taylor away with her plea to help Kevin move Mike's old beer refrigerator to my mother's. Hal's computer could wait. I had just been given the chance to solve the murders in one fell swoop. *He never bothered to backup data until a few weeks ago?* Now why would he decide all of a sudden to start backing up at the same time everyone started to die? There must be something on that DVD he thought was mighty important. My guess was that it was a record of Born2fish meeting him at the house. All I needed to do was find where he kept the DVD backups and make a copy of that meeting.

I tried the large file-folder drawer first, thinking he may store them there instead of files. No such luck. He actually used the drawer for files and a few porn magazines. I was tempted to look through the other drawers – not for DVDs but just to snoop – when I remembered the file cabinet in the hidden closet. I left the desk and opened the concealed door of his security system.

Surveillance systems were something new to me. They would have been a complete waste of money for my little cabin - most of them cost more than anything I owned. It would be like renting a safe deposit box to safeguard my rejection letters. Besides, I already had the best security alarm money could buy. I had Fred. But even though I had never programmed a system like the Surveillance Net 1000, it didn't look any more difficult than a TV remote. I would have to play with it if I had time before Taylor came back.

The file cabinet was locked, so I went back to the desk to search for a key. It wasn't in the top-center draw, so I did a Kinsey Millhone trick and felt under the bottom of it. I had read enough Grafton novels to know where to look for hidden keys. Kinsey, Grafton's infamous PI, would have been proud. The key was taped right where she would have found it.

All I found for my clever impersonation of the alphabet sleuth was more girlie magazines and some old VCR tapes. How he managed to watch those was another mystery. Did he have a hidden tape player somewhere? Next, I checked out a box of computer paper in the corner. I've used empty boxes for storage. Maybe Hal did, too. Bingo. There were five DVDs in the box. They were labeled 6-1, 6-2, etc. I took the disk that read 6-1, as it must be the first week of June, and Mike died on the fourth.

Once back at Hal's desk, I inserted my pilfered DVD into the computer. Then I thought better of it and pushed the eject button. There would never be time to copy the disk. I removed it and returned it to its jewel case. Then I slipped the case in a pocket of my laptop carrying case. I would have to find a way to return it later – hopefully before Hal returned from his trip. Now all I had to do was delete any record of my spyware program, and I could once more sleep at nights.

My little spy was still running. It hadn't been deleted after all. Then I saw why it wasn't sending me any data. Hal's internet connection wasn't working. My program had not been able to connect to me and had been using most of the system resources trying. No wonder the computer was so slow. I immediately stopped my Trojan and copied its log files to a flash drive I had inserted into a USB port. I deleted the program and every trace of its existence. I started to check what had happened to the internet connection when I heard a car outside.

Just as I finished, I heard the front door open and smelled the scent of expensive perfume. "Hi, Amy. I didn't expect you. I thought you were chained to that hospital," I said in a voice that did nothing to hide my surprise.

"Only when Hal's home," she said without a hint of catching me off-guard. "Where's Taylor? I didn't see his truck."

"He went to help move a refrigerator for my mother. I would have gone too, but I thought I'd better fix this computer and get Hal off my back."

Amy came up behind me and looked over my head at the computer. Then she put both hands on my shoulders and started giving me a massage. "Did you find what the bastard did to slow it down?"

Her little massage was starting to get me aroused. I just sat there like a golden retriever and couldn't say a word. I half expected to see my leg start to shake the way Fred does when I rub his back. Words finally found their way out of my mouth. "Looks like some kind of spyware he must have picked up from a download. I killed it and am running a malware check as we speak. This could take a while, but please don't stop. That feels so good."

She stopped with her massage, so I turned around in the swivel chair to face her. It was the first I'd looked at her since she came in. She looked so sad, yet at the same time, she was trying to smile. "Are you okay, Amy?"

"It's been a rough day, but thank you for asking, Jake." She was looking at me in a way I've only seen in movies: the kind of scene where the girl has fallen for her lover. "I'll get changed and meet you on the deck. I hope you don't mind Budweiser; I don't have any Colorado beer."

"Taylor won't be back for a while," I rose to my feet and softly took her head in my hands. Then, without another word, I bent down and kissed her. She didn't resist or act surprised.

When we finally stopped for a breath, she took me by the hand, led me out of the office, and to the curved staircase leading to her bedroom.

***

Fred woke me late the next morning, wanting to go outside and do his thing. "Okay, Fred, alright already." I got up just when Amy was about to kiss me again in my dream. "Couldn't you hold it for a few more minutes?"

I opened the door to the lower level deck, and Fred quickly ran down the stairs to his favorite patch of ground, where he started his circling, sniffing, and circling. He finally did his thing after he found the perfect spot. It made me want to do the same, so I headed toward the bathroom where I had installed a toilet a few days earlier. I had no need to circle the room. I knew where the bathroom was without smelling every spot on the carpet to find it.

I looked at my face in the mirror and wondered what Amy saw in me. The face staring back at me reminded me of the hunchback in The Beauty and the Beast. It wasn't that I was bad looking. But my three-day beard, and hair that hadn't seen a barber in months, should have been enough to make her run screaming for help. I was so glad she didn't.

Our little tryst was fantastic, while it lasted. We had finished with the bed and were in the shower when Taylor returned with Kevin. I don't know if they believed my excuse of fixing the upstairs toilet, and I really didn't care. All I could think about was Amy. I even had a hard time concentrating on the DVD when I showed it to Megan later.

Fred was already watching Megan in the kitchen when I flushed and joined them. "Good morning, Sleeping Beauty," Megan said. She was making French toast and sausage while Fred waited patiently for her to burn the sausage.

"Now I know what woke Fred," I said. "That smells great."

Megan soaked another slice of bread in her egg batter then threw it in the skillet. "How'd it go with the DVD last night? I'm sorry I couldn't help, but you were making me dizzy with the fast forward, then reverse, then fast forward again and again."

"It's the only way to find what we want without spending days watching them," I said while taking a cup from a hook under one of the upper kitchen cabinets. I chose one with the picture of a John Deere tractor she had picked up at a garage sale. "Too bad the fool didn't set the date on his system or we could have fast forwarded to the date Born2fish was supposed to meet Hal."

"I take it you never found it then?" she asked.

"No. I finally gave up when I realized I didn't have the June disk after all. He must have labeled the disk with the month he removed it from the system, and that makes the video over a month old."

Megan flipped over the toast in the pan and looked at me strangely. "How on earth did you figure that out?"

I poured my coffee and went back to sit down. I slowly took a sip just to create a little suspense. "That clip you pointed out of the Paddlefish snaggers. You know, where those fishermen were swinging their poles back and forth like they were trying to snag something."

"Spoonbill," she said. "We call them Spoonbill."

"The article I googled called them Paddlefish," I said grinning. "But regardless, your snagging season on those monsters is in the Spring. From March fifteen until April thirtieth. That means Hal labeled April's recordings as June. I had assumed 6-1 was the first week of June, but June must have been when he did the backup. My guess is he copied everything on the hard drive until he got to what he wanted. The meeting with born2fish is probably on the last disk."

"I should have caught that. Mike use to go every spring," she said, looking like a kid who just flunked a math test. "So are you going back for June?"

"As soon as I figure out a way to get back in. In the meantime, are you going to cook that so only Fred will eat it, or do I get some first?"

"Fred needs to learn to eat his own food. This may be our last meal for a while unless one of us gets a job pretty soon, so I hope you enjoy it."

I finished my coffee and made a show of the empty cup. "Damn if you don't sound like Natalie. But don't worry. I bought us a little more time last night after watching the DVD."

Megan came over with the coffee pot and filled my cup. "And just how did you do that, Mister Chauvinist?"

"I borrowed twenty thousand on my 401K. If we watch our money, it should be enough to catch up your payments and get us by a few more months," I answered. "You can pay me back when you sell the house."

"Jake," she started to say before throwing her arms around my neck to hug me. "You're the best brother in the whole world." She said between sobs.

Fred loved the burnt French toast and sausage. Meg and I settled for some pop tarts and scrambled eggs. A combination I don't ever recall seeing on a four star menu.

We had just finished our breakfast when we heard Taylor's truck. The boys had stayed at Taylor's since Hal was on the road. Megan pretended to look at a watch on her wrist that didn't exist. "Whatever got those two up so early?" she asked.

Kevin was the first one to walk into the kitchen and went straight to the refrigerator. Taylor sat down at the kitchen table next to Fred and patted him on the head. "Good morning, Mrs. Carver. Jake," he said.

"Thank you Taylor," she answered. "Aren't you going to say 'good morning' too, Kevin?"

"We're all out of energy drinks, Mom," he said while staring inside the refrigerator.

"Yes, I know. You'll have to settle for coffee until I can get to the store," she answered. "I didn't expect you guys up before noon. What's up?"

"My dad came home this morning and started a big fight with Mom," Taylor said. He now had Fred's head between his hands and was rubbing Fred's ears. The boy didn't seem to be the least bit upset.

"Yeah, we had to get out of there," Kevin said after pouring the last of the coffee.

Megan's expression turned solemn at the news. "Is she okay?"

"Where's the sugar, Mom? There ain't no sugar in the bowl?"

Taylor stopped petting Fred and turned to Megan. "Yeah, she'll probably go to grandma's in Clinton. That's what she usually does when they get into it."

Megan got up, went to her pantry at the far end of the kitchen, and came back with a nearly empty bag of sugar. "What happened to get him so mad?" she asked.

Kevin left his cup on the counter and took a seat at the table. I saw he wasn't going to make another pot of coffee, so I got up and started rinsing out the pot. I wanted to ask about Amy but decided to just wait and hear what the boys had to say first.

"Dad came back from his trip in a foul mood and started calling Mom names," Taylor said. He didn't look at anyone in particular – just stared out the sliding glass door. "He's not my real father, you know. Mom says my real father bolted when he found out she was pregnant, and Hal came along just in time. The SOB never lets her forget it."

Megan filled the sugar bowl, then put three spoonfuls in Kevin's coffee before throwing the empty bag in the trash. "Why doesn't your mom just leave him?" she asked when she returned to the table and gave Kevin his cup.

"She loves that freaking house. Sometimes I think she loves it more than me. Says she'll lose everything if Hal walks out," he answered, then started to rise from his chair. "Is it okay if I go out on the deck to have a smoke?"

"Yeah. This coffee tastes like shit anyway, " Kevin said and slid his cup toward Megan. "Then I gotta get some sleep."

Fred followed the boys out to the deck. Maybe he thought they might be hiding a treat in their pockets, or more likely, he was hoping for another ear massage. Next to food, there is nothing a Golden Retriever likes more than having someone rub his ears.

Fred started barking the minute he went through the open door. I had just finished with the coffee pot, so I went out to see what he was barking at. "What is it, Boy? Don't tell me we have another intruder." I said as I looked to see what he was growling at. I couldn't believe my eyes.

A huge bald eagle was perched in an oak tree overlooking the lake. It couldn't be more than fifty feet away, and it had turned its head toward us. I swear I could see it blink. It must have heard Fred, for it spread its wings and swooped down toward the water before catching an updraft. It was amazing to watch the beautiful creature fly with hardly flapping a wing.

"Quite a sight, isn't it?" Megan had joined me on the deck. "You should be here in the winter. We have dozens of them come down from the north because our lake hardly ever freezes over. That's one of the locals. We have several pairs that never leave."

Fred ran down the stairs after the eagle. He would stop every few steps and bark at it while it circled to gain more height. I looked over at Megan and saw her smile for the first time this morning. "Do you need a cashier's check or will a personal check do? My bank has a branch in Sedalia if you need the cashier's check." I asked her.

Her smile faded to a frown. She must have realized what I was asking. "My bank will put a ten day hold on a personal check. A cashier's check would be better."

"I need to make a trip up there anyway. There's a sale on tires at that tire shop across from my bank, so I'll take the motor home. It's going to need them for the trip home."

"You can't leave now, Jake. You're so close to getting the proof we need to prove Mike didn't kill himself."

I looked to see if Taylor had overheard her. He and Kevin had gone to the far end of the deck to be downwind from us. "Better keep it down," I said in a near whisper, nodding toward the boys. "I'm not leaving yet. I just wanted to get the old girl in shape to drive. I can't keep borrowing everyone's car forever."

Megan ignored my pleas to lower her voice. "You ought to trade that gas-hog in on something more useful. Why do you even want that beast?"

This time Kevin must have heard her. "Are you selling your motor home, Uncle Martin?" he asked, flicking his cigarette off the side of the deck and joining us.

"Kevin!" Megan yelled. "Do you want to burn down the house?"

"Don't have a cow, Mom. You know nuthin burns here. Mike tried every Spring to burn the ticks and could never get the weeds to burn."

"That was Spring, Kevin. We haven't had any rain for a week. Get your ass down there and find that cigarette."

"Okay. Okay," he answered. "Come on, Taylor. Let's get out of here before I get grounded." Taylor doused his butt in his now cold coffee and followed Kevin down the stairs.

"We're gonna take the boat, Mom," Kevin called out when they reached the bottom of the stairs. His cigarette had landed on the path and was still burning. He stomped on it and ground it into the dirt. "Maybe we'll go on over to Taylor's and get something to eat. At least his dad won't give us no shit about smoking."

"Don't go too far," she yelled back. "It must be just about out of gas." Then she turned back to me. "So what's next? Have you thought about how to get the other DVD?"

"Another reason I want to drive up to Sedalia. Remember that beat-up truck we saw in the lot where I rented my car - the one with the roofing company sign? I need to see if they rent it out."

Megan's expression turned blank. "What on earth do you want with a roofing truck?" So I told her how I was going to commit a felony breaking and entering.

Megan thought my idea of impersonating a roofer was insane. I had explained how the only door without an alarm was the glass door in the master bedroom that led to a private deck. A deck that was only accessible from the master bedroom or a ladder. All I needed was to wait for Hal to leave on another business trip and then pretend I was a roofer fixing the flat roof that was both a deck and shelter for their screened porch below. She had asked how I knew the door wasn't secure with some remark about 'what was I doing in Amy's bedroom.' I made a lame excuse about 'casing the joint,' which I could tell she didn't believe. She still had her doubts about my plan when we both left the house. I gave her my debit card, so she could drop by the ATM and get some grocery money, and I left for Sedalia in my motor home.

Fred couldn't go with me to Sedalia because of the heat. The cab-air in the motor home wasn't working, so I left him at Megan's with central air-conditioning to keep him cool. I had all the windows open and almost missed the telltale message beep of my cell phone because of the wind noise. There was a call from Amy and another one from Sergeant Bennet.

Amy didn't answer when I called back, so I left a message, then reluctantly called Bennet. "Hi, Jake," he answered. *This was a first*, I thought. *He always called me Mr. Martin before.* "We recovered your credit card. A couple in Kansas tried to buy gas with it, and it didn't clear because you had been smart enough to cancel it. They left without paying and were picked up by the Kansas Highway patrol twenty minutes later."

I had nearly forgotten how Bennet didn't buy my story of being robbed. *So now you believe me?* I thought. "That's great, Sergeant. I don't suppose they still had my cash?"

"No. No cash in the report. Of course Kansas is keeping the card for now. It's evidence. I just thought I'd give you a head's up in case you get subpoenaed as a witness."

After hanging up with Bennet, I tried Amy's cell again. "Hi, handsome," she answered. "I was beginning to think you forgot me already."

"Forget the girl of my dreams? No way. I've been trying to call all morning, but my service doesn't work at Meg's." I didn't let on that I heard about her argument with Hal.

"I suppose Taylor told you Hal came back."

"Yeah. Are you okay?"

There was a slight pause before she answered. "I get a break in an hour. Can you stop by the hospital, and we can get something to eat? I really need someone to talk to."

"I was going to my bank in Sedalia, but there's a branch in Clinton. So I'll stop by after the bank. Sure you're okay?"

This time, the pause was longer. She must not have covered the mouthpiece completely; I could hear a man's voice. "I've got to go, Jake. See you in an hour."

The minute she hung up, I began to have doubts. It was the same feeling of insecurity I'd had before I'd found Natalie with someone else. *This will never work*, I told myself. *It's probably some old coot asking for his medicine. And I'm jealous of that?* I tried to let it go and took a left at Highway C in Lincoln when I saw a sign pointing to Clinton.

Getting Megan's check for five thousand from the bank turned out to take a lot longer than I had expected. Although I had the three different forms of ID they needed, they still acted like I was trying to scam them. It wasn't until they called my branch manager, at my insistence, that they issued the cashier's check. By then I was late for my date. When Amy didn't pick up my call, I went straight to the hospital.

Sitting in the parking lot was Hal's Mercedes. My blood pressure went up ten points. I sat in my motor home, trying to think. I knew Amy drove the SUV just as much as Hal, so I was probably jumping to conclusions. *But what if it was him?*

My question was answered before I could get out of the motor home. Amy and Hal came out the Emergency entrance and headed for the Mercedes. They were holding hands.

***

Fred was waiting for me on the front entry, guarding a package from UPS when I returned. "How did you get out here, Freddie?" I asked when I went over to pet him. Then I noticed that Taylor's truck was gone, and realized the boys must have come back after Megan and I had left. Fred wasn't used to Missouri's heat and humidity, and he was panting like a rabid hound. He even had foam dripping from his jaw. I needed to get him cooled off before he had a stroke. I picked up the package and opened the door.

He headed straight for his water bowl in the kitchen. I yelled out to see if anyone was home. There would have been hell to pay if the boys had still been there, but unless someone was dumb enough to steal Taylor's truck, I knew I was calling out to an empty house. Then I dropped the package on the table and went over to the refrigerator to grab a beer. The fridge was still empty except for a couple of beers, which meant Megan had not been the one to leave Fred out in the heat.

Fred came over by me and laid his head at my feet. The package was for me. I knew it had to be the floppy drive I ordered off eBay, so I made a mental note to check out the floppy from the recycle yard later. There was no rush. I needed to take care of my dog more than I needed to play with a computer at the moment. "Want to go for a swim, Old Boy?" He was up in an instant, wagging his tail and barking at me. Whoever said dogs didn't have the intelligence to speak never owned a Golden Retriever.

Before I was halfway down the stairs, Fred beat me to the dock and jumped in the lake. Megan's pontoon boat was parked in its slip, and the lift was at the bottom. That seemed strange. It wasn't like Kevin to walk up the stairs when there was an easier way up the hill. I was still thinking about who could have taken it down without going back up when I caught up with Fred. He was back on the shore with a rock he must have found at the bottom of the water. "Give me the rock, Freddie," I said, reaching toward his slimy muzzle.

After a little tug-of-war, he gave me the rock then raced toward the end of the dock. He should have played football. He knew where to catch my forward pass and was right on his spot waiting for it. I decided to play a trick on him and threw it in the other direction, closer to the shore. He was on it in a heartbeat.

The rock landed in the same place we had found the intruder's footprint several days ago. But now, the lake was nearly two feet higher, and the print had to be washed away. "What do you have there, Boy," I said when Fred came up with something other than a rock. Fred made me go through his keep-away game before he finally relinquished his prize. It was a waterlogged cell phone.

It didn't take two seconds to realize what we had. "Good Boy. This must be what our trespasser was looking for," I said. "Let's go back to the house and dry this thing out. If we can get it working, you may have just solved the case."

It stood to reason that the killer dropped his phone when he was feeding Bill Atkins to the fishes. I finally had some tangible evidence to prove or disprove my theory that Bennet was Hal's stooge. Even if I was wrong about Bennet, I will have a pretty good idea who the killer is. Of course, there wasn't much hope of the phone working again. But I knew the data on its SIM card was another story. Worst case, I would get another phone exactly like it and switch SIM cards.

Fred ran up the path to the lift and waited while I played catch-up. I got in the lift, and he took the seat next to me, acting like a kid on a carnival ride. I swear he was grinning in anticipation of the ride to the top. I too was enjoying the slow ride up the hill. It reminded me of the cog-wheel tram up the side of Pike's Peak back home. Allison was a curious ten-year old the last time I made that trip. She was still at an age where her father was the smartest man alive. My melancholy day-trip vanished half way up the hill. I could see the sliding door to my room was off its tracks and lying on the ground.

I stopped the lift at the lower-level deck and ran over to my room. "Is this how you got out, Freddie?" His excitement on the tram had been replaced by fear. His tail was down, and the hair on his back was standing straight up.

CHAPTER 17

I seriously doubted that whoever broke-in was still here. He must have come and gone by boat, or the lift wouldn't have been at the dock. But I wasn't taking any chances, and I stood outside the open door frame to check out the room before I entered. Fred stayed back several feet acting like a whipped puppy. "The coast is clear, Fred, let's see what they took." He didn't follow me when I stepped into the room.

I was expecting to see the type of damage my mother had from her break-in, but I didn't see anything out of place. The sheets on the bed were pulled out at the corners, and the blanket half on the floor, exactly the way I had left it. Then I looked under the bed and saw my computer was still where I hid it. Hiding something under a bed was not the safest place – I knew that. I just wanted to keep it out of Kevin's sight. The kid had a tendency to think any piece of electronics was made just for him.

Fred finally joined me, but he still had his tail between his legs. "Don't worry, Old Buddy, the jerk is gone," I said as I knelt on one knee and took his head in my hands. "Did he hurt you?"

Fred leaned his head sideways. It was his way of asking me to rub a particular ear. I obliged and kissed him on the top of his head, then began checking him over for injuries. He must have scared the burglar away before the intruder had a chance to ransack the house. My fear now was that he had kicked or hit Fred to make him so terrified.

Fred smiled at the attention he was getting and started to wag his tail. Only a dog owner could tell it was a smile. Most people would think I was bonkers to describe his expression that way, but it was a smile nonetheless. When I was satisfied that the only thing wrong with Fred was his ego, I put the door back on its tracks, took my computer, and headed for the kitchen. Something told me there was a connection between this break-in and my mother's. I figured I could check out the floppy from the recycle yard while the phone was drying out.

The damage to the sliding door had been superficial. The burglar had simply lifted the door up and off its track. I had made a mental note to get a security bracket for the door, so it wouldn't happen again. It was a simple fix but not something most door manufactures seem to care about or they would supply one with the door.

Fred and I were back in the kitchen, working on installing the floppy drive, when he heard someone at the front door. His tail was wagging, so it had to be someone he knew. "Is that you, Jake?" Megan called out. "Want to help me with these?"

"Give me a minute," I answered. "I'm in the middle of something."

She came into the kitchen carrying a couple of paper bags full of groceries. Evidently, she must have bought them at the only store in town that still did things the old fashioned way and still gave a choice between paper and plastic. "What's that mess you have on the table?" she asked, placing the bags on the kitchen counter.

I clicked the 'Finish' icon on the installation screen for the floppy driver and turned to answer. There was something different about her. "The floppy drive came today. Maybe now we can find the guy who stole Mom's air conditioner," I answered. "What did you do to your hair? It looks good."

"I hope you don't mind, Porky. I used your card to get a new do. Mom made me do it," she said, making an upside-down happy-face. It was her way of acting hurt ever since I could remember. She would lower her head so slightly and pretend to pout like a baby. Damn, if it didn't work.

"No. That's fine. Natalie always did that when she was feeling down, too." I hid my irritation the best I could. "How's Mom doing? I take it you stopped by her place?"

"Mean as ever. We went shopping together at the little store by her house. That's why I got my hair done. She made one of her comments about it. You know how she can be so critical. By the way, she's wants you to call her. She says she's been trying for a couple of days to get you, but you don't answer your phone."

"She's probably been dialing the wrong number again. I'm starting to worry about her, Meg, I haven't had any calls from her, or they would have shown up on my call list."

Her faked pout turned into a soft smile. "Well, you better call her the first chance you get. But I'll warn you. She wants you to finish cleaning out the garage," she said, and then shifted her eyes to the table. "So what's with your cell phone? Why's it covered in mud? Did you drop it in the lake?"

"It's not mine. Fred found it by your dock. I'm letting it dry out before I try to recharge the battery. But I think you better get something to drink and sit down. You won't believe the day we've had."

Worry lines appeared on her forehead. They made her look ten years older despite the new haircut. "Was there a problem getting the check?"

"No, you're okay," I answered to calm her down when I saw fear in her eyes. "But you will still need that drink."

"After the groceries. I've got stuff out there that's going to spoil in this heat if you don't get off your butt and help me." Then she turned and headed for the door.

Fred followed her, but I knew he wouldn't be much help. So I quit what I was doing and went to give her a hand. True to her word, the back of her Jeep was full. She had even lowered the back seat to get all the bags in. It was a wonder my debit card cleared – this load must have cost hundreds.

Once we got all the groceries in the house and put away, I was able to get back to reading the floppy from the recycle center. Megan put a cold Keystone and a half-empty bottle of Merlot on the table and sat next to me, so she could watch me work my magic. While waiting for the computer to boot, I started telling her about my day. I began in reverse, starting with the break-in seemed to be the most important event of the day. I hated it when someone tried to tell me something important, and they had to recite an entire saga before getting to the point; so I told her about the sliding door before explaining how Fred found the phone. Her bottle of wine was empty by the time I told her Fred must have scared off the would-be burglar.

"Thank God for Fred. My house might have been trashed like Mom's," she said in response to my watchdog saving the day, raising her empty glass in a salute.

"Well, maybe Fred shouldn't get all the credit. It might have been the UPS man, too," I added while working on the spreadsheet from the floppy. I decided to sort the entries by date and narrow down the list to sales after my mother's break-in. "There's a good chance he might have rang the doorbell when our intruder was breaking in." I looked down at Fred for confirmation, but he wasn't even listening. He was curled up on his side and snoring.

While Megan went back to putting the groceries away, I continued with my reverse story telling. She would nod and say things like "Wow" and "No kidding" until I got to the end of my story, or should I say the beginning. That was when I said I thought the phone belonged to Bennet.

"Did it ever occur to you that the phone might have fallen out of Bill's pocket when he was dumped by my dock?" she said, coming back to the table for her empty bottle. "And I don't see how you can make it work. Last time Kevin dropped a phone in the toilet, I had to buy him a new one." Before I could answer, she was off to the pantry where she kept her trash can.

Her remark caught me off-guard. The thought that it might belong to Bill never occurred to me. I stopped in the middle of reading the list and looked at her with new respect. "Not bad for a rookie. I suppose it's possible... Holy shit! Look at this."

"Ron Nixon," she said after coming back to see what got me so excited. "And look at the date. That's when Mom was staying here because she didn't want to go home yet."

"Makes you wonder how he ever got a job as a security guard," I answered. "Everyone I've talked to says he's bad news. So it doesn't surprise me he would stoop to stealing from a widow only days after her husband died, but how did he ever get clearance to guard that museum?"

Megan gave me her obtuse look. It was the kind of expression one uses when trying to explain a simple fact to a child for the tenth time. "I think I told you that before. According to Mike, Ron's never been arrested since he was a teenager. Not that he shouldn't have, from what I've heard. I guess the juvenile record doesn't show up on a background check."

"Well that's about to change. I do believe trashing someone's house is considered a felony – even in Missouri."

Megan went back to the refrigerator and took out a bottle of Chardonnay. "You want another beer while I'm in here?"

I'm no James Bond. I had no idea if it was acceptable to mix wines that way, so I bit my tongue before I showed my enology ignorance. I did notice, however, that the bottle was already open, so at least she wasn't wasting good wine. "Sure. Might help to cool me down before I decide to go out and beat the crap out of that asshole."

She came back with my beer and sat down across the table from me. "Maybe you've had too many of these, Porky," she said, holding the beer just out of my reach. "Why is it that men always want to fight first? You don't know it was Mom's air conditioner. He might have been selling scrap he picked up from the demolition of the museum."

"Yeah. And I might have been a world-famous physicist, "I answered, dismissing her brilliant insight. She was right again. I just didn't feel like letting her know. I would need a lot more to hang Nixon than a record of him selling scrap.

She narrowed her eyes and looked straight at me. "Einstein would have been nothing without his wife. Did you know she was a mathematician and physicist, too? She went over his papers with a microscope and found all his mistakes. He would have been shit without her."

"Wasn't she his first cousin?" I asked. "This is getting creepy, Meg."

"No. That was his second wife. His first wife was a second cousin."

"And we make jokes about our neighbors in Arkansas. Where did you learn all this? I don't remember you ever being a student of history?"

Megan's cold stare started to soften. "Some show on TV, but that's not the point." She stood up from the table and went back to the Chardonnay she had left on the kitchen counter. "The point is, you can be as big a bastard as Einstein. Give a girl some credit once in a while."

Now it was my turn to smile. "It's a man thing, Meg. If I gave you the credit, I'd have to turn in my man card. But before I do that, we need to find out who Fred's phone belongs to. If it's Bill, you get the prize. And if it's Bennet's, I'll promise not to gloat."

She filled her glass and put the empty Chardonnay bottle in the trash. "Won't it take a while to charge it?" she asked.

"Scratch that scenario," I answered and began removing its SIM card. "It uses the same service as my phone. There is a good chance its card will work on my phone." Then I got lucky; the card was compatible with my phone. I crossed my fingers while the phone went through its startup cycle.

"I thought you couldn't get a signal from here?" Megan had come up behind me to watch my magic. I had been so intent with the phone that I didn't hear her and almost dropped it.

"I can't. This is data stored on the chip," I said as I selected the call list menu. "Do you have something I can write with? I need to copy these numbers then I'll run them through a reverse lookup on my computer."

She went to the counter and opened the drawer where she stored the kitchen clutter. "Will this do?" she asked, handing me a small pink notepad trimmed in flowers.

"As long as I don't have to show the list to anyone," I answered, and I began writing down the numbers from the Status menu. "Hand me your house phone, would you?"

"Who you going to call?" she asked.

"Maybe we will get lucky and the voice mail will give away the owner's name," I said while calling the cell phone.

Megan went back to the other side of the table and sat down. She put her elbows on the table and her head in her hands, waiting for the call to complete. "My money is still on Atkins," she said.

I pressed the speaker button, figuring it would save time by not having to repeat the message. All I got was a phone company recording stating that the customer had not yet set up his mailbox. "I'll do a reverse lookup from my computer later, but let's check out his call list first." I knew it would be tedious. My phone stored over sixty recent calls. Chances were, Fred's phone did too. Megan lost interest when she saw me going through the list. "This is making me thirsty," she said as she left the table. "I'm gonna open another bottle. Do you want some?"

"No. I'm still working on my beer, but thanks anyway," I answered, writing down the numbers, along with the time and dates, on Megan's pink paper.

"That's odd. There's only a dozen or so calls," I said when I got to the end of the list.

"Maybe whoever owned the phone didn't use it much," she said.

"Or maybe he deleted his call list every day or so," I answered. "Some people do that when they have something to hide." I finished writing the last call when my phone complained about its battery running low.

"I need to run downstairs, get my laptop, and put my phone on its charger. Hold on, and I'll be right back." I expected my shadow to follow me, but Fred was still asleep under by my chair and didn't hear me leave.

***

Of the twelve or thirteen numbers in the call list, only four were unique. Once I got my phone recharged, I needed to check out the phone's data usage and billing statement. But first, I needed to use the bathroom and unload the four beers I had since seeing Amy walk out of the hospital with Hal. It was a ritual that always helped clear my mind as well as my bladder.

I knew I was getting close to solving the puzzle of Mike's demise. Whoever lost the phone by Megan's dock must have done so when they dumped Bill's body. And it didn't take a paperback detective to connect that person to Mike's murder. Unless Megan was right, and the phone fell out of Atkins' pocket when he was dumped. *But why would someone come back looking for the phone if that was the case? And if the perpetrator was Bennet, as I thought earlier, wouldn't there have been calls to his office?* I had just zipped up when the door opened behind me.

"When did you start using the toilet, Fred?" My shadow must have woken up and went looking for me.

"Woof," he answered. I knew him better than I knew my own kid. It was his, 'I want out', bark.

I finished without taking the time to wash, and let him out before he decided to use my bathroom instead of his. Then I went over to the bed to fetch my computer from its hiding place.

Megan was at the kitchen counter, struggling with a wine cork, when I returned several minutes later with Fred on my tail. "Did you fall asleep down there?" she asked just as the cork popped loose and wine started to flow out of the bottle.

I nearly threw my computer on the table and went over and grabbed a handful of paper towels. "We had to make a pit stop." I began wiping up the spill, and then I stopped cold when I noticed the price tag on the wine bottle.

I never was much of a wine expert, but I already knew just by the cork that it cost more than any wine I would buy. "Forty-five dollars! Megan, what were you thinking?"

She gave me the defiant look she used to give our father when she was caught doing something she wasn't supposed to do. "Cheap wine gives me a headache. And what do you care how I spend my money. I told you I would pay you back every dime, so please don't start acting like Mike."

Fred went under the table when he heard us raise our voices. I hadn't seen him do that since Natalie and I would have our fights. It made me realize that it really was none of my business how Megan spent the money I loaned her. "Sorry, Sis. It was sort of a shock is all."

Without saying another word, Megan poured herself a large glass and left the kitchen. I reached down and patted Fred on the head. "It's okay, Boy. She'll cool down once she has a drink or two." I said it loud enough so Megan could hear, then went back to my computer.

The first number I typed into the reverse-lookup webpage was the cell phone itself. The results claimed to know the owner and for only three-ninety-five, or twenty-nine dollars a month for unlimited access, they would tell me who owned the number. The same held true for the next number. Only the last two were listed in a public directory, and hence, free information. One was for the Pig's Roast, and another whose name sounded familiar but didn't ring any bells. I was about to cough up the ransom for the privilege of seeing the unlisted numbers when my computer started complaining about a low battery. *What was it with these batteries?* I thought. *Just who were they trying to protect?*

I shut down my computer and went over to the kitchen counter. I took the bottle Meg had left and joined her on the deck. She saw the bottle in my hand. "Don't bother. I haven't cooled off yet."

I filled her glass anyway. "I'm sorry about that remark, Meg. I must get it from Mom. Look at us – it's just like we're teenagers again."

"More like we're married. Ug. Gag me with a spoon. I need to throw up. What a terrible thought. Married to your own brother," she said before taking a sip from her glass. Then, after a long pause, "Did you find who owns the phone?"

"Not yet. I went to one of those free lookup sites, and my computer died just as I was about to enter my credit card number. I guess the credit gods were telling me not to do it."

Megan gave me a weird look. We were kids checking out a two-headed snake the last time I saw her make a face like that. "Why did you need a credit card if it was free?"

"Oh, the lookup is free all right, but not the information. I sure do miss the good-old-days when the internet really was free. Now everyone wants to charge you for everything. Next thing you know, they will be watching with a webcam and charging you if you pick your nose."

"So, we don't know any more now than we did before Fred found the phone?"

"They did give me two names and addresses. They haven't started to charge for information that can be found in a phone book. At least not yet. No doubt that is coming once they buy out the companies that print the phone books."

She put down her glass and ran her hands through her hair. It was more of a grab-and-pull than a combing motion. "Are you going to tell me what you found, or do I have to listen to you gripe about your stupid internet all night?"

"One call to the Pig's Roast and another to a Ferguson on Cedar Ridge Drive. According to the phone, they were both on May fifteenth."

"Could you use my computer? It's not a fancy laptop like you have, but the batteries never go dead."

Before I could answer, we both heard her kitchen phone ring. "I better get that, it might be Kevin," she said, and then left me on the deck to fetch the phone.

The phone must have woke Fred. The stress of my shouting match with my sister earlier had put him to sleep. It's no wonder dogs don't need psychiatrists; they sleep away their problems. He came out the door when Megan went in. He headed straight for the stairs without acknowledging me. I watched him go down to the first level then head for a tree while I listened to my sister's conversation. "Yes, Mother. I'll tell him. No, I have to wait for Kevin. He isn't answering his phone either. Love you, too. Bye."

I could see Megan through her patio door. She didn't come back to the deck after hanging up the phone. She was walking in the other direction, toward the bathroom on the other side of her great room. It didn't take me more than a minute or two to figure out what she and Fred were doing. That epiphany came when I realized I needed to go, too. I was tempted to do it off the deck, but I didn't want to chance Megan coming back before I finished. So I did the civilized thing and went down the stairs to my lower-level bathroom. I needed to put my computer on its charger anyway.

When I came back up the stairs, both Fred and Megan were sitting at the deck table. "Mom said to tell you that she's going to have to hire someone to clean up the trash in her garage if you don't get your butt over there right now," she said before I could even sit down. "Those were her words, not mine."

"Megan, I can't drive. I've had too much to drink. Besides, it's too late. The dump won't be open."

She giggled and pointed to her empty wine bottle. "I ain't exactly the poster girl for alcoholics amomonis either." She tried her best to speak with a straight face. "But don't worry, I told her the boys were out in Trailer's fruck, and you wouldn't be able to borrow it 'til somorrow. So she'd have to wait unless she wanted to get her van ditty." Then she broke out laughing.

I couldn't help myself and started laughing as well. "I better sleep this off if I'm going to drive tomorrow. I'd ask Fred, but he's had too much to drink, too."

Megan must have thought that was the funniest line she had heard all day. I swear she was cackling as Fred and I took our leave.

Once I fell to sleep, I had the strangest dream. Now I know why ancient oracles would put themselves in a drug-induced trance before asking the gods for answers. The alcohol from too much beer did the same for me. I remembered who the Ferguson's were.

CHAPTER 18

The next morning, I woke at the crack of dawn with a headache and the stale taste of beer in my mouth. I wanted to go back to sleep, but as usual, Fred wanted out. I let him out, and I went to the bathroom. Brushing my teeth failed to get rid of the beer taste, so I went up to the kitchen to make some coffee. To my surprise, Megan was already at the table.

Her hair was a mess, and she had not yet put on any makeup. "Coffee's almost done," she said when saw me. "Thought I better get up when I heard your furry alarm go off. The boys came home last night, and I didn't want you waking them to borrow the truck."

"I must have slept right through it. I never heard them," I answered as I went over to the dishwasher to retrieve two cups. My sister had a bad habit of using the dishwasher as a cupboard. She refused to put away the dishes after washing them. I filled two cups without waiting for the coffee maker to finish. I liked mine black. But I knew she would want cream and sugar for hers, so I retrieved them before sitting down.

"Thank you, Porky. You'll make some lucky girl a nice husband someday."

I gave her my imitation of a snarl. I learned to lift the corner of my upper lip the way Elvis did back in the day, but with me, it came out looking mean. "The truck can wait. I think I found another piece of the puzzle last night. I need to see who owns that cell phone. I do believe he murdered the Fergusons."

"Who?" She gave me her blank look again.

"Remember the retired coin-dealer couple from Liberty?" I paused just long enough to build suspense. "Where the husband supposedly killed his wife because of her terminal cancer then shot himself. He called them from his phone just before he murdered them."

"The husband called himself before he murdered his wife?"

"No. Not the husband. Don't you follow me? The owner of the cell phone called to see if they were home. He must not have got an answer and got caught breaking into the old couple's house. Then he shot them, and he made it look like murder-suicide."

Megan got up and fetched the coffee pot. "You must still be a little sleepy," she said while filling my cup. "That's quite a dream."

"I'm wide awake, Meg. But it was so real. It was like I was watching an old black-and-white movie. I could see him sneaking up to the house and lifting their sliding door off its tracks, just like yours. Then Ferguson catches him going through a desk – I guess he must have been in the home office by now – and Ferguson recognizes him. Ferguson has a gun in his hands – he must have brought it from his bedroom, you know how dreams are. Then the scene jumps to the burglar with the gun, standing over Ferguson. The wife comes into the room, and the burglar shoots her too."

"Did you see his face?" she asked now that I had her focused on my story.

"No. Typical Alfred Hitchcock. The whole thing took place in near darkness."

Megan put down her cup and got up from her chair. "I'll call Mom and tell her Taylor's truck broke down. We've got to see who owns that phone."

***

I had expected Mother to be furious when she heard I wasn't coming as planned. But she bought Megan's story of the truck being out of commission and said she'd have Triple-A come over to fix it. Megan told her I was already working on it and should have it fixed in time to still make it to the dump. I had missed the conversation and got the news after I returned from the lower level with my computer.

"If you don't feel like going, Jake, I suppose I can call her back with another story," she said as we waited for the computer to boot.

The little hour-glass finally went away. Now I had to wait for a wireless connection. "It's okay. I might as well get it over with before she disowns me," I answered.

When the icon in the bottom tray showed three bars, I opened a browser and went straight to a pay-to-snoop reverse-lookup page. I entered the number belonging to the phone. Megan was now standing behind me, watching like a dealer at a blackjack table.

"Ronald Nixon?" I said a little too loudly. Fred raised his head and surveyed the room to see what all the excitement was about. He had been lying by my chair, keeping a watch out for more burglars, or whatever it is dogs think they're doing when they guard us. He laid back down once he saw we were safe.

"So much for hanging Bennet," I said. "If the phone was lost by Atkins' killer, this eliminates Bennet as my prime suspect. Guess I wanted it to be him so bad, I never considered the most likely suspect. Nixon must have killed Bill for the SBA money."

Megan returned to her chair and raised her nearly empty coffee cup. "Congratulations, Sherlock. I knew you could do it. Once we show this to the sheriff, he can arrest Nixon, and I can finally get my insurance." Then she took a drink of her cold coffee and made a terrible sour face. I thought she was going to spit coffee all over the table.

I tried not to laugh but failed miserably. It was all I could do to speak. "God, I wish I could post a picture of that face. YouTube would go viral."

Megan's pucker turned into a pout. "You could have warned me. I got so excited that I forgot it was cold." Then she smiled and went to the sink to empty her cup.

"Sorry about that," I said, now that my laughter had subsided to a mere chuckle. "But don't celebrate yet. Where's the connection to Mike? All we know is that Ron probably murdered Bill and the Fergusons. We have nothing to show he killed Mike, too."

Megan rinsed out her cup before filling it with hot coffee. She held the cup with both hands then looked at me. "I guess you're right. I assumed whoever killed Bill also killed Mike." The lines around her eyes seemed to deepen. "So what now, Jake? None of this makes any sense. I don't see how you can connect all the murders to that phone."

"Maybe the last call on the list will connect the dots for us," I answered and typed the last unknown number into the web page.

She returned to her chair and took a sip from her cup before setting it down on the table. "I'll bet it's Hal."

I stopped typing and looked up at her in amazement. "Hal?" I asked.

"Think about it, Jake. If Nixon did kill the old couple for their coins, who would he sell them to?"

"Good point, Miss Marple," I answered and resumed with my reverse lookup. "That would make a lot of sense if you're right." I hit the submit button and waited to see what my four dollar investment would yield. "My God," I said. "It is Hal."

***

Taylor's truck was on empty when I left Meg's house by myself. I would be on my own cleaning out my mother's garage. Fred wanted to come. He begged me to take him with me; the July heat was too much for his thick coat, so I left him in air conditioned comfort while I braved the heat with nothing but hot wind coming through the truck windows to cool me off. I didn't bother waiting for Kevin and Taylor to get up. Megan had told me they wouldn't be able to help. They had met a couple girls the day before, and the boys had already made plans to take them out on the pontoon later in the afternoon. The humidity must have been off the scale, and I was wishing I was back home in the dry mountain air when the truck ran out of gas.

I threw the transmission into neutral and crossed my fingers. There was no sign of a shoulder. Luckily, I was on the downside of one of Highway Seven's roller-coaster hills and spotted a driveway halfway up the next hill. I just needed enough momentum going downhill, so I could coast to the driveway. I was almost there when I spotted a dark car coming up behind; it had to be doing over seventy. I turned on my flashers and prayed he wouldn't hit me. I made it into the driveway, without a second to spare, when the car threw on its brakes and skidded to a stop. It was a shiny-black Mercedes SUV.

Hal didn't bother to get off the road. He parked half in the driveway and half on the road. If another driver were to come by, he would have to swerve into the oncoming lane to miss the Mercedes. As he started walking toward me, I noticed Amy in the passenger seat. "Where's Taylor?" he asked without bothering to ask if I was okay.

"He's not here, Hal. He let me use the truck, so I could finish at my mother's. Guess he forgot to put gas in it. I ran out."

Hal gave me a disgusted look. "Well, you better come with us. I'll drop you off at the Pig's Roast and call Triple-A." Then he turned around and waddled back to his car. He was so overweight that he actually walked like a duck.

Hal was still working his way back to his side of the car when I slipped into the back seat. Amy had already turned to say something to me, but I spoke first. "Hi, beautiful. I hope you don't make a habit out of picking up strangers off the road."

I think I almost made her laugh. But before she could react, Hal opened his door, and she quickly turned away. "Damn it's hot out there. I'll sure be glad when our plane lands in San Diego. You know they have the best weather in the country there, Jake. Always seventy-two degrees and no humidity."

"You leaving on another business trip?" I asked.

"No, not this time. The wife and I are taking a little vacation. Thought we'd make it like a second honeymoon, check out some properties while we're at it. Something by the Ocean. Maybe in Carlsbad or Del Mar."

Amy had lowered the makeup mirror in her visor and was checking her lipstick. "Megan said Taylor could stay with you guys for the week," she said to the mirror when she saw me watching her. "He practically lives there anyway."

"Yeah. That's why I was a little upset back there, Jake. Last I heard he was going out on Meg's pontoon. I thought he had lied to me," Hal said.

Amy turned toward him, started to say something, but must have changed her mind. She went back to the mirror and rolled her eyes so I could see. Then Hal went on, oblivious to the dirty looks from his wife. "I'll have to drop you at the Pig's Roast. I don't want to miss our flight. It's over two hours to KCI, and the traffic up there is terrible. Oh, and don't worry about Triple-A. I've got a Premium membership that covers all our cars. They'll even give you the gas to get you going again.

"Speaking of the devil's den," he continued as he pulled up into the restaurant's parking lot. "By the way, Jake, how would you like to make a few bucks while we're gone?"

"As long as it's not babysitting."

I saw Amy crack a smile over that remark. Hal just frowned. "Ha," he answered. "No. I heard you're some kind of handyman."

"It pays the bills until I can find a programming job."

"Well, assuming you're a better handyman than a programmer, I was wondering if you wouldn't mind taking a look at the roof over our sunroom. The damn thing has leaked ever since they put it on, and I can't get them to come back and fix it."

I didn't know whether to hit him or thank him. He really hit home with his wisecrack on my programming abilities, but I couldn't believe my good luck. He was giving me the rope I needed to hang him with. "Sure. Anything for a neighbor. Can Taylor let me in to check it out? I will need to see where the water is coming in. There's usually a telltale stain where it is leaking."

"Sorry. No can do. The house is locked up tighter than Fort Knox. I changed the code so he won't be having any parties while we're gone. Bennet will be on him in a New York minute if he tries to get in. Can you try to fix it without going inside?"

I wasn't about to miss out on the opportunity over something as simple as a security system. "No problem," I answered with my own tired cliché and proceeded to leave the car. As I closed the door, I caught a glimpse of Amy watching me. It was all I could do not to reach over and kiss her goodbye.

I watched as they drove away after leaving me on the side of the highway. He didn't even take the time to drop me at the front door. I waited for the Mercedes to disappear over a hill and then started toward the bar. There were only a couple of cars in the parking lot. That, I knew, would change in less than an hour; the lunch crowd would soon begin. The place was called the Pig's Roast for good reason; they had great barbeque ribs.

When I entered, it didn't take long to adjust to the light. Though there was little in the way of lighting, the blinds on the window tables were all up. There was a couple at one of the tables, and Tonto was sitting at his favorite bar stool. I took a seat next to him and patted him on the head. Sam was at the grill, but when I sat down, he turned. "I was beginning to think you went back to Colorado, Jake. How have you been?"

Tonto turned his head, so I could rub his ears. "Nope," I said, "just trying to stay out of trouble."

Sam flipped the burgers on the grill, added some cheese and onions, and then came over to the bar. He reached under the bar, opened a Coors, and handed it to me. "On the house, Buddy. I never had a chance to say how sorry I am about your father. He was a good man."

"Thanks, Sam. I appreciate that. And thanks for the beer. I need it after being out in this heat." Tonto must have loved the ear-rub. His eyes closed to near slits, and he began to purr.

Sam looked down at his cat and shook his head. "Traitor," he said to Tonto then turned back to me. "Have you been walking?"

"No. I was driving Taylor's truck when it ran out of gas. Hal came by and gave me a ride, said he'd call Triple-A, then dropped me off here."

"Hold on Jake. I need to talk to you. Just let me take care of those two." He went back to the grill and finished preparing the burgers. I started to get hungry. My usual fare of McDonald's Doubles was nothing like the burgers he was making. He slathered the Kaiser rolls with mayonnaise, placed the thick patties with their cheese and onions on one slice, and a thick slice of tomato and lettuce on the other half. He finished off the plate with fries and a dill pickle.

I continued to rub Tonto's ears with one hand while raising the cold bottle of beer to my lips with the other. While I sat there wondering what Sam had to say, Johnny Cash was singing about a boy named Sue in the background. About the only topic we had in common was Linda, so I figured he wanted to bring me up to date on her latest boyfriend. The front door opened just when Sue got his ear cut off. It was a guy wearing a long sleeved shirt rolled up to the elbows. He had his name embroidered underneath the Shell Oil logo. "Are you Jake Martin?" he asked when he saw me at the bar.

"Triple-A?" I asked.

"Yeah. Hal Morgan said I'd find you here. Don't mean to rush you, but I've got a shit load of calls. Never fails when it gets hot. Cars start to vapor lock, and the idiots keep grinding on the starter until the battery goes dead."

"Boy, you guys are fast," I said, getting up to leave.

I looked over at Sam, who was still waiting on his customers. "I'll stop by later, Sam. I can't wait to try one of those burgers."

Before he could answer, two more couples entered. He waved then hurried back to the bar as I followed the driver out the door.

***

When I pulled up to her house, Mother was in her garage with the door open. I parked in the street because her minivan was in the driveway. She stopped whatever she had been doing and came to the front of the garage. Her hair was tied up in a bun and covered with one of Dad's old baseball caps. Her face was covered in a painter's mask, and she was wearing one of his old long-sleeve shirts and work gloves. "Are you trying to die of heatstroke, Mom?" I asked, halfway up the driveway. The temperature had risen even higher now that it was mid-afternoon. It must have been close to a hundred.

She pulled her mask down and away from her face, so she could talk. It was one of those paper things held in place with rubber-band straps. "I've got rats in here, Jacob. I'd rather have heatstroke than die from some kind of rat virus. This would have never happened if you had cleaned up this mess sooner." The tension on the straps was too much, and they broke, snapping her in the face.

I tried not to laugh at her startled reaction. She had the look of a person caught completely off guard. "Sorry, Mom. But I'm here now, so why don't you go inside and cool off. I'll finish up in there."

She removed the mask completely, then my father's gloves and shirt. She was wearing one of Dad's oversized tee-shirts under his work shirt. It was soaked in perspiration. "You better come in the house and cool off too, Jacob. You'll need the keys to the van anyway, so you can back that truck up to the garage," she said while rubbing an invisible wound on her face. Then she turned to go back into the house.

I took a quick look into the garage before following her. The boys and I had removed all of the broken furniture and cabinets weeks ago. Only a pile of black trash-bags remained. Though I was at least ten feet away, I could smell the stench. It was no wonder she had rats. Someone must have put out raw garbage in one of the bags.

My mother kept her keys on a key-rack just inside her door. Some people never learn. After having her house ransacked, I would have thought she would try to make it a little harder for a burglar. All a burglar had to do was break a pane of door glass and reach in for the keys. I took her car-keys off the hook and called out to her. "I better get started, Mom. The dump closes at four."

I bumped my head on the top of the van's door frame as I tried to get in the driver's seat. Mother had the seat too far forward for my six-two frame. I reached under the seat, feeling for the adjustment lever, and felt something sticky. It was a roll of duct tape that had become soft and gooey in the heat. I placed the tape on the passenger's floor-mat and went back to search for the seat lever. Once I had the seat set to where my legs weren't up to my chin, I got back out of the car and headed toward the garage in search of a rag to wipe off the glue on my hand. Mother would have what she called a 'hissy fit' if I got the mess on her steering wheel. That's when I saw the hose Fred had retrieved from the truck during our initial cleanup.

The glue used in duct tape must be the stickiest glue made. Although the tape on the hose was long gone, dirt had stuck to where the tape had been, and in a flash, I saw the truth. I went to the rear of the van and got down to check the tailpipe. It too had the residue of duct-tape glue.

CHAPTER 19

When I put the garden hose into the tailpipe, I could see it was only long enough to reach the back of the minivan. On a hunch, I opened the tailgate door and saw where there was a crease in the rubber gasket that seals off the door. I placed the hose in the crease. It wasn't a tight fit, but it collapsed when I closed the door. I went back in the garage and fetched the PVC pipe I had seen earlier. After slipping the hose through the pipe and placing it back on the gasket, I shut the minivan door again. This time, it was a near airtight fit. I removed the hose and turned to see my mother, standing a few feet away, watching. Then, before either of us could speak, Megan drove up and parked behind Taylor's truck.

My mother looked over at Megan, and then she turned back to me. "I wish you hadn't done that, Jacob. Some things are better left alone. But bring your sister inside, so she can hear why we did it, too." Then, without saying a word to Megan, she turned and went back to the house.

"What was that all about?" Megan asked when she met me in the garage. She was dressed a lot like Mother. She had on some of Kevin's old jeans and a tee-shirt with a picture of the Ramones. I was surprised to see Kevin liked a band from my generation.

"She just added another piece that doesn't fit the jigsaw puzzle. You better let her tell it," I said and went into the house.

When we joined her in the kitchen, our mother was crying softly. There were some sandwiches and lemonade on the table. She must have come out to tell me about them, and then saw me checking out her minivan. "Your father only did it for Megan," she said when we both sat down. "I didn't even know about it until he called me to help him. You won't tell anyone, will you Jacob?"

Megan first looked at our mother before she turned to me. "What's going on, Jake? I feel like I just came in to the middle of a movie."

I sat up in my chair and reached for one of the sandwiches. I wasn't trying to be melodramatic, but it must have seemed that way. "This isn't the time to play Charlie Chan. What the hell is going on?" she asked.

"I'm sorry, Meg. Mike really did commit suicide. Father staged the accident to cover it up."

Megan's eyes seemed to grow larger. "What? That's ridiculous. Daddy couldn't have done that," she said then turned her attention to our mother. "Is that true, Mom?"

"Yes," she answered without looking at Megan. "He borrowed Mike's truck that day to take the lawnmower to the shop. When he returned the truck, he found Mike in your garage inside the minivan. It was still running, and he had a hose running from the exhaust pipe into the van."

"But why didn't you tell me?" Megan asked.

Mother looked up at Megan. She had stopped crying, and I could see the look of self-righteousness returning. "He knew you wouldn't get a dime of the insurance if they found Mike that way, so he put him in his truck, drove it over by the dam, and made it all look like an accident. We didn't want to involve you, in case we got caught."

"Which also explains why the suicide note didn't show up until Megan was arrested for murder," I said to Megan. "Our parents must have destroyed the original, and then Mom wrote another to cover your ass."

"Jacob! Please don't use that language in front of me."

"Sorry. But I am right? Aren't I?"

"Not quite," she answered, lowering her eyes again. "I wanted to burn the note we found with Mike, but your father insisted we keep it. Thank god I listened to him. It was the one thing that saved Megan from being charged with murder."

Megan sat stone quiet. Her eyes went from me, back to my mother, then back to me. After what seemed like enough time for the realization to take hold, I spoke up. "I wish you had told us sooner, Mother. Megan could have taken that low-ball offer on the house and moved on with her life, and I could have gone home weeks ago instead of wasting my time playing detective."

Megan finally spoke, "Does that mean you're planning on leaving, Jake?"

"I was planning to go home next week for Allison's birthday anyway. Now, I don't see any reason to come back here. I can give what we know about Nixon to Bennet and head out of Dodge. After what he did to mom's house, I'd like to see Nixon hang, but now that we know he didn't kill Mike, there is no need for me to stick around."

"You can't tell Bennet about this!" Mother said in a high-pitched voice.

"No, Mom, don't worry," I answered while getting up to leave. "I won't tell him about you and Dad. I was referring to some dirt Megan and I found on Nixon. I'll let her fill you in. I need to take your trash to the dump before it closes." I bent down and kissed her on the top of the head. "It's our family secret, Mom."

***

I barely made it to the dump before they closed. Bennet should have been out on patrol. He could have made his quota of speeding tickets. Taylor's truck may look old, but under the hood, it had a massive four-hundred-sixty cubic inch V8. I made the hour drive to Sedalia in thirty some minutes. It was thirty minutes well spent. It gave me time to think before turning over the cell phone. I realized that Bennet might not be the best person to disclose what I knew about Nixon.

Ever since I came to town, Bennet had been trying to crucify me. I didn't have a clue why. But I decided I'd better not give him a smoking gun that he could use against me. My safest bet was with Rosenblum. I decided I'd drop by his office with Nixon's cell phone and the floppy disk from the recycle center. That way, I would be two states away when Bennet found out I had been withholding evidence.

I didn't break any speed records on the drive back to Megan's. There was no need to get back anytime soon. She and our mother had also had time to think, and God only knew what they had decided to do about the evidence we had on Nixon. When I made the turn onto Highway Seven and saw the sign for the Pig's Roast, I remembered Sam had tried to tell me something when I had left with the tow-truck driver earlier. It was a great excuse to prolong the confrontation with my mother and sister.

When I entered, there were still several customers sitting in the dining room and a few more at the bar. The sunlight, now that it was past the horizon, came through the lakeside windows, but it didn't light up the place much. In a few minutes, it would die out and only the dim lights of the table lamps would illuminate the room. I thought I spotted Linda serving in the dining room. Dim light can play tricks that way. After I took a seat at the bar next to Tonto, I realized it had been wishful thinking. The cat had no problem with the light and recognized me instantly. He was on my lap before I barely sat down.

"That old cat has really taken to you, Jake." Sam said while sliding a bottle of Coors across the counter.

Tonto pushed his head up against my hand. I took the hint and started rubbing his ears. "Just like my dog. They love it when someone scratches their ears," I answered while reaching for the beer with my free hand. "By the way, what was it you wanted to tell me earlier?"

Sam took a moment to check out the other customers before answering, and then he hit himself upside the head. "Damn. I almost forgot again. I must be getting sometimers. I have something for Megan. It's back in the office. Hold on, I won't be a minute."

I pretended to laugh then took a long sip of my beer. I needed to change position on the bar stool. Tonto had fallen asleep in my lap, and I didn't want to disturb him. I quietly turned the stool away from the bar toward the diners. I was checking out the new waitress when Sam returned. I swung around a little too quickly and woke Tonto.

The cat jumped off my lap, slowly walked over to the end of the bar where he had a small pet bed, laid down, and went back to sleep. "Damn cat thinks he owns the place," Sam said. He handed me a folded piece of paper. He then looked over at Tonto, who was rubbing his back against the end of the bar. "You don't need another pet, do you?"

"I wouldn't mind, but my sister and my dog might have a few objections. Megan's allergic to cats, and I'm not sure how Fred would react. I don't think he would appreciate me bringing home a cat," I answered while I unfolded the paper. "What's this, Sam?"

Sam smiled before answering. "I put together a list of investors who can help Megan. I think I told you that, before the bust, I used to be a mortgage broker. These are a few people I know who won't try to low-ball her. They'll give her a decent price."

I looked up from the note, but before I could say anything, several construction workers came in the front door and headed toward the bar. Sam was already on his way to wait on them. I refolded the note, finished my beer, and got up to leave. I fished out a five dollar bill from my wallet and placed it by my empty bottle. I put Sam's list in my wallet and headed for the door, just as the construction crew took seats at the bar. One of them nudged Tonto with his boot. The cat hissed at him then turned and slowly walked toward the back room.

***

The sun was at my back the next morning as I drove past the Pig's Roast, heading toward town. I had left the house right after letting Fred out and before anyone woke up. I figured that, by the time I finished breakfast at the Rusted Kettle, the local hardware store would be open. I had promised Hal I would fix his roof, if I could, so I needed to get some plastic roofing cement and a roofer's trowel. If the job required anything more, I would tell him to find someone local who could put a new roof over his sunroom.

Passing the Pig's Roast reminded me of Sam's list. Megan was not a happy camper when I had given her the list of investors. I realized now that I should have waited. She had already put away a full bottle of her favorite Chardonnay. On the other hand, the house would be back in foreclosure if she continued to spend the money I lent her on everything except the mortgage, so I convinced myself that I did the right thing.

The Rusted Kettle was packed when I entered. All three of the non-smoking tables at the rear were taken, as were all the front tables. I was about to turn and leave when a woman at one of the front tables started waving at me. "Jake, come sit with us," she said. I recognized the couple who had given me a ride after my run-in with Bennet.

"Hello, Sharon," I said when I went over to her. "And how are you doing, Harley?" I asked her husband. He turned to greet me, but stayed seated.

Harley put down his cigarette and offered me a shaking hand. "Haven't seen you since the funeral. Your mom tells us you've been working like a dog getting her house back in shape. That's a real crime what they done to it."

"Christ sake, Harley. At least let him sit down before you start talking him to death," Sharon cut in. She moved her plate next to her husband and went around the table to sit by him. "Take my chair, Jake, so you don't get your ear talked off sitting next to the old coot."

The cloud of smoke above the table made me want to beg off. But I sat down across from the couple anyway. "Thanks Sharon. I didn't expect the place to be so crowded this early."

"Gotta make hay while the sun shines, Boy," Harley cut in. "We ain't like those sissies in the city who can't get going 'till they've had their so called brunch. What gets you going so early?"

"Harley!" Sharon said. "That wasn't very nice."

Harley gave his wife a blank look, "What? What did I say?"

"It's okay, Sharon," I said. "No offense taken." Then I looked over at Harley who looked like he still didn't understand the insult. "I need to finish up a few odd jobs before I leave for home. Thought I'd get some roofing cement then stop at my mom's house to get my dad's ladder. First on my list is a little roof repair."

"Did that bastard ruin your mother's roof, too?" Harley asked.

"Harley! Must you swear all the time?" Sharon asked.

"Sorry, Mother. I guess calling Nixon a bastard ain't strong enough. How about I call him a son-of-a-bitch instead?"

I dropped the menu I had picked up from the middle of the table. It was one of those plastic-coated single-page menus. "Nixon? How did you know Nixon trashed my mother's house?"

Harley must have known he now had my attention. He leaned forward, holding his cigarette inches from my face. "Hell, Son. Why else would he disappear the way he done?"

I instinctively leaned back in my chair, retrieving the menu to wave the smoke from my face. "He left town? Do you know when?"

Harley made a show of snuffing out his cigarette in the ashtray on the table then narrowed his eyes. He paused just long enough to create some suspense. "I think the SOB knew Bennet was on to him and left right after robbing your mother. The rumor is that Bennet tracked down the missing copper from the museum. The bastard took all the flashing and gutters from what was left of the roof and sold it for scrap. Back then, they made buildings to last. Not like that cheap plastic and tin they use for gutters now-a-days." Harley reached for his cigarette pack in his shirt before continuing. "I hear they have to notify the cops, just like the pawn shops now, when anyone brings in a suspicious load. They say he got a couple thousand for it. Bennet was on him like a hound on a coon. Must have missed him by only a day or so."

I felt like asking Harley when pawn shops started buying copper, but I knew what he meant and didn't try to correct him. I didn't know what to say, and luckily, I didn't have to. The waitress must have thought I was flagging her down by waving the smoke away from my face with the menu. "What can I get you, Honey?" she asked when she came to the table with a pot of coffee in one hand and a cup in the other.

"Just coffee, please," I answered. "I need to get going and make some hay while the sun is still shining."

***

Mother had spent the night at Megan's, so when I stopped off to get my father's ladder, I didn't worry about waking her. She was also another reason I had left Megan's so early. I didn't want to rehash the conversation from the night before. She didn't want us to turn in the cell phone or floppy disk. She was afraid that any investigation might uncover her deed of staging Mike's accident.

My father's ladder was nearly covered by weeds. They had entwined themselves between the rungs of the ladder, making it extremely difficult to pick up off the ground. It looked like I needed to add cutting the grass and weeds around my mother's house to my list of chores. On a hunch, I decided to check his garden hose as well. I felt a sense of relief when I found it still connected to the faucet on the back of the house. It didn't come close to matching the hose Mike used to commit suicide.

The drive back to Hal's house didn't take long. This time I passed the Pig's Roast without hesitation; my thoughts were still on what to do with Nixon's cell phone. Bennet had already discovered Nixon was selling scrap copper, so I didn't need to worry about the floppy any longer. It would serve no purpose telling him something he already knew. But I couldn't ignore the cell phone. It clearly implicated Nixon in murder, and I could be in real trouble if I sat on that information.

The porch light was still on when I parked in Hal's driveway. It made me laugh to myself. To spend all that money on a fancy security system and then leave the porch light burning was like putting an ad in the paper that no one was home.

After untying the ladder and lifting it out of Taylor's truck, I went around the side of the garage with it balanced on my shoulder. It was a heavy, twenty-foot, aluminum extension-ladder. In my quest to keep it balanced on my shoulder, I didn't notice the short hose sticking out from a faucet on the side of the house. I tripped and fell flat on my face. When I got up to brush myself off, I saw a security camera tucked under the roof's eave. I saluted the camera with my middle finger and mouthed a few choice words for it to see. When I bent back down to pick up the ladder, I saw the hose that had tripped me. There was no doubt it was the missing part of Mike's hose.

I left the ladder and went back to the truck. I had to think where I wasn't being watched. "Why would Mike take a hose from Hal's, then go home and kill himself?" I asked myself. "Unless, it wasn't Mike," I answered. "And whoever it was must have been seen by the camera."

CHAPTER 20

At this point, any sane person would have simply called the sheriff and told them what they had found. But it wasn't a question of sanity. There was still the possibility that Bennet was involved somehow. If that was the case, all he had to do to cover his tracks was get the DVD and destroy it. I had to see that DVD before he did. It was time to fix a roof.

As I went back to work, I thought about the irony of the roof. I recalled how I told Megan I was going to check out the roofing truck in Sedalia, so I could break in and then got sidetracked by Amy asking me to come to her rescue. I had abandoned that plan, and the consequences of breaking and entering, after Fred found the cell phone. Now here I was, ready to commit the felony after all. But this time, I didn't have to pretend – I had been invited.

Hal must have thought burglars didn't carry ladders to work and decided not to wire the upstairs windows to the security system. I knew that from my previous visit. Megan had a laugh at that insider knowledge – she surely must have guessed how I came about that privileged information.

The house was built on a slope, with the back decks facing the water, making the second story decks three stories high because of the walkout basement. My ladder was only good for twenty feet - at least ten feet short of my goal.

I had to first climb the stairs, with my ladder on my shoulder, to the first-story deck, then set it up to get to the upper deck. I didn't even try the doors on the first deck, for I could see a security sensor through the glass. Opening the door would send a silent alarm to the security company, which would in turn call the sheriff.

Although the French doors on the deck over the sunroom didn't have any sensors, they were locked. I couldn't simply lift the door out of its tracks like the burglar at Meg's did; however, I couldn't believe my luck. The carpenters had installed the doors with their hinges facing out so the doors would swing out instead of in. I simply popped out the hinge pins and removed a door. Then I unlocked the deadbolt, replaced the door on its hinges, and went inside. I quickly went down the stairs to Hal's office and stopped cold. The monitor on his desk had six different camera views. One of the cameras was looking at the back of the house. It must have taken a video of me removing the French doors.

I had no problem erasing the evidence of my breaking-and-entering. After going into the hidden room where Hal kept the surveillance system, I pressed the back button on the recorder and found the video showing me removing the door and deleted it. Then I went over to the boxes where Hal kept the backup DVDs. I already knew I couldn't trust Hal's labels and wanted to make sure I got the right one, so I took the four remaining disks. Now all I needed to do was figure out a way to disable the system long enough for me to make a clean getaway. All my effort would be for naught if the cameras caught me leaving the house through the master bedroom.

The six cameras were connected to the back of the security console. Fortunately, they were labeled, so I pulled the wire to the camera covering the back of the house. I didn't remove it all the way. I left it plugged into the jack just enough to disable the camera and make it look like it had come loose. It amazed me how clever I could be at times. I closed the hidden door and returned to Hal's office. There was a red alarm icon flashing on the security monitor.

Calm down, Jake, I told myself. The alarm was probably intended only for Hal and the security company. A burglar would not have known he set off the alarm until the police showed up. The security company would more than likely make a call to the house before contacting the sheriff. Would there be a code I would need to answer if I pretended to be Hal? If I failed to supply the code, or didn't answer, how much time did I have before the sheriff arrived? *Think, Jake, calm down and think.*

My first impulse was to run out the door and get away as fast as I could. Then reason took over. Once the security company called in the alarm, I would have at least half an hour before the sheriff would show, and then, they would almost certainly review the video before they did that. My first task had to be to disable the video recorder, so I shut down the computer that controlled the cameras. That would prevent the security company from remotely un-deleting my break-in. Now if they tried to review the recording or my escape, they would be out of luck. Of course, nothing would stop someone from rebooting the system. I thought about taking the recorder with me, but then they would know for sure there was a burglary. I needed to make it look like a malfunction. The speaker from Hal's surround system should do the trick.

I ran into the media room and disconnected the bass speaker from the surround-sound system. Returning to the surveillance room, I removed the back cover of the speaker cabinet to expose its heavy magnet. I then ejected the removable disk drive from the recorder, removed it from its caddy, and passed it over the magnet several times. After returning the drive to its caddy and inserting it back into the recorder, I tried booting the system. Perfect, the hard drive would not boot. I had erased the boot sector and hopefully all the data on the drive. Now anyone would think the system simply malfunctioned. *Not bad for a novice burglar*, I thought. Then the phone started to ring while I was putting the speaker back in place. I froze. *Should I answer it and pretend to be Hal?*

"This is your captain calling. You have won two free tickets to the Bahamas; however, you must return our call within the next twenty minutes to claim your prize."

***

When I pulled into its parking lot, The Pig's Roast was a welcome sight. Though I had made a pact with God to walk the straight and narrow after leaving Hal's house, I didn't think that included a drink to calm my nerves. The dreaded call from the security company never came – at least not while I was in the house. My escape had been uneventful, except for tripping over the garden hose again in my haste to get away.

Linda's replacement was on duty when I took my seat at the bar next to Tonto. "What can I get you, Sweetie?" she asked. Her outfit was skimpier than anything Linda ever wore.

When I answered, I tried my best to look her in the eyes. "Coors please. And could I use your phone? My cell doesn't seem to work out here."

She bent down to get my beer from the cooler under the bar. I felt like a pervert, but I couldn't help but stare when she leaned down. She opened my beer, wiped the wet bottle with her bar-towel, and smiled as she handed it to me. "Sure, Honey. It's at the end of the bar. Over there by the cat's bed."

Maybe she saw me blush when she caught me looking at her ample breasts. But the light was dim, so I acted like nothing happened and went to the phone. Megan picked up on the second ring.

I was still nursing my beer when Megan walked in. The barmaid had left me alone, so she could wait on the lunch crowd that was already starting to fill the tables in the dining area. Except for Tonto, Megan and I had the bar to ourselves, so I told her about my adventure. Tonto didn't miss a word.

Megan seemed to light up the dim bar when I told her the garden hose was a perfect match to the one found in Mike's truck. "Then Mike didn't kill himself," she said. "Do you really think the DVD will show who did it?"

Before I could answer, Bennet walked in with two other deputies.

CHAPTER 21

Bennet and his deputies took a table toward the front and acted like he didn't recognize Meg or me. It was just as well; I would have confessed before he could read me my rights.

The waitress saw the deputies, too. She quickly finished taking an order at one of the window tables and headed toward the deputies. Bennet and company had already selected a table close to the bar. "Well hello, Handsome," she said when she made it to their table. "You're late this afternoon."

Bennet smiled at her and took the menu she handed him. "Had to check out a false alarm, Jen. Those boys in Kansas City think we have nothing better to do than play nursemaid to their security systems." He gave her back the menu without looking at it. "Can you make me a quick burger? I've got to be in court this afternoon."

Megan poked me in the ribs. I turned on my barstool to see why. "Don't stare at them," she whispered.

I ignored my sister, turning back in time to see the waitress pretend to pout before addressing the other deputies. "How about you fellas? You want a burger too?"

When he looked up at the waitress, the deputy facing me saw me watching. "Miss, could we have our check when you get a chance?" I said, hoping he would think that's why I had been looking in their direction.

"Be right with you," she answered in an irritated voice without looking at us. My ploy must have worked. The deputy ignored me and picked up the conversation with the waitress.

***

Fred was waiting for us in the driveway. I couldn't remember a time when he had been so happy to see me. "Did you miss me, Boy?"

He answered by catching me off balance, knocking me off my feet, and planting a wet kiss on my face.

"What about me, Freddie? Don't I get a kiss too," Megan said between laughs.

Fred stopped kissing me long enough to turn his attention to my sister. It was enough to get Fred off me, so I could get to my feet and brush myself off. "Looks like the boys forgot to let him back in again," I said, looking at Kevin's empty parking space. "I wonder how long he's been out here?"

"They must have put him out for this," Megan said, waving a business card at me that she had found by the lock box. "It's from one of Sam's investors. He says he'd like to make an offer on the house." It was like someone flipped the mood switch. Her cheerful smile turned to a frown. She put the card in her purse, fished out the keys, and let us in the house.

I went straight to the kitchen with Fred at my heels while Megan went to her office – presumably to call the investor. I busied myself with filling Fred's water bowl and getting a couple of beers from the refrigerator, all the while trying to listen to Megan's conversation through her open office door.

"Let me think about it." I heard her say. "I'll call you back tomorrow and let you know."

"Well?" I asked when she joined us in the kitchen. I could see she was on the verge of tears.

"Let's go out on the deck and drink those, Jake," she said, pointing at the beers.

I followed her out the sliding door, and Fred followed me. He must have sensed the change in her mood; his tail was no longer wagging. "The offer is less than what I owe," she said after taking a long drink. "He says I can probably get the bank to do a short sell, whatever that is, and at least not go into foreclosure."

"It's where the bank agrees to take less than what you owe and not come after you for the difference. I believe it's a black mark on your credit but not as bad as foreclosure."

"Who the hell cares about my credit rating? The bastards can foreclose for all I care before I walk away losing everything I put in this place." She started to cry.

Fred was as upset by her outburst and tears as I was. He laid his head on her lap, as if to say it would be okay. He couldn't talk, so I found the words for both of us. "Just tell them no, Meg. I still have my life insurance I can borrow against. It should keep the bank off your back for a few more months."

My words of comfort opened the flood gates. I would never understand women if I lived into the next century. "What'd I say?" I asked Fred as Megan ran to her room.

Instead of running after her, like I used to with Natalie, I decided to let it go and check out the DVDs I stole from Hal. Fred and I were in the kitchen, watching the surveillance video on my laptop, when Megan rejoined us half an hour later. I was in the process of watching Nixon cut the garden hose. "Are you sure it's the same hose?" she asked while looking over my shoulder at the computer screen.

"No doubt about it. Watch this," I answered and clicked on the fast-reverse icon. When it reached the point where I wanted, I clicked on the forward button. We could see all six camera angles, each in a different frame. Nixon and Mike were seen on the deck camera, and an SUV could be seen coming down the driveway in another frame. My computer didn't have the right software to select individual frames, so we couldn't hear the audio on any of them. Mike was pointing a shotgun at Nixon, and the two seemed to be arguing. Megan and I watched Linda leave the SUV, and then we saw her on the deck camera. Mike must have seen her, too. When he turned to look, Nixon grabbed the gun out of Mike's hands and hit him over the head with it. The deck camera captured it all in high definition color video.

Because she was behind me, I couldn't see Megan's expression, but I heard her gasp when we saw Nixon dragging Mike's limp body to the minivan and putting him in the passenger seat. Then we saw him go to the side of the garage and cut the hose. The camera kept recording, for nearly a minute, after Nixon had driven off with Mike slumped over the minivan's dash. The time stamp on the next video showed that half an hour had passed. This time, we saw Nixon and Linda return. He got out of her car and went around the house, out of the camera's view. Then she left. A few minutes later, we saw Nixon at the dock, leaving in his boat. It had the words 'Bass Tracker' written on the side in letters only a blind person could miss.

Oddly enough, that was all the video there was. I had expected to see Hal show up, but I couldn't find it on any of the DVDs. He must have destroyed any trace of his presence to protect himself.

I turned around to say something to Megan. Tears quietly rolled down her cheeks. "We should give this to the sheriff," I said. "I could send him an anonymous copy from a 'concerned citizen' or something like that. I don't relish spending twenty years in a Missouri prison for burglary."

***

I spent the next day getting ready for my trip home, and Megan went into town to take our mother to church. Or maybe it was the other way around. Megan wasn't much of a church person, but it was easier than listening to our Mother nag. It also gave me time to think things through. The next morning, we took the DVD to Rosenblum.

I had decided to give him the original and keep a copy for myself. The thought of being tracked down by some hidden electronic code on the DVD had kept me up most of the night. I remembered reading that was how they caught the BTK killer a few years back. He had sent them a floppy disk that was traced to a computer at the church where he did some volunteer work – or something like that.

At first, Rosenblum was a little put out when we barged into his office unannounced. But his attitude quickly changed after we managed to get him to watch the video. "And all this time, I thought it was Hal," he said, when we saw Nixon drive away in his boat.

Megan had been watching the lawyer watch the video. "I'd like to see the insurance company claim Mike killed himself now," she said, grinning.

Rosenblum returned her smile with a frown. "I wish it were that easy, Meg. Until I can get the coroner to change the death certificate, they won't give you a penny. And he won't do that based on what I've seen here. How do we know Nixon didn't take Mike home to sleep it off? We don't see him actually kill Mike, do we?"

Megan's quit grinning. It looked like she might start crying, so I jumped in, "Come on, Ira, you know how the system works. Put a little pressure on those guys, and you'll have a confession before the sun sets."

"You watch too much TV, Jake," he answered. "But you do have a point. I'll ask the DA to have the sheriff work on Linda. I think she's our best bet. Now all I need to do is find a way to give this to Bennet. I know his first question will be where did I get it from?"

***

Rosenblum didn't have to answer any of Bennet's questions after all. The crafty lawyer went to his friend Simons, the judge, and Simons called his friend, the sheriff, leaving Bennet out of the loop.

The sheriff checked the phone records then put out a warrant for Nixon and arrested Linda at her grandfather's house. When the DA threatened to charge her as an accomplice to murder, Linda confessed. The DA pointed out that any handwriting expert would show Linda wrote Mike's suicide note. Her confession confirmed my suspicions. Mike had gone to Hal's to sell him the coins, and

Nixon had somehow found out about the meeting and got there first. That beautiful cursive script of hers was her undoing.

Linda claimed no knowledge of how Mike ended up in the lake. The last she had seen him or Nixon was when Nixon put Mike in the minivan and drove away. She suggested that Nixon must have put Mike in his truck and then staged the accident. Rosenblum told us not to worry. He was sure the DA wouldn't press charges against our mother if the truth came out when they caught up with Nixon.

It didn't take Rosenblum long to have Mike's death certificate changed. Fred and I, shortly after, left for home in our motor home. We took the long way back by traveling the old US highways and avoiding the freeways. There wasn't much waiting for me back home. I just had to make it before Allison's birthday; that wasn't until December, so I got the idea to take our time and travel the blue highways.

The blue highways were, according to a book I had read several years ago by the same name, the old US highways that were the main roads across America before the freeways. The author of that book, William Least Heat Moon, had made it seem like a trip back to when life was not so hectic and dog-eat-dog. I would have to cross Kansas again to get back to Colorado and anything was better than the boring trip over Interstate Seventy. Like most of my hair-brained ideas, this one came to me out of nowhere, so I changed my route for no reason other than it sounded like a good idea at the time.

My first mistake was in trying to use modern technology to take me back sixty years. My GPS had us traveling down US 50 toward Wichita. Highway fifty shared the road with I-35 for over a hundred miles. Mister Moon would have been very upset.

After turning off the GPS in Emporia, and consulting the map given to me at a Kansas rest area, I saw Highway 50 would give me a clear shot to Colorado without passing through any large cities. It wasn't until I was back on the road less-traveled that I realized I was being followed.

CHAPTER 22

Whoever was following me had been clever enough to stay far enough behind that I didn't notice him on the busy freeway from Kansas City to Emporia. I only realized he was following me because of his Missouri plates. I had seen those plates before. The first three letters were my daughter's initials, AEM. I remembered seeing the plates back in Sedalia when I first had the stupid idea to take US 50 to Colorado.

"We've got company, Fred. Should I try to shake him?" My furry traveling companion looked out his window and barked. I thought for a moment that Fred actually understood me until I saw I had just passed a McDonald's.

"How about something to eat? Are you hungry for a McDouble?" Now I really had his attention. He started to drool.

I made a quick U-turn and pulled into McDonald's parking lot, and I almost hit the car in front of me because I was watching in my rearview mirrors for the SUV with Missouri plates. I saw the big SUV slow down then drive on just before I saw the car in front of me. Fred flew forward when I slammed on my breaks.

"You okay, big Fella?" I asked. He answered by wagging his tail without losing sight of the restaurant. His training to recognize the golden arches would have made Pavlov proud.

I couldn't go through the drive-up window with the motor home, so I parked in the rear and walked back to the restaurant. Fred could guard the motor home, and I covered my back by watching the street for the SUV. He, or I suppose it could have been a she, didn't return. I ordered four McDoubles and fries and went back to the motor home where Fred and I ate our gourmet meal. If we were being followed, it had to be the CIA using their latest stealth technology, for we never saw the big SUV again after leaving Emporia. My mind soon went on to other thoughts when I got a call from my sister.

"Hi, Porky. Are you guys home yet?"

"No. We decided to take the scenic cruise. We won't be home for a couple of days. What's up?" I asked.

"I got an offer on the house," she answered. "It's still less than I wanted, but money won't be an issue much longer. Ira got the insurance company to come through. We're going down to Springfield tomorrow to pick up the check."

"We? Ira's going with you?"

"It's not what you think, Porky. He has some business in Branson, so he offered to go with me in case the insurance company gives me any trouble."

"What about the offer? Are you going to take it?"

"Depends on Mom. If I can talk her into going back to Colorado. Anyway, that's not the main reason I called."

"Oh?" I answered. I hated it when she did this to me.

"They found the gun Nixon used to kill Bill."

"By your dock," I said.

"Almost exactly where you said it would be. They bought your theory that Nixon had been searching for it around my dock after dropping it when he dumped Bill's body. Bennet even said you were pretty smart to figure out the shoes belonged to a cop. Of course, he had to add that a security guard wasn't a real cop."

"Bennet said that? What kind of drugs have you been taking Meg? Bennet hates my guts," I said. "I take it they haven't found Nixon yet?"

"Not yet. Ira thinks it's only a matter of time before he shows up."

***

Megan had her insurance check by the time Fred and I made it home. She sent me more than enough to cover all I had lent her. I was finally able to send Greg Junior the balance on what I figured I owed for the motor home and catch up all my bills. With a little luck, I could scrape by at least a year until I finished my novel or found a job. I didn't like all the loose ends I had left back in Missouri. I didn't know if they would ever convict Hal of selling illegal prescription drugs or if the gold coins would ever be found. I figured that would all come out when they were able to catch Nixon. He had disappeared before the warrant was issued.

Yes, life was good again and back to normal. Until déjà vu struck with another two-o'clock call from my mother. "Jacob, it's your Mother."

"I figured that, Mom. Who else would call me at two in the morning?"

"Don't be so smart with me, Jacob. Your sister is in bad shape."

"Calm down, Mom. What happened?"

"Nixon showed up at Meg's door, demanding his coins. When she pretended she had no idea what he was talking about, he beat her and tied her up, then tore up the house looking for them. Kevin and Taylor showed up just in time before that terrible man had his way with your sister. That coward ran away when he heard Kevin's car, but thanks to Kevin's quick thinking, he got the license number. That's how we know it was Nixon."

"Where is Meg now, Mother?"

"She's sleeping. I would have called you sooner, but it's been so hectic with the police and all."

"Do you need me there, Mom?" *Please say no*, I thought.

"No. She should be okay. They wanted her to see a doctor, but Amy checked her over and said it was just superficial."

232

"Amy? Amy's there?" I asked.

"She and Taylor have been staying with Meg, you know."

"What about Hal? Is he there too?"

"No. They split up after you left. Just Amy and Taylor. And the boys can fix what that terrible man broke. All he did was knock a few holes in the walls and steal some CDs, so we don't need you here." She answered.

"CDs or DVDs, Mom?

"I don't know. They're all the same to me. What difference does it make anyway, Jacob?"

"A big difference, Mom. But just one more question. Did Nixon's plates start with the letters AEM?"

"How did you know that, Jacob?"

"ESP, Mom."

The phone went silent. I thought she had hung up on me, but then Megan came on the line. "I hope Mom didn't scare you, Porky. You don't need to come back – the bastard barely scratched me."

"You sure? I can be there by tomorrow."

"No. Don't do that. Ira's taking me to Saint Louis with him to some kind of convention. I won't be here. You stay put and take care of Fred, or have him take care of you, as the case may be."

"Ira?"

"I've got to go now, Jake. Thank you for everything. Love ya." Then she hung up, leaving me in the dark about her new relationship with Rosenblum. There wasn't anything I could do, but now I knew who had been following me on my trip home.

Fred had slept through the entire phone call and only woke when I hung up. He began to growl.

"What you hear out there, old Fella?" I asked as he stared at the door.

Mother's call had me spooked, so I grabbed the twelve gauge shotgun I kept in the closet. I kept it loaded, unless Allison was visiting, but I kept the chamber empty. I quickly pumped it once to put a shell in the chamber then clicked off the safety. If someone was out there ready to break in, they would soon be hamburger.

The sound of the cocked gun must have scared off my visitor. Although Fred was barking too loud to hear clearly, someone or something had been out there; I thought I could hear it running down the gravel driveway. My first impulse was to let my ferocious guard dog loose. Then, when I saw him hiding under the coffee table, I had second thoughts. My table wasn't glass, so he must have known he would be safe.

I turned on my flood lights and peeked out the window. No one was there. I went out the back door and circled around the house. Fred had found the courage to join me and was now by my side. We were about ready to go back inside when I happened to shine my flashlight on the motor home. The door was swinging open.

Living in the foothills of Denver has its advantages, but it also has its problems. We get more than our share of critters this far from the city lights. I've seen deer, elk, black bear, and raccoons. There was even a mountain lion a few years back that had attacked and killed several of a neighbor's llamas. But I've never seen an animal that could open a locked motor home door.

"If you're in there, Buddy, you better come out before I fill you full of buckshot," I said, and waited for a response. It didn't come.

I shut off my flashlight and quietly crept around the side of the motor home, peering in the dinette window. I couldn't see any movement, so I took a chance and turned on the light. Still nothing. By now, my heart was racing. If there had been someone in there with a gun, I would have been dead. The motor home skin could barely stop a rock. It would have been no match for a bullet.

Fred started to growl again, and I could see the hair on his back standing straight up. I shut off my light again and dropped to the ground thinking there had to be someone in there. I was expecting a shot at any moment. Instead, I heard the sound of a car start down the road, and tires spinning on the gravel.

Fred took off running after the car. He wasn't fooling anyone. Now that the sissy knew he had no chance of catching the intruder, he thought he would show me what a great guard dog he was.

My heart slowed down to only two hundred beats per minute, and I picked myself up off the ground and went into the motor home. It had been trashed. My first thought was Nixon and how he had trashed Megan's house looking for 'his' coins. But that was impossible. Even Superman could not have flown over seven hundred miles in such a short time.

Fred came back about the time I had the motor home put back together. The intruder hadn't trashed it as bad as he could have. Maybe he didn't have the time. All the drawers had been pulled out and one of the top cabinet doors would have to be fixed, but otherwise, it would be okay. "Come on, Boy, let's go back to the cabin. I'll call the sheriff in the morning."

I didn't call the sheriff, but I did call my mother back. "Jacob, what is so important you had to call me at five in the morning?"

"Isn't caller ID great, Mom?" I answered. "Sorry to wake you. I thought you would still be up."

"Well, I wasn't. I've hardly had any sleep the last two days, and now you go and wake me."

"Mom, when did Nixon break in and beat up Megan?"

"Yesterday. What does that have to do with waking me up?"

"What time yesterday?"

"Yesterday morning. Why?"

So much, I thought, for my superman theory of travel. Nixon had over twenty-four hours after leaving Meg's.

"Thanks, Mom. You've been a big help. I'll call you later and explain." Then I hung up and called 911.

The sheriff in Colorado was too busy to send anyone out to take a report until the next day. It was late afternoon before a deputy came around.

"You need to get some plates on this thing," he said when I showed him the motor home. "That temporary sticker expired a week ago."

"Thanks for pointing that out, officer. I'll take care of it tomorrow. Is there any way you can get a print from it to see who broke in?"

He laughed like I had told a real funny joke. "Not unless someone was murdered. We don't have the time or resources to follow up on these petty crimes. About the best we can do is take a report for your insurance company."

"I told you back in the cabin, I think I know the guy who did this, and he is wanted for murder."

"I'll tell my sergeant. But I don't see how he could get all the way from Missouri in only a day. Not if he's driving. And he couldn't fly if there is an all points out for him back there, as you say."

"It's only a twelve hour drive, Officer, less if he speeds," I said

"Sorry, but with all the budget cutbacks, we just don't have the resources. Is that your dog?" he asked.

"Yeah. I think he scared the guy off before he could do more damage."

"Better get a license for him and keep him in the yard. We don't allow unlicensed pets in the county anymore." The deputy went over to pet Fred, then stopped when Fred's ears went back and his back hair turned to porcupine quills. "Does he bite?"

"No. It must be the uniform." I replied.

The deputy got back in his Jeep and started his motor. "I'll give this report to my sergeant and ask him to see what he can find out about this Ron Nixon. Maybe, we can beef up our patrols in the area if we think he's headed this way. But if I was you, I think I'd get back in my motor home and go somewhere."

I thought my imitation of a detective had ended in Missouri. Now it looked like I was back in business. It was obvious the local law wasn't interested in my problem anymore than the police in Truman had been interested in looking for my mother's burglar. Of course, there was no mystery here. It had to be Nixon looking for those damn coins. There was no doubt I was in grave danger and the only protection I had from a guy who had killed at least twice was a shotgun and a dog that would run for the nearest coffee table at the first sign of a threat. Then I came to my senses; I decided to take the deputy's advice. Fred and I were long overdue for a father and son fishing trip.

Summer is short lived in the Colorado high country, and Fred and I hadn't caught a single brown trout all year. We needed to get into the mountains and catch our share before it was too late. It was the middle of July, and snow would be falling up there before we knew it. My plan was to take the motor home and camp at one of the State or National campgrounds, then backpack into the wilderness. Nixon, if he was dumb enough to follow us, would be ill prepared for the fickle weather above ten thousand feet. But as the deputy had warned, I would need to get the plates on my motor home before I went anywhere. Our escape to the high country would have to wait another day. It was too late to drive into town for the plates.

Fred and I were sitting on our deck with our beer, trying to decide if we should stay the night or get in the motor home and head for a campground closer to town. Actually, I'm not sure how much Fred thought about having his throat slit in the middle of the night. He was more interested in biting the bubbles from the beer I poured on the deck. I had just opened another beer when my cell rang.

"Where have you been, Porky? I've been trying all day to get you."

"I'm surprised you got me now. How come you didn't call the house phone? You know I hardly get a signal up here on my cell." I answered.

"I did. It's out of order. Didn't you pay the bill?"

"Must be the squirrels again. They're always eating through the wires, but enough about my phone. How are you doing? I thought you were going to Saint Louis with Ira?"

"Tomorrow, that's why I called. I wanted you to know before I left, Bennet got a call from your sheriff and said you had been vandalized."

"I'll be. He did follow up on my report."

"Bennet told him about Nixon and ..." The cell phone cut off before she could finish.

I tried calling Megan back, but I couldn't get a signal. It was getting dark, or I would have walked up the hill and tried again. That seemed to work sometimes, but it too was hit and miss.

"Guess I'll have to get off my butt, Fred, and see what's wrong with the house phone," I said and gave him the rest of my beer.

Meg was right. There was no dial tone at all. It was a cordless phone, so I checked the adapter and then the phone jack. Everything seemed to be okay, so I went outside to check the wiring.

The phone wire ran from the eave of my roof to the utility pole at the end of my drive. We didn't have the luxury of underground utilities in my neighborhood. That was a convenience for the rich folk along Upper Bear Creek. The not-so-rich, who lived off the dirt roads, had to contend with frequent phone and power outages. This time, it wasn't the squirrels, not unless they started carrying wire cutters. The line, where it entered the junction box on my house, was cut cleanly off. I could have fixed the cut line in less than ten minutes, but if Nixon was out there with a rifle, I would be dead meat. He must have sneaked back when Fred and I were on the deck. Then again, he might have cut the phone line when he ransacked the motor home. Either way, that line could wait until morning.

"Don't even think about going to sleep tonight," I told Fred once we went back in the cabin and bolted the door. Then I checked my shotgun, made sure I had a shell in the chamber, and turned off all the lights. We sat there listening for over half an hour before I fell to sleep.

The sun was already up when I woke. It must have been around seven in the morning. My trusted sentinel was sound asleep at my feet. I must have been dreaming, for I thought I had heard something out there. It had to be a dream; Fred, even with a hangover, would have heard it much sooner than I could. Then Fred woke up and started to growl. Soon his growl turned to barking, and he was doing his porcupine imitation again. Someone was on our front deck.

CHAPTER 23

I went to the side window while Fred went to the front door. His barking should distract whoever was out there long enough for me to get a peek out the blinds.

"Jake," the intruder called out. "Jake, it's me, Hal. Are you in there?"

"Am I ever glad to see you. I thought for sure it was Ron Nixon, coming to slit my throat," I said as I opened the door. "What are you doing in my neck of the woods?"

"Filling in for a friend who's sick. My company flew me up from San Diego last night to meet his clients tomorrow. I had some time to kill, so I thought I'd look you up. And here I am. Is that thing loaded?" he asked, pointing at my shotgun.

"Sorry. We had a scare yesterday," I answered, putting the gun next to the closet after setting the safety. "Nixon broke into my motor home yesterday, and I think he may come back."

"No kidding? Well, I can see why you would be on edge. He must still be looking for those stupid coins."

"Evidently. He broke into Megan's two days ago, looking for them. Why he thinks I would have them is anybody's guess," I answered. "I was just about to make a pot of coffee. Would you like a cup?"

Hal surveyed my one room cabin, then sat down on the couch. "Taylor told me about the incident at your sister's. I'm glad she's okay." Then, as he got up and went to the sliding door leading to the deck, he changed the subject.

"Fantastic view you have. I can't believe there's snow on that mountain already," he said.

"That's Mount Evans. One of our fourteener's. They usually have snow all year round." Then I almost dropped the coffee pot. I happened to glance out the kitchen window at Hal's car.

"I thought you said you flew in last night, Hal? What's up with the Missouri plates?" It was a big SUV. The plate started with the letters AEM.

"Really? I never noticed. Someone from Missouri must have dropped it off at the rental company." Hal had maneuvered himself between me and where I had put the shotgun. I was sure he knew I had figured out it was he, and not Nixon, who had paid me a visit.

"Guess that happens all the time," I said, as I opened the drawer where I kept the kitchen knives and forks.

"Close the drawer, Jake." He had my shotgun and was pointing it at me.

"You're too damn smart for your own good, Jake. Why didn't you leave last night when you had a chance? Now I'm going to have to kill you, too."

I wasn't surprised. "By too, I assume you mean Nixon?"

"Damn, Jake, you are good. How did you figure that out?"

Hal must not have known about the safety on my gun: I could see it was still on. I had to keep his attention off the gun until I could jump him. "I just remembered where I saw your plates before. And I don't mean when you followed me from Kansas City to Emporia. Your partner in crime must have been Nixon. That was his SUV Linda was driving on the day Mike was murdered, so if you are driving it now, after admitting to a murder, it can only mean one thing. You must have killed your partner."

"Way to go, Sherlock. Want to tell me why I killed Nixon while you're at it?"

"That one is simple. I'm surprised Bennet didn't catch on by now. You've been replacing prescription drugs with Mexican counterfeits. Mike and Bill must have bank rolled your operation with the business loan, and when the truck got seized, Mike panicked. You paid him off with your collection of double eagles, and when he found they weren't worth anywhere near his fifty grand, he came looking for blood. You beat him to the punch with your hired gun, Nixon."

I continued talking as I inched closer to the gun. "I assume you paid Nixon off with the promise he could have the coins."

"Not bad, Jake. No wonder Amy likes you so much. Except you're wrong about the coins. It's not quite that simple."

"Oh, what did I miss?"

"They weren't my coins. At least, not until I paid Bill and Nixon to get them for me."He must have seen the confused look on my face. "Guess you're not so smart after all, or you would have guessed where they came from."

Then I remembered the news article. "You paid them to steal the coins from the Fergusons? Is that what started all this?"

His eyes wandered to the shotgun and then quickly back to me. I saw him feel for the safety and turn it off. "Looks like you missed your chance, Bud. You could have jumped me there."

"At least have the decency to tell me before you kill me. Did they kill the old couple and make it look like a murder-suicide?"

"Hell, why not. You can tell the story to everyone in Hell, so I'll be a legend when I join you. Ron killed them. The old man caught them in his bedroom and shot Atkins. Ron got the gun from him, and then he shot the old man and his wife. When he called me to tell me what happened, I had Ron dump Bill's body by Mike's dock. Mike had figured out, or maybe Bill had told him, that Bill had bankrolled my drug deal. Mike was threatening to tell Bennet if I didn't give him back his money, so I thought I'd frame him for killing Bill. At least you got some of it right." Hal moved away from the door and closer to the kitchen, all the time, making sure the gun was aimed at my head. "Sit down, Jake. This may take a while. Got anything to drink in here?" he asked and opened my refrigerator.

"Help yourself. I'll take a beer too, if you don't mind."

"Sure. Even you deserve a last meal," he said and laughed. He put the beer on the kitchen table and took a seat on the other side, then motioned with his free hand for me to sit at the table.

"Ron was scared shitless and ready to run," Hal continued as I popped the top of the can. "I had to go back there myself and set the scene to make it look like a mercy killing. Did a pretty good job, don't you think?"

"You would have made Agatha Christie proud." I saw Fred out of the corner of my eye. *Not now, Freddie*, I thought, *not until I hear all the story.* He looked like he was ready to jump Hal, so I moved over to hold his collar.

Hal raised the gun, but he didn't stop me. "I paid off Nixon with most of the coins and kept the good ones for myself. The idiot thought he got the best of the deal, not knowing what a Carson City was worth."

"At least a hundred thousand," I answered. "Then you had him kill Mike to shut him up?"

"No. I had nothing to do with that. I kept Mike at Bay with a promise to pay him off with another deal I had going. Anyway, the fool, Nixon that is, went and hid his coins at the museum where he worked as a night guard. Can you believe he cut into a support beam when he hid them in the walls."

"Nixon is responsible for the building collapse?"

Hal smiled. Not a friendly smile, but one you'd expect to see from Jack the Ripper. "Looks that way."

"So that's how Mike got the coins. He found them when he was hired to help tear the place down. I always knew the story about Jesse James was BS." I moved a little closer, pretending to hold Fred back. I was almost close enough to grab for the shotgun. "Is that why you had Mike killed? You wanted all the coins."

"Aren't you listening, Jake. I told you, I had nothing to do with that. And the coins I gave Nixon weren't worth that much. He'd be lucky to get enough to cover the gold in them. It was that idiot Ron. He got Mike to meet him at my place, pretending to be me when I was out of town. He tricked Mike into thinking I wanted to buy them. But it's getting late, Jake, so tell me where you hid my DVDs. Too bad you won't live to tell your story, but if you behave and tell me where they are, I promise I won't go after the rest of your family. Otherwise, they're next." He raised the shotgun and aimed it at my face.

"Bennet has them. Surely you know that by now," I said while trying to get closer to the gun. I wasn't going to go down without some kind of fight.

"Don't take me as some kind of fool, Jake. You only gave him the last one. I want the other four you kept. And don't come any closer unless you want to feel what it's like to be a chicken without a head."

I had nearly forgotten about them. Now I realized Meg and I should have watched them, too. "Did we miss something, Hal?" I asked as I stopped inching toward the gun. "They're still in my computer case. It's in my bedroom over there."

Hal turned toward my bedroom. I had a split second to grab for the gun before he pulled the trigger, but Fred beat me to it. Not that my best buddy came to my rescue because he was a trained attack dog; Fred's keen ears heard the siren before we did, and he knocked Hal over in his haste to reach the coffee table. The gun went off, putting a huge hole in my ceiling.

The distraction of the sheriff was all Hal needed to bolt out the door. Unfortunately for him, the deputy had heard the shot and returned fire when he saw Hal with the gun in his hands.

It was only later that I found out how the deputy showed up when he did. Megan had tried to tell me, before my cell went dead, that Bennet had found Nixon at the bottom of Truman Lake, not far from where Mike was found, and that Bennet had already figured out it was Hal. It seems Bennet had been working with the DEA for several weeks. They had been on Hal's trail for months.

When Bennet heard about my break-in, he called the Colorado sheriff. After the phone company verified the line had been cut, the local sheriff decided I was in imminent danger and dispatched an officer to my house. Luckily for Hal, the officer was a lousy shot and missed all the vital organs.

"Thanks a lot, Fred. I should have killed you when I had the chance." Hal said as the paramedics put him on a stretcher.

Fred wagged his tail as if to say, "You're welcome."

EPILOGUE

Hal won't be bothering anyone for some time. He got three life sentences, plus fifty years, for his part in the 'Black Widow Murders.' He saved himself from lethal injection by telling the DA everything he had told me.

The coins did eventually show up. Meg never cared much for her pontoon and sold it to Linda's father. He found the coins in the live well under the seat. He gave them to their rightful owners: the children of the murdered coin dealers. The reward was enough to put a down payment on the Pig's Roast, and he gave the place to Linda. Sam went back to selling mortgages in Kansas City.

My angel, Amy, married a doctor after taking a job at a prestigious hospital in Saint Louis. Rosenblum managed to get her an annulment from Hal on the basis that they never consummated the marriage. Taylor went with her, and the last I heard, he had gone back to school to become a medical technician.

Megan had a small wedding at the Broadmoor in Colorado Springs, saving me another trip to Truman. Ira asked me to be the Best Man, and I obliged. I thought about asking if Fred could carry the ring, then remembered Ira didn't care much for dogs. Mother sold her house in town and moved in with Megan, so she could raise Kevin properly. It remains to be seen how Ira will like living with his new mother-in-law. The newlyweds are still on a world cruise.

My plan to turn my adventure into a novel kept getting distracted by almost anything that came along. The latest distraction had been the movie I rented, called *Harry and Tonto*. Harry was an old man whose only friend in the world was his cat, Tonto. I wiped my eyes when Tonto died, and I turned off the television to let Fred out in the snow.

Snow comes early in the Rockies, and this year is no exception. There was already several feet on the ground and more was expected overnight. Fred loved it. I stood at the bay window of our little cabin, watching him burrow in the drifts and pop out the other side as though he were chasing a rabbit. He was no longer a puppy, yet he could still act like one. With some luck and a prayer, he would be there for me in my old age.

96342134R00141

Made in the USA
Lexington, KY
19 August 2018